"I can't be your hero, Melissa."

Sebastian took a step toward the door.

She raised her chin. "I'm a modern woman. I don't need to be saved."

"Everyone needs to be saved eventually."

She moved until she was standing barely an inch from him. Up this close, it was impossible to avoid the full impact of his presence. Strong and capable. Sexy. Way too sexy.

She cupped his cheek and he didn't pull away. *That was good. But not enough.* Gently she brushed her thumb across his skin. The whirl of emotions in his gaze touched her. In a way, they were similar.

She saw his fear. Determination. Loneliness. Yearning.

The last made something inside of her clench, for she knew what it was like to want that much.

"Do *you* need to be saved?" she whispered.

Dear Reader,

June brings you six high-octane reads from Silhouette Intimate Moments, just in time for summer. First up, Ingrid Weaver enthralls readers with *Loving the Lone Wolf* (#1369), which is part of her revenge-ridden PAYBACK miniseries, Here, a street thug turned multimillionaire on a mission falls for the enemy's girlfriend and learns that looks can be deceiving! Crank up your air-conditioning as Debra Cowan's miniseries THE HOT ZONE will definitely raise temperatures with its firefighter characters. The second book, *Melting Point* (#1370), has a detective heroine and firefighting hero discovering more than one way to put out a fire as they track a serial killer.

Caridad Piñeiro lures us back to her haunting miniseries, THE CALLING. In *Danger Calls* (#1371), a beautiful doctor loses herself in her work, until a heady passion creates delicious chaos while throwing her onto a dangerous path. You'll want to curl up with Linda Winstead Jones's latest book, *One Major Distraction* (#1372), from her miniseries LAST CHANCE HEROES, in which a marine poses as a teacher to find a killer and falls for none other than the fetching school cook…who hides one whopper of a secret.

When a SWAT hero butts heads with a plucky reporter, a passionate interlude is sure to follow in Diana Duncan's *Truth or Consequences* (#1373), the next book in her fast-paced miniseries FOREVER IN A DAY. In *Deadly Reunion* (#1374), by Lauren Nichols, our heroine thinks her life is comfortable. But of course, mayhem ensues as her ex-husband—a man she's never stopped loving—returns to solve a murder and clear his name…and she's going to help him.

This month is all about finding love against the odds and those adventures lurking around the corner. So as you lounge in your favorite chair, lose yourself in one of these gems from Silhouette Intimate Moments!

Sincerely,

Patience Smith
Associate Senior Editor

Please address questions and book requests to:
Silhouette Reader Service
U.S.: 3010 Walden Ave., P.O. Box 1325, Buffalo, NY 14269
Canadian: P.O. Box 609, Fort Erie, Ont. L2A 5X3

DANGER CALLS

CARIDAD PIÑEIRO

Silhouette®

INTIMATE MOMENTS™

Published by Silhouette Books

America's Publisher of Contemporary Romance

SILHOUETTE BOOKS

ISBN 0-373-27441-6

DANGER CALLS

Copyright © 2005 by Caridad Piñeiro Scordato

Visit Silhouette Books at www.eHarlequin.com

Printed in U.S.A.

Books by Caridad Piñeiro

Silhouette Intimate Moments

Darkness Calls #1283
Danger Calls #1371

*The Calling

CARIDAD PIÑEIRO

was born in Havana, Cuba, and settled in the New York metropolitan area. She attended Villanova University on a presidential scholarship and graduated magna cum laude in 1980. Caridad earned her *Juris Doctor* from St. John's University, and in 1994 she became the first female and Latino partner of Abelman, Frayne & Schwab.

Caridad is a multipublished author whose love of the written word developed when her fifth grade teacher assigned a project—to write a book that would be placed in a class lending library. She has been hooked on writing ever since.

When not writing, Caridad teaches workshops on various topics related to writing and heads a writing group. Caridad has appeared on Fox Television's *Good Day New York,* New Jersey News' *Jersey's Talking* with Lee Leonard and WGN-TV's *Adelante Chicago,* as well as being one of the Latino authors featured at the first Spanish Pavilion at the 2000 Chicago BookExpo America. Articles featuring Caridad's works have appeared in the *New York Daily News,* Newark, New Jersey's *Star Ledger,* South Florida's *Sun Sentinel, latinolink.com, Variety Yahoo! Online News,* and *Waterbury Republican-American.*

Caridad has been married for over twenty years, and is the mother of a teenage girl.

To all my friends at New Jersey Romance Writers for their support and encouragement. In particular, many, many thanks to Irene, Lois, Kathye, Anne, Patt, Mary, Shirley, Chris, Nancy, Ronnie and Ann for their caring and helpfulness. For more information on this wonderful group of writers, visit www.njromancewriters.org.

Prologue

Westchester County, October 2004

The body twitched convulsively on the floor of the cage before death stilled its movements.

Only two more rats to go and the active cell strain would be gone, leaving just the frozen samples and the journal taken from Dr. Frederick Danvers's lab nearly a year ago. Not that either had been of much use. The journal contained no instructions on how to prepare the frozen cell samples for use in test subjects. Multiple attempts to activate the preserved strain using standard lab procedures had been dismally unsuccessful. There was little of the precious live sample left. In addition, the journal had not provided any clues as to the origin of the unusual cell strain so that more could be obtained. The project was close to failure.

A nudge with a finger to the dead rat's body—just to make sure, since one had given a rather nasty bite once. A postmortem examination would hopefully yield some knowledge. If it didn't, there was only one way left to secure what was needed to further the experiments. One very unpleasant way.

Unfortunately, such means were sometimes necessary when the possibility of reward was immense. And what greater prize could there be than the promise of immortality?

After all, who wouldn't want to live forever?

Chapter 1

Westchester County, November 2004

Death would not be ignored that day.

It was in the bite of the chill wind as it ripped through the bare branches of trees, wailing plaintively. It was in the somber darkness of the clouds as it began to rain, as if they, too, were weeping.

Melissa Danvers stared down at the graves of her parents. A little more than a year ago, the ground had been too hard to bury them. Now a carpet of green, dulled by the frosts of fall, covered the earth where her parents rested. But there was still no peace for Melissa. There were too many things left unsaid and unresolved.

She murmured a prayer beneath her breath as the cries of the wind grew in intensity. Melissa almost didn't hear the rain turn into sleet that beat a *rat-a-tat-tat* against her umbrella as she concentrated on the graves. She wondered what it had been like for them in those last moments before their car left the road and hurtled down the incline. Would they be alive if she had called the police when they hadn't arrived according to schedule? Had they suffered for hours before they were found, or had their deaths been quick?

A particularly forceful gust of wind grabbed at her umbrella. Sleet stung her face and she shivered. A second later, he wrapped a strong arm around her. Looking up, she met the gaze of her family's oldest and dearest friend. Of the man who had been so many things to her—surrogate brother, fairy godfather, protector. Now, he was all the family she had left.

"You okay?" Ryder Latimer asked as he drew her close.

She leaned into the comfort of his solid presence, which blocked the buffeting winds and provided her stability, much as he had most of her life. "I'm hanging in there. And you?"

Ryder stared down at the ground. Icy rain dripped from the brim of the fedora onto his face, but he seemed not to care. He looked paler than usual and Melissa worried that this outing was taxing his strength. He had yet to fully recover from the injuries he had suffered a few months before while assisting his FBI agent lover with a criminal investigation. "Are you feeling all right?"

He nodded and, without looking at her again, said, "I should have done more."

"There's nothing either of us could have done," she replied, although her heart was heavy with remorse.

Ryder said nothing else, but she sensed that he shared her guilt. He had turned down an invitation to accompany her parents for a quiet weekend in Vermont. If he'd been driving instead of her father... She stopped herself, unwilling to begin the blame game again. Especially with Ryder, who had always been there for her. She also had to be his support now.

He handed her red roses and she laid one on each grave, pausing to pass her hand over the wet, spiky grass. Softly, beneath her breath, she said another goodbye to a mother and father she had never really known.

Ryder also laid a flower on each grave. After he was done, he took her elbow and hurried her to the limo that waited to return them to the Manhattan apartment they shared.

As she neared the car, the driver popped out of his seat and came around to open the door. She struggled with the umbrella for a moment, then slipped inside. A second later, Ryder sat in the seat opposite her and tossed off his hat.

She met his dark gaze, remembering a similar moment on the day her parents had been buried. He had been troubled then, as well. She hadn't understood why until she had opened the envelope brought to the graveside ceremony by her father's attorney.

With vivid recall, that day came alive again as they sat in silence while the limo pulled away.

The envelope had been old, its age apparent from the brittleness and rich yellow color of the heavy parchment. There was a patina on the envelope's surface, as if it had been handled often.

Ryder had clearly known what it held. He'd told her it was her destiny, but nothing could have prepared her for what was contained in the neat, precise words of the letter: a legacy from an ancestor dead for well over a century.

On that day, she'd had to deal with her parents' deaths. But then again, virtually everyone everywhere had to confront death and accept the inevitability that one day, death would come for them, as well.

Only fate sometimes interceded in ways hard to imagine.

On that day, Melissa had been forced to realize that fate had changed not only what she believed about death, but the very nature of her existence. She could no longer just be a physician dedicated to saving lives. Fate had charged her with being the companion and physician to Ryder Latimer, a one-hundred-and-forty-year-old vampire.

After the shock of it, she realized every Danvers before her had answered the call. Honor demanded she do no less. Since Ryder had always been there for her, for her family, she had felt compelled to repay him for being her champion.

In the time since then, she'd slowly learned just what her duty to Ryder entailed and how difficult it was. Handling things that couldn't wait until the sun was weak enough for Ryder to emerge. Obtaining the blood necessary for his feedings. Giving him medical assistance when the sun, garlic or a lack of blood taxed his system.

In the last few months, it had been an even more exacting burden. After his injuries, he'd been too sick to tolerate even the weakest of sunlight, which had made him a virtual prisoner in their apartment. He'd required extra blood and medicine in an effort to help his recovery. His lover, Diana Reyes, had assisted Melissa on many an occasion, but she lacked the medical skills to deal with Ryder's more complex needs. That was solely up to Melissa and it kept her almost constantly on edge. Both mental and physical exhaustion had become part of her daily routine.

For a brief moment, the burdens of her life had been eased by a chance encounter with Diana's younger brother Sebastian. In just one night, he'd provided her a glimpse into the kind of life she had come to think wasn't possible—one where she wasn't alone. But one night was all it had been. With daylight, Melissa had been troubled by the idea of sharing the secret of Ryder's existence and the commitment to keep him safe. And by the idea of sharing herself.

Ryder, she thought and looked at him again. He had closed his eyes and seemed to be resting. Although he was normally pale by human standards, his skin seemed almost bloodless today. She worried again that he had pushed himself too hard. As if sensing her prolonged perusal, Ryder opened his eyes and met her gaze.

"I'm okay," he said, and Melissa wondered if mind reading was one of his vampiric abilities. Or did he just know her that well?

"You don't look okay."

"I'm doing fine—"

She cut him off with an angry slash of her hand. "You're *not* fine. It's been over two months, and you're still weak. I'm worried."

"You shouldn't be. I'm healing slowly, but I *am* getting better," Ryder insisted.

Melissa couldn't argue that he appeared stronger and was doing more every day. But he still wasn't healthy enough for her taste. "Your strength and energy levels—"

"I've never been hurt this badly before, except for…" His voice trailed off, broadcasting his reservations.

With a wave of her hand, she urged Ryder to clarify.

He dragged his fingers through his dark hair, his frustration obvious. "Except for when I was first turned. Your great-great-grandfather, William, tended to me until I seemed to get better."

"Seemed to? It's like being pregnant, Ryder. Either you are or—"

"I got toothy," he said harshly and locked his gaze with hers. "I got hungry and I got wild and the fangs emerged. You don't want to know what I was like then."

His hands were clenched tightly by his side. Melissa reached out and grasped one fist. "I know what you were like then, from reading the first journals. But now…" She hesitated, unsure of how to continue without treading on very treacherous ground.

The journals her ancestors had kept could be an amazing source of information regarding Ryder's vampirism. She'd managed to go through about a dozen before one of them had been stolen from her office.

"One of the journals is missing and you're uncomfortable that I've asked you to approach Sebastian for help?" Ryder questioned.

"Am I that easy to read?" she wondered aloud.

Ryder chuckled and said, "A big hint, Danvers. Poker is not your game."

Melissa shook her head in amusement, then brought up the argument they'd had often since someone had broken into her office a few days ago and stolen one of the Danvers's memoirs. "We can keep the journals safe by ourselves. We don't need to ask anyone else for help."

Ryder shook his head. "No, we can't. At a minimum, we should ask Diana for her advice. As for Sebastian, his skills would be invaluable."

Though she was uneasy about bringing Sebastian back into her life, she knew Ryder was right. Those journals were too important to risk. They needed copies—encrypted, impossible-to-steal copies. Because Melissa was convinced there was information in her ancestor's notes that could help her heal Ryder faster.

Her father had concocted a mix to counteract the effects of too much sun and other poisons on Ryder's system. What was left of the mixture had saved Ryder's life two months ago. And with today's medical advances, she hoped she could make a difference. Perhaps even find a cure.

Then Ryder might not need her as his constant companion. She could have a life with… Sebastian again came to mind, as he did too often lately.

"I stopped hoping for a cure a long time ago," Ryder said quietly, again reading her thoughts. "I don't want you to have your hopes dashed, as well."

But they've already been destroyed. She suddenly wanted to lash out at him. Ever since she'd discovered her duty, as next in the Danvers line, her hopes and dreams had virtually disappeared. Somehow she'd persevered, creating the illusion of normalcy in much the same way Ryder adopted the semblance of humanity. The sham had worked for a little while. But now there were recent happenings in both their lives that suddenly made her wonder *What if?*

For starters, Ryder was in love with a human and, from what she could see, the feeling was very mutual. Of course his relationship with Diana hadn't progressed to the living-together stage. The marriage thing seemed out of the question. But *what if* Diana was here to stay? Would that free Melissa of her duty?

And if it didn't, and Melissa somehow suspected that it didn't, what about *her* life? What about the possibility of love?

Only, she reminded herself, no one had mentioned love that night, only sex. Which, with Sebastian, had been... She wouldn't call it a mistake, but it had certainly been unplanned. Spontaneous. Well, at least the first time. The second and third... Being a modern, mature, *Sex and the City* kind of girl, she knew that one night with a man did not a romance make. But in the very few and very infrequent free moments since then, she'd wondered whether a second or third or fourth date with Sebastian might change things.

After the craziness of such thoughts, logic would return and she would acknowledge that what had happened that night had been simple transference. Or at least that's what one of her psychiatrist friends would call it. She'd taken the caring shown by Sebastian toward his sister and toward Ryder and transferred it to herself. With her parents' recent deaths and Ryder seriously injured, she'd been vulnerable, starved for affection. It had resulted in a very pleasant interlude.

But that was all it had been or ever could be. In addition to the constraints of being both a doctor and Ryder's companion, she wasn't ready to trust her heart to anyone. She might not ever be ready.

It's not as if she'd learned how to trust—how to love—from her parents. They had been emotionally distant, at best. Her mother had been a physically frail creature, needing most of her husband's attention and having little patience for the inquisitive and energetic child Melissa had been. Her father's time had been taken up by his medical practice. And, of course, as she had learned at his death, by Ryder and his demands.

Later, medical school and her residency had curbed what was left of her personal life. Her few encounters during that time had intentionally lacked emotional investment. Since becoming Ryder's companion, her social life had become nonexistent.

Except, of course, for Sebastian.

But if she was ever to have any life at all, Melissa had to take control of things. To have control, she needed more information than what was currently at her disposal.

She wrapped her arms around herself, more than a little uneasy about the path she was about to embark upon. She wasn't someone who normally challenged the status quo, but maybe a year with a vampire—and that one night with Sebastian—had left her feeling a little rebellious. For too long, she had followed without question. Guarded her heart to avoid being rejected. In spite of her protests against seeking help to safeguard the journals, she had no doubt the possibility of a normal life was worth the risk. Even if that help—that risk—came from Sebastian.

When she spoke, the strength of her conviction was clear. "I'll go to Sebastian tomorrow, but for the other… I'm not asking permission, Ryder. I plan on scouring those journals for any hint of a cure. With or without your help."

"And nothing—"

"Nothing, not even getting toothy, is going to stop me."

Chapter 2

Sebastian Reyes had a problem. Or rather, his new client had one. They had gotten the SQL Slammer virus because someone in their IT department forgot to shut down Port 1434. He entered the user name and password he had been provided, cleared his client's firewall and remotely accessed their network. With a few keystrokes, he had a patch going to fix the issue.

He grabbed three squeeze stress balls and pushed away from his desk, where his computer was monitoring the progress. He tossed the first stress ball high into the air, followed it with the others, juggling them to pass the time while his computer ground away. As he walked around, stress squeezies flying through the air, Sebastian occasionally shot a look at the monitor where a large dialogue box announced how much of the patch was finished.

Not much longer, he realized, pleased his new computer and server setup were working so well. Even though the dot-com bust had finally reached the company for which he had been working, resulting in its bankruptcy, he'd recently sold one of his computer games. And he'd turned the frequent requests from former clients—such as the frantic call regarding the virus—into a consulting business for those who needed their networks operating, and the private things on their systems remaining private. So instead of doing the nine-to-five office routine, he worked out of the apartment he shared with his FBI agent sister, Diana, writing new games and monitoring for performance and security issues. Plus he got to do other fun things, like hacking into the systems of clients and other consultants to make sure everything was in working order. Nonconformist that he was, he loved the hacking best.

All in all, he couldn't complain. At twenty-eight, he was making a decent living with less stress, and he was his own boss. He smiled, tossed the balls around, then stopped his juggling as he noticed the patch was complete.

Sebastian laid the squeeze balls on the desktop and ended the remote session just as the doorbell rang.

He opened the door and stopped short.

Melissa Danvers.

Dr. Melissa Danvers, vampire keeper, still looking as stunning today as she had nearly three months ago when she'd first dropped that bombshell on him. He'd thought it a shame someone so very beautiful was a crackpot, until his sister confirmed that Ryder Latimer was a vampire.

"Hi. You're the last thing I expected to see," he said, wondering what she was doing on his doorstep, but pleased nonetheless.

She held her Coach purse before her and nervously fingered the straps, looking decidedly prim, proper and uneasy. But that uneasiness couldn't dim her beauty. For months, he'd tried to convince himself his recollections of her had been suspect, colored by the tension and danger of the night they had shared.

They hadn't. Wheat-blond hair framed an oval-shaped face that was classically beautiful. From the straight, slightly pug nose to a heart-shape mouth with lips…

Don't think about those lips, he warned himself. *Just keep it simple. Meet her gaze directly and firmly and…*

Only the blue of her changeling eyes was a stormy gray tonight—the color of trouble. So he shouldn't have been surprised when she said, "I have a problem."

"A problem?" Panic raced through him. There was only one problem he could think of that would bring her to *his* door. They'd taken precautions when they'd made love that night, but of course, nothing was foolproof. His gut tightened with concern. He was barely capable of taking care of himself, much less a child or a wife. His father would have…

He refused to think about the chastisement that would have been sure to come from his father, if he'd still been alive. Sebastian was no longer the hesitant little boy always striving for his *Papi*'s acceptance. He was a grown man, and he knew what he had to do.

He motioned Melissa into the apartment, then closed the door behind her and strove for a totally-in-control kind of voice. "Wrong. *No problema.* Whatever you need, Melissa. Are you Catholic?"

A shocked expression crossed her patrician features. "Forthright, aren't you? And no, I'm Episcopalian."

He squared his shoulders and, with what he hoped seemed like bravado, nodded. "I'm a responsible kind of guy. And you're smart. Attractive. And—"

"Healthy. See. I have all my teeth," Melissa said with some bite and forced her mouth wide open to display her perfectly white and straight teeth.

Sebastian narrowed his eyes as he considered her carefully. "Do you always hide behind a joke?"

She shook her head, as if chastising herself, and her shoulder-length hair swayed with the movement. "We're getting off on the wrong foot. I'm sorry. It's not a personal kind of problem. I need your techno-knowledge."

Sebastian released a long breath and was surprised that mixed in with the relief was a little regret. Maybe even a bit of anger. Three months of not being able to stop thinking about her and the only reason she was on his doorstep now was because she needed his expertise. "So I guess what happened between us was—"

Melissa held up her hand to silence him. "Please don't be offended, but I thought we both knew that it was a result of the danger and—"

"The tension. Right. Nothing else." He had known someone like Melissa would have no interest in someone like him. They were too different. It was why he hadn't called her after their night together. It was why he shouldn't have been thinking of her all this time. He stuffed his hands into his pockets—he was too tempted to move a stray lock of her silky blond hair from her face. That would be wrong. So totally wrong.

"What kind of computer help do you need?" He struggled for a neutral tone.

When her gaze met his, something big and dangerous flared to life inside him. She hesitated, seeming to recognize what he was feeling. "Actually, I'm rethinking this."

Despite her statement, she took the seat Sebastian offered and settled herself on the black leather couch in the living room that doubled as his office. He sat before her on the coffee table. Leaning forward, he braced his elbows on his thighs and clasped his hands together. He was fighting a losing battle not to touch her. "Why don't you let me be the judge of that?"

Melissa paused again, clearly troubled. With a nod of her head, she explained. Sebastian patiently listened to her description of the Danvers family journals and how one had recently been taken from her office. That didn't give him a clue as to why his help was needed until Melissa finished by saying that Ryder and Diana thought someone should scan the remaining journals as a safeguard.

He gave a careless shrug. "Scanning is easy enough to do. But someone could still snatch the one machine with the images. Unless you encrypt the files and the database. Put the pieces at different secure locations."

Melissa smiled. "That's why you're the best person for this job. You know exactly what we need to do. And you already know Ryder's secret."

"It would take a day or—"

Melissa quickly jumped in. "It needs to be foolproof. No one can hack into this."

From the tone of her voice, Sebastian gathered there was something she wasn't telling him. It bothered him that she wasn't being totally honest. "Not giving me all the details, are you?"

She flushed and shifted nervously. "I'm not really sure—"

He moved off the table and sat down next to her. "And I'm not sure I want to be dragged into something without all the information."

The stain of color on her cheeks deepened and she looked away. Sebastian lost the battle then. He cupped her chin and applied gentle pressure until she faced him. Her skin was smooth and warm beneath his fingers. As soft and silky as it had been the night they… He ripped himself from those thoughts. They were a dangerous distraction. "If there's more, I need to know."

Giving him a tight smile, Melissa shied away from his touch. "I'm not sure there's more yet. But there are too many things that seem to connect."

"Like?" he pressed.

"Ryder's secret. The missing journal. The car crash that killed my parents more than a year ago. It's just too many things happening too close together." She looked down at her hands as she spoke. They were clasped together tightly, her knuckles nearly white from the pressure.

"I'm sorry. I didn't know your parents were dead." Sebastian reached out and covered her hands with one of his. "Have you talked to Diana about your suspicions?"

Again Melissa eased away from his comforting gesture. "Ryder and I told her about the crash. And the journal. She's not sure we should be worried, but thinks it can't hurt to get some more information. We gave her the details we had."

Sebastian considered all that Melissa had revealed, and all that she hadn't. She was unsure around him. That was clear from the way she withdrew every time he tried to make some overture. He knew from their night together, she wasn't used to being close to people, not even in a friendly way. Could they work together, given what had happened between them? And she obviously believed there was a possibility the journals—and the people connected to them—were in danger.

With the exception of his sister, Sebastian kept away from emotional complications. Maybe it was selfish, but the life he had chosen spared him from dealing with the expectations of others, his father in particular. Sebastian had found his own way and was happy with it. He wasn't sure he was prepared to be anyone's champion.

"I need to think about this."

Her head jerked up and her eyes widened with surprise. "You're not sure you can do what we want?"

Sebastian rose. He rocked back and forth on his heels as he said, "Tech stuff is a slam dunk. I'm a whiz at that. But the rest—"

Melissa jumped up off the sofa. "Whatever happened before, it won't happen again." She stressed that promise with an emphatic slash of her hand.

He wished it were that simple. "Well, thanks for that little ego boost," he quipped and, before she could answer, continued. "I'm not sure I want to be involved. I kinda like my solitary life. Plus, being a hero is more up Diana's alley than mine."

"B-but you helped before. When Ryder was hurt," Melissa said.

Sebastian shrugged. "No choice then. You needed me—"

"We *need* you *now*. There's no one else we can trust with Ryder's secret."

He wasn't going to leap without thinking about it first. His father may have believed him to be thoughtless in his rebellion, but in fact, Sebastian's decisions had always been studied and logical. Right now, logic was telling him that it made no sense to become more involved in Melissa's life.

Melissa, with her by-the-book personality, was a challenge to the comfortable world he had created for himself. She was also a possible danger to his safety, if it turned out she was right and the crash that had killed her parents hadn't been an accident. And worse, although he didn't want to admit it, she was a real risk to his heart, regardless of everything else.

He didn't want to seem callous, but it made no sense to carry on with the conversation until he'd had time to consider everything without the pressure of Melissa hovering nearby. She was a distraction he didn't need. He motioned to the door and Melissa hurried to it, the lines of her body tight with anger.

As she stepped out, he gently grasped her arm. "I didn't say no, Melissa. I just need to think about it."

With a curt nod, she strode off. He lingered by the door, watching her go, wishing he could have immediately said yes. Despite his mixed emotions, something about Melissa Danvers intrigued him.

When Sebastian closed the door he'd intended to try out an amended version of his latest game. But as he took hold of the joystick and loaded up the program, his mind drifted back to Melissa.

Forcing himself to concentrate, he made sure the changes requested by the computer game manufacturer were working.

He was just completing the first level when he heard the grate of a key in the lock. "Well look who's finally home."

"I have an early morning," Diana answered as she entered the apartment.

Sebastian gave her a puzzled look.

"Ryder's still weak. He needs to rest—"

"And he's not about to get it with you around," he said with a knowing grin.

Diana smiled and grabbed the squeeze balls from the desk. She juggled them at a speed well beyond what Sebastian could manage. But then again, Diana never did anything at normal levels. Including picking a boyfriend.

"Show-off," Sebastian teased and Diana playfully tossed the balls at him in response.

Sebastian managed to catch them all as his sister peeked at the screen. "What are you working on?"

Rising, Sebastian blocked Diana's view of the monitor, leaned on the edge of the desk and crossed his arms. "Hacking into classified FBI files to see what's new with my sis and her furry friends."

She crossed her arms and stood before him, impatiently tapping one sensibly-soled foot. "Ryder's not furry."

"Oh, yeah. That's right. He's just life-challenged?" He cocked an eyebrow.

Diana tried to see around him, but Sebastian dodged left and right, blocking her view. With a huff, Diana finally said, "You're not hacking me, right? I mean, I know you could do it, but you didn't. Right?"

He grinned and stepped aside to show her the frozen scene in the game. "I could, but I won't because you'd have to bring me in." He held his hands out in front of him, pretending he was about to be handcuffed.

His sister slapped his hands away. "Cut it out, *hermanito.* Concerned brother slash hacker extraordinaire that you are, you wouldn't put me in that difficult a position."

Sebastian joined her on the couch as she kicked off her shoes. He watched his sister intently as he said, "Things are tough enough, aren't they? What with Ryder and stuff."

Diana met his gaze squarely. "I'm assuming Melissa came by?"

"She did. Explained her problem. I'm not sure what to do," Sebastian admitted.

"About her or the project?"

"The project and nothing but the project."

"Funny. My radar hinted the two of you had connected."

Sebastian tried to laugh off the suggestion. He was hesitant to admit he and Melissa had shared a night together. "Yeah, like a wrong number kind of connect."

Diana rose from the sofa and placed her hands on her hips, drawing open her suit jacket slightly. She scrutinized him much the way she would a suspect. "Guess I was wrong."

"Yep. Major League error."

His sister smirked, confirming she recognized the lie for what it was. She playfully chucked him on the chin. "Little bro, you may fool some women with that pretty-boy face, but not this girl."

Ruefully shaking his head, Sebastian said, "We've been through too much together, huh?"

And wasn't that an understatement of gigantic proportions? In the year after their father's death, Sebastian had tried to help his sister cope with the pain. His sister had always been the strong one—until their father had been killed and Diana had fallen apart.

Diana had entered a dark and dangerous world, and Sebastian had thought he could somehow keep her from totally going over the edge. So he'd gone with her to clubs for those who liked to live precariously; been by her side on many a late night. Tried to make sure that in the numbing haze created by one too many tequila shooters, Diana did nothing that would harm her.

The defiant streak inside of him had responded to the make-no-excuses, take-no-crap kind of life. In that blurry world of alcohol and angry music, he'd finally discovered peace. He'd realized there was nothing wrong in walking his own path, rather than toeing his father's line. His *dead* father, who he'd never been able to please anyway.

Rebellion suited Sebastian and gave him a place where he was free of his pain. But the freedom had been an illusion, and a dangerous one at that. The partying and drinking had only numbed his guilt over never having lived up to his father's expectations.

It had taken great strength to untangle all the conflicting emotions within himself, to deal with Diana's pain, and his own, and find a way back to who he really was. It hadn't been easy, but it had made him a stronger man.

Years later, he had finally accepted that he could never have been the son his father wanted. The best he could do was be his own man.

"There's a lot going on now, and I've dragged you into it again, haven't I?" There was an edge of anguish in his sister's voice that Sebastian hated to hear.

"You love Ryder and he makes you happy. I would never wish anything different for you."

"But you want something different for yourself?" she pressed, apparently hearing something behind his words.

"I want the Happily Ever After, but with someone simple."

"Someone not like Melissa—is that it?"

Sebastian was finding it difficult not to confide in his sister since they'd never kept anything from each other before. He didn't want to start now. "There was something between us," he said, although he didn't quite know what to call the night he and Melissa had shared.

"Something, huh? You think you can just make that something go away?"

"I'm trying, although it's not easy," he stated flatly. "There are other things in my life that keep me busy."

"Like your games? And your hacking?" Sebastian flinched as he heard the echo of his father's words lashing out at him. *Like father, like daughter.*

Diana must have realized she'd struck a sore point, for she apologized instantly. "I didn't mean to condemn."

"Didn't you? You sounded just like him. RoboCop redux."

Her color paled at his rebuke and her generous mouth thinned into a tight line. But she still reached out and laid a hand on Sebastian's leg in an effort to soothe the sting of her words. "*Hermanito*, I'm sorry. It's just you and I are so different that way."

"Don't I know it. Didn't Dad tell me often enough that I should be more responsible? That I should care about school more." His sister started to speak but Sebastian silenced her with an angry wave of his hand. "You know what I remember best about Dad? Besides watching him die in your arms?" He paused, although he expected no answer to his question. "I must have been thirteen or fourteen. I was playing a game up in my room and Dad came in. He sat beside me, watching the screen but not talking. I tried to explain the rules, but after a few minutes, Dad mumbled something about wasting time playing games when life was so much more important."

"He just couldn't understand you," Diana said, much as Sebastian expected she would. He adored his sister and trusted her judgment, but Diana had never grown beyond her hero worship of their police-officer father. She didn't realize that while being a champion to others, their father had often put his family second and ignored a son who was totally different in temperament and interests.

"Do you think Melissa could understand me?"

"I haven't thought about it," Diana admitted.

"She's uptight and über-responsible. I'm a no-strings-attached kind of guy." He looked away from his sister. He didn't want her to see his confusion or his guilt. Despite his best efforts these last three months, he hadn't been able to forget Melissa.

More than most, he knew the hardship of conforming and being bound by another's conventions. Sebastian sensed that Melissa's life was not her own, that she needed an escape from the burdens she bore. He wanted to ease the weight off her shoulders. He hadn't felt that way in a long time—as if he could help someone else. Be someone worthy for her. But he'd both disappointed and angered her tonight with his hesitation.

Funny how much it was like the situation with his father all over again.

After a long silent moment he turned to face his sister, not knowing what to expect. Certainly not the little Mona Lisa-like smile on her face. "Seems to me you've been thinking about it way too much, *hermanito.*"

Sebastian stood, took a breath, about to tell her that he didn't want to talk about it, when Diana surprised him by saying, "I've got to get some sleep. *Hasta mañana.*" She rose and gave him a quick kiss on the cheek.

"'Night, sis." How could she understand him so well? Sometimes better than he understood himself.

After Diana walked into her bedroom and closed the door, it was impossible to concentrate on the mock investigations and battles of his game.

If he had any sense, he would stop wondering about Melissa. But it was difficult, given the impression she'd made. Months ago, she had been strong enough to confront his sister and convince Diana to look for a missing Ryder. When faced with Ryder's injuries, Melissa had been capable and unafraid. But after the crisis was over, the pain hidden behind her competent façade had called out to him. He'd tried to soothe her emotional wounds, and they'd ended up making love.

Not that he considered himself shallow, but he *had* noticed more than her vulnerability. Melissa's eyes—*dios,* but he could spend hours looking into her changeling blue eyes. A deep, dark slate-gray with worry. Bright and sparkling with bits of aquamarine when she was happy, as she had been in those unguarded moments the morning after.

She had a dimple when she smiled, and although her smile was sometimes hesitant, as if she didn't experience it often, it lit up a face that was stunning in a healthy, blond, California-girl kind of way.

Sebastian couldn't deny that he'd remembered on more than one occasion what she had tasted like when he kissed her. How her compact, curvy body had felt pressed to his. What she looked like without her…

He groaned as his nether regions sprang to life as they did way too often when he thought about Melissa. He heard a door opening, sat up slightly and grabbed a pillow, which he placed on his lap to hide his erection. A second later, Diana strolled into the room.

She was rubbing her hands together, as if she had just put on some lotion, and she had changed into her pajamas. "Still up?" she asked when she noticed him on the couch.

Oh, he was up, but not in a way he'd admit to his sister. "*Sí*, still awake. Trying to figure out a problem."

Diana gave him a puzzled look, her brows furrowed together. "Need help?"

Sputtering, Sebastian quickly replied, "No, thanks. I think I've figured out what to do." And the truth was he suddenly knew where to begin.

Chapter 3

Melissa had been with her patient for the last hour, trying to be of comfort as the young girl went through her first treatment for a rare blood disorder. There was a crick in the small of Melissa's back from sitting in the chair by the girl's bedside and, after, helping shift her into another bed so she could return to her room.

It didn't matter that Melissa had missed lunch. She hadn't really been hungry, and her fifteen-year-old patient was nervous and needed a little support. Besides, Melissa's afternoon was light, appointmentwise. She could grab a quick bite later, before rounds. As she reached her office, she heard the phone ringing and raced inside.

"Dr. Danvers."

"Hello, Doc," Sebastian said.

Anger rose up in her as she recalled their encounter of the night before. Color her stupid, but she'd been counting on him to help without hesitation. "Have you made up your mind yet?"

"Direct and to the point. Right, Doc?"

Melissa shook her head at her own abruptness and tried to smooth things over. After all, she needed this man's assistance. "Please don't call me *Doc*. It always makes me feel as if I should be balding and hanging out with six dwarves. I'm short, but not that short."

Sebastian chuckled and she was able to picture his grin in her mind. That was not good. She shouldn't be remembering that much about this man. "Melissa, then. I wanted to talk about the help you needed. Maybe even share a latte kind of boost."

"I could use some caffeine," she said, although what she was more interested in was his answer to her request. "There's a pretty good coffee shop right near the corner of 60th and York."

"I can meet you there in about ten minutes. Does that work for you?" Sebastian asked.

"I'll see you then."

It was one of those weird summerlike December days in New York City. Midseventies with a bright blue cloudless sky. Melissa made the short walk to the coffee shop, enjoying the weather. It was something she rarely got to do.

As promised, Sebastian was waiting outside. He wore faded black jeans that were snug against his lean legs and a black *Buffy the Vampire Slayer* shirt, bearing a picture of the blond superhero and assorted monsters. The first time she had met him, he had sported a *Star Wars* T-shirt.

Today's shirt, featuring one of her favorite shows, made her smile. Some vampires, Ryder excluded, might find the show politically incorrect toward the undead. Although she had never met another vampire. When she'd questioned Ryder, he'd hinted that others like him existed in Manhattan. He'd also made it clear he preferred to avoid their company. Melissa hadn't pressed the issue at the time. Someday, however, they might have to revisit that issue.

Sebastian grinned as he caught sight of her. His smile

caused an unexpected lurch in the middle of her chest. Melissa suddenly felt like a self-conscious thirteen-year-old instead of a liberated thirtysomething woman. "Hi."

"*Hola*," he replied and made no motion other than to hold his hand out in the direction of the shop. She wasn't sure why that disappointed her. She'd been expecting a handshake, a hug or one of the other typical greetings people who knew one another shared.

But then again, she and Sebastian didn't really know each other at all.

Inside the coffee shop was fairly quiet as the afternoon lunch rush was over and the midafternoon coffee break surge had yet to start. It took only a minute for them to place their orders.

"You look wiped," Sebastian said. "Why don't you grab a seat? I'll bring our coffees over when they're ready."

Melissa nodded and walked to the front of the shop, where there was a bench seat and table near a window facing York Avenue.

While waiting for their orders, Sebastian looked her way. She smiled nervously, then glanced down at her outfit, suddenly wishing she had changed. The white lab jacket and hospital scrubs were big on her petite physique, giving her a too-youthful appearance. Of course, that might not be such a bad thing considering Sebastian was several years younger than her—in his late twenties at the most. Also, someone had told her once that the pale blue color of the scrubs made her eyes look a crystalline blue. She wondered if Sebastian would notice, then forced such thoughts from her mind.

The only thing between them was Sebastian's help with the journals. Nothing else. Certainly nothing like what Sebastian had done with her and to her during their first meeting. A little bit of heat flared to life at the recollection of that night. She fanned her hand before her face to cool it.

A second later, he walked over with their lattes and she fumbled a bit as she took the large cup from him. "Thanks."

When she looked up into his eyes, she noted amusement. She was about to ask him what was funny, when he said, "You're not used to people caring for you, are you?"

It was unsettling that he could be so right. "Are you always this perceptive?" she challenged, trying to erect some kind of barrier to his insight. She didn't like being so transparent. *Poker face*, she reminded herself.

Sebastian only smiled and motioned to the bench with the hand that held his coffee. "May I join you there?"

Melissa realized for the first time that there was very little room beside her. Unfortunately, there was also no chair nearby. To refuse him would seem rude. She shifted to the edge nearest the window and inclined her head in invitation.

When he eased down beside her, his broad shoulder brushed against hers. His denim-covered legs were not as close, but still too near. She was finding it hard to ignore him. He was attractive, with his gleaming dark hair and eyes accented by well-defined cheekbones. His skin had the kind of tanned color that didn't fade in the winter. And his lips…

Don't think about those lips, she warned herself and forced her thoughts to something else.

Like the fact that he wasn't tall. Barely five foot ten, but his leanly muscled body gave the sense of greater height. His sculpted arms were bared by his short-sleeved T-shirt. She had tried to put his physical strength out of her mind, but now, with him nearly on top of her, it was hard not to appreciate how compellingly masculine he was. Even harder to just sit here beside him and stare. She grabbed her cup with two hands and shimmied closer to the edge of the bench. He smirked wryly.

"Don't flatter yourself," she said.

"I guess I invaded your space, huh? Sorry. I'm Cuban. We're physical with…" He paused, as if searching for the right words. Finally he said, "Friends and family."

"Well, have MCI take me off your list," she replied sharply, then shook her head. "I'm sorry. That was harsh."

Sebastian gave a careless shrug, which stretched the fabric of his shirt across the width of his shoulders. He took a sip of his latte. "But you're right. We're not family…or friends. Still, you want my help."

She was grateful he was enough of a gentleman not to mention their night together. Things were uncomfortable enough. She examined his face but couldn't read his mood like she had the other night. "We're not friends *yet*," she said, realizing how weird it was that she had known this man intimately, but didn't really have a clue about him.

"There's time for you to make my list," he said. "What about you and Ryder? Have you been friends for long?"

She stared at her coffee and avoided his gaze. "Ryder's more than a friend. He's all the family I have."

"I guess you've known him a long time?"

"All my life."

Motioning with his hand, Sebastian asked, "All your life as in—"

"Forever." Melissa took another sip of her latte.

Sebastian cocked his head, seemingly perplexed. "Didn't you notice that, well, Ryder didn't get any older-looking?"

Out of the corner of her eye, Melissa glanced at him. "No more than I wonder about Dick Clark every New Year's Eve."

Sebastian laughed. Melissa joined him and rolled her eyes, realizing just how unbelievable her whole situation must be to an outsider like him.

"And you've been his keeper… Do you think we can call you something else? Like his companion, maybe?"

"A rose by any other name—"

"Do you resent it?"

"It's what I have to do."

"Why?" he challenged with a cocky shrug.

"Because it's my duty. Because my family has honored that call for nearly six generations." Suddenly she had the urge to leave. The conversation was exposing too much to a virtual stranger. This meeting was supposed to have been about him helping, not about her. "Come to think of it, it's time I returned to the hospital."

She began to rise, but Sebastian laid a hand on her arm and applied gentle pressure to keep her beside him. She stared at his hand and followed the line of his muscled arm until her gaze met his. "I have to—"

"No, you don't. In fact, rumor has it that the only two things you have to do are die and pay taxes. Only I guess you don't have to die, do you?" His voice trailed off at the end, as if he, too, realized what an awkward situation they were in.

"If you're like Ryder, time doesn't matter." But it mattered to her and to this man sitting beside her, looking at her way too seriously and with too much compassion.

"I respect what you feel about honoring your family's loyalties, only—"

"It's an outdated concept in today's world, where anyone can do anything and not worry about the consequences?"

As if she hadn't harshly interrupted, Sebastian calmly continued, "I know how hard it is. I just wish that you could find some peace with that duty. With what you want most for *you*, in here." He emphasized that statement by pointing to the spot above his heart.

Melissa struggled for something to say, something that could break the connection she was experiencing with him, only she couldn't find the words.

At her prolonged silence, he finally said, "When did you find out what Ryder was?"

"I'm not sure I like all these questions," she replied softly.

Sebastian laid a hand on her arm. "I just need to know more before I commit."

Seeing that he wasn't going to give up, Melissa relaxed against the back of the bench. Sebastian removed his hand from her arm. Funny how she sensed the absence of it. Of the quiet strength in his long slender fingers. "I found out about Ryder a little over a year ago. When my parents died."

"Is that when—"

"I became his…personal physician," she answered and shot a quick look at him to gauge his reaction.

He smiled as she acquiesced to his earlier request, but then he became serious once more. "You resent it, don't you?"

"Broken record time. I think you asked that already."

He held up a finger. "But *you* didn't really answer."

Maybe she hadn't answered because she didn't want to discuss it. Especially not with Sebastian. She had given him her body, but she was afraid of giving him more.

"This is the point where I should realize this is something you'd rather not discuss," he said.

Melissa hated the tension between them. Trying to ease the strain, she adopted a lighthearted tone. "I would very much appreciate a change of topic."

He smiled sadly, but the sadness faded as he leaned his head against the padded bench, clearly thinking about something.

Melissa was suddenly impatient to hear what he would say next, and realized she *liked* that he was unpredictable.

"Okay, so let's talk about your favorite kind of food."

The very abrupt change in subject threw her, but brought a hesitant smile to her lips. "And why would we want to do that?"

He turned the full force of his gaze on her. Her heart did that funky thing again in the middle of her chest.

"So I know what kind of restaurant to take you to."

His interest shouldn't have pleased her. She didn't have time for a normal life. She couldn't become involved with him. He was carefree, fun…young. Not the kind of guy who'd want to live her kind of life. Despite that, she found herself exercising a rarely used skill—flirtation.

"What makes you think I'd want to go?" She bestowed on him her best come-hither smile. Or at least, she hoped it was that and not a grimace. Her smile muscles felt stiff.

Sebastian scrutinized her face, obviously unsure of where he stood, before shooting her a quick grin. "Let's just say that I know you want to go, but that you also want to keep it all business. So we will."

"We will what?" she asked, perplexed.

"Keep it business. You can tell me more about the journals while I think about what equipment we need and how I'll program things."

She shouldn't have been disappointed. He was doing the right thing, just as he had done the morning after. He hadn't pressed, almost as if he'd realized she was uncertain about all they had shared the night before. Instead, he'd been tender and concerned, tracing the dark circle beneath one eye and excusing himself so she could rest.

She suddenly wanted to know more about this complex rebel with a gentle touch and a heart that… She stopped herself. She shouldn't be thinking about things of the heart. She'd never been good with emotion and now, as Ryder's doctor, there was even less space for that in her life. "Maybe you should just come over to the apartment and do whatever you need to. That might be better."

After a long pause, he said, "I could bring food so we could eat while we talk. So is it Italian?"

Melissa chuckled at his stubbornness. "Yes. With lots of garlic. And garlic bread. Maybe even Parmesan garlic salad dressing."

He laughed. "It's tough caring for a vampire, isn't it?" he said.

Melissa nodded. "So about this *business* meeting…"

Chapter 4

Sebastian struggled with what to wear, not sure of the message he wanted to send. If he had been meeting a client, he'd replace the T-shirt and faded jeans with more suitable attire. Of course, since Melissa had not mentioned remuneration, and even if she had he would have refused it, he wasn't quite certain she would fall into the client category.

He grabbed an *X-Files* T-shirt but didn't put it on. After all, he wanted her to take him seriously, even if the only kind of relationship they had was a professional one. At least for now. Sebastian couldn't help hoping the good doctor was battling a personal desire having nothing to do with work.

The T-shirt suddenly seemed juvenile. Or was it the ghost of his father whispering in his ear? Tossing the shirt aside, he rifled through his closet and finally settled on a sharply pressed pair of khaki slacks, a cream-colored button-down shirt and a russet suede blazer to chase away an early winter chill.

After he was finished, he examined himself in the mirror.

The colors of the shirt and blazer looked good on him. And he was glad he'd gotten a haircut. His hair was cropped short around his ears, but left longer at the top. He'd removed his earring and the bracelet and rings he normally wore. He looked neater, more put together. *More respectable*, the annoying voice in his head urged.

Sebastian ignored it and walked the few blocks from his apartment to Little Italy. He picked up the meal he had ordered earlier, complete with mozzarella-topped garlic bread. After, he flagged a cab on the narrow street in front of the restaurant, and the taxi made great time in getting to Ryder and Melissa's apartment on Sixty-Sixth Street, right off Second Avenue.

Sebastian took the elevator to her floor after being cleared by the doorman, vaguely recalling the layout of the apartment building. More clearly, he remembered that Melissa's bedroom was on the first floor of the duplex while Ryder lived on the penthouse level. Sebastian hadn't spent more than a night there, but it had been a night that had indelibly seared itself into his memory.

Alerted to his presence by the doorman, Melissa was already waiting. She wore a pair of trousers and a sleeveless lace blouse. Both were black. The blouse had a deep V-neck with small scalloped lace along the edges. *Fairly sedate*, he thought, until she turned to walk into the apartment and he saw the back of the blouse. It was nothing but a sheer panel of lace that exposed the creaminess of her skin. He bit back a groan. There was nothing underneath the blouse besides her.

Melissa tossed him a knowing smile as he followed her. She was testing him. Seeing if he could keep it just business.

It should have annoyed him. It didn't. He liked her spunk.

"I figured we'd eat in here. Keep it simple," she said, leading him past a modern-looking formal dining room and into the eating area of a spacious state-of-the-art kitchen.

"That's fine. You can tell me what kind of computer equipment Ryder has while we eat. After, you can show me a journal or two." He placed the plastic bag of food on the black granite counter and slipped off his blazer. When he removed the take-out aluminum pans from inside the bag, the pungent aroma of garlic wafted into the air.

Melissa closed her eyes, inhaled deeply and smiled. "Good thing Ryder's not home."

"So the garlic thing's not just legend?" He finished laying out the pans and began to uncover them. "Dishes?" he questioned.

Nodding, Melissa opened a cabinet and removed various plates and bowls. She handed them to him and said, "Garlic does strange things to Ryder. In small doses, he can deal with it. If he were to ingest a large amount of it…" She shrugged and snagged a piece of mozzarella-topped garlic bread. "Hmm. Delicious."

"Don't fill up on the bread. There's the salad with garlic Parmesan dressing as requested. Scampi with roasted garlic. And last but not least, grilled chicken with pesto. As a side, we have linguini with marinara sauce, for a slight change of pace."

Melissa popped the last bit of garlic bread into her mouth and smiled. After she finished chewing, she said, "I like a man who's true to his word. Would you like some wine with dinner? Ryder has a great collection."

"Ryder drinks wine? I thought vampires only drank—"

"Blood? Hollywood stereotypes," Melissa teased, tsking and shaking her head. She walked to a small wine cellar built into the wooden kitchen cabinets then turned a few bottles to expose the labels before pulling one out.

"Red seems appropriate," she said and held the bottle out for his approval.

Sebastian uncorked the wine while Melissa forked some salad into bowls and prepared another set of plates with a little bit of each of the main courses and the pasta.

Once they were seated and the wine poured, Sebastian raised his glass and offered a toast, "To working together."

Melissa raised her glass, but was quick to clarify, "I don't think there will be much *together*, Sebastian."

She doth protest too much, he thought. She was building defenses right before his eyes.

He knew the price to be paid for erecting such barriers. He'd kept his father away with the walls created by his defiance. Behind those walls, he'd avoided hurting people who expected more of him than he was able to give.

"Understood, Melissa. Just business." He held up one hand as if in surrender, although giving up was the last thing on his mind.

Sebastian's too-quick acquiescence surprised her because of the disappointment that came again, much as it had at the coffeehouse the other day. Disappointment implied that she'd hoped he'd take this opportunity to rekindle… No. To rekindle one had to have kindled in the first place. Their night of sex apparently hadn't lit any fires for him. But that's the way she wanted it, wasn't it?

"Fine," she said and nodded as if to confirm it to herself. "Ryder will cut you a check—"

Sebastian stopped her again by raising one hand. "I won't take money for helping. Especially since I'm doing it for my sister."

"Oh." This time her disappointment cut deep. She didn't rate, obviously, but why should that surprise her? She hadn't rated with her parents, either. "What about the equipment you need?" she asked, hoping her dismay wasn't apparent.

Sebastian chewed his scampi thoughtfully before replying, "I'm not rolling in the dough, so I will let Ryder reimburse me for that. I'm assuming he can afford it," he said, motioning to everything around them with his empty fork.

"Money isn't an issue. At least, as far as I know," she replied, then turned her attention to the food while Sebastian asked questions about the journals and their sizes, Ryder's existing computer, peripherals and Internet connections. She answered as best she could and advised Sebastian when he would have to ask Ryder for more information.

Dinner was just about finished when the apartment alarm chirped, signalling Ryder's return.

Ryder walked into the kitchen and stopped in his tracks, Diana behind him. "Whoa. If you wanted me to stay away, all you had to do was ask."

Diana smiled at her brother and greeted Melissa with a nod of her head. "Have the two of you decided what to do?" Diana asked as she paused in the doorway, briefcase gripped tightly in her hand.

Sebastian shot Melissa an uneasy glance. "I have a basic idea of what I need for the project. I guess we can start…" He paused, waiting for Melissa to fill in the blank.

"As soon as you confirm the equipment you need and do the programming," she finished.

"We should try to do that as soon as possible," Ryder advised.

It was obvious to Melissa from Ryder's tone that something was up. "You have more information?" she asked as she grabbed her plate and started clearing the table. Sebastian rose and joined her, removing the remainder of their meal and leaving their glasses and the half-empty bottle of wine.

Diana opened her briefcase and removed an assortment of papers. "I looked at the reports and made a call or two. There are a number of things that just don't connect."

"It wasn't an accident, was it?" Melissa asked and plopped down heavily in her chair, her knees suddenly rubbery.

"Nine-one-one received a call from a pay phone reporting the accident. Crews were dispatched immediately, but there were no motorists at the scene when the police arrived."

Melissa knew Diana was only trying to be complete with the facts, but there was just one thing she wanted to hear. "Can you skip to—"

"The real four-one-one," Sebastian finished for her and she gave him a grateful smile.

"I contacted the initial officer on the scene and asked why he hadn't requested medical assistance." Diana hesitated and looked at Melissa uneasily as she finished, "He said that when he felt for a pulse the bodies were cold. He knew immediately there was no reason for paramedics, but there was no way the bodies—"

"My parents," Melissa lashed out.

"*Perdoname*," Diana apologized before continuing. "Even though it was chilly, from the time of the call to the arrival of the police, to be cold your parents had to have been dead for some time."

Since the day the journal had disappeared, Melissa had wondered whether there was some connection to her parents' crash. Even though some medicine and prescription pads had been stolen, too, it made no sense for a drug dealer to steal a musty old journal. Nor had it made sense for her normally cautious father to speed down an icy and dangerous road. Perhaps her father had discovered something someone didn't want him to know. She thought she'd convinced herself she'd be able to handle any revelation about their deaths, but she'd been wrong. She gripped the table to stop the way her world seemed to be spinning.

Sebastian laid a hand on her shoulder. "Are you okay?"

"I need some air."

Melissa raced out the door before Sebastian could react. He looked at Ryder. "Don't you think you should see if she's all right?"

"She just needs some time alone," Ryder responded.

Anger surged through him at Ryder's too-pat answer. "Melissa's been alone for too long." With that, he pushed away from the table, shoving it so hard that wine sloshed over the lip of Melissa's nearly full glass.

He stepped through a set of French doors on the main floor that opened onto a small balcony where Melissa stood. She'd wrapped her arms tight around herself and her head hung

down, her chin almost on her chest. It was as if she wanted to
disappear into herself. He placed a hand on the glass of the
sliding door, wishing he could touch her with that gesture. A
moment later her shoulders started to shake. He couldn't handle that.

Sebastian walked up behind her. Large soundless sobs
racked her body.

It twisted something inside him to see her in such pain. He
laid his hand on the gap between her neck and shoulder. At
his touch, she turned and leaned into him. He wasn't sure what
to do for a moment. He had so many reasons for wanting their
relationship not to get personal. So he stood there awkwardly,
hands raised in midair until he finally did what his heart knew
to be right. He wrapped his arms around her and held her
tightly. He bent his head and rested it against the top of hers.
At that moment, whatever restraints she had left broke free.

She eased her arms around him, gripped his shirt in her fists
and buried her head against his chest, murmuring, "I'm sorry.
I'm so sorry."

He grasped the back of her head and tunnelled his fingers
into the thick wealth of her hair. "Shh. There's nothing to be
sorry about."

She kept crying and repeating those words over and over
in soft tones. He held her until her distress abated and the sobs
racking her body subsided into small hiccuping breaths. When
she was finally calm, she pulled away from him and her gaze
met his. Her eyes were a gleaming sapphire, bright with tears
still waiting to be shed. He cupped her face, wiped his thumbs
across the wet trails on her soft warm skin. It seemed only natural to move his finger a fraction of an inch, trace the outline
of her lips with his thumb. He bent his head until the spill of
her breath bathed his lips.

Her lips were satiny. Flavored with the salt of her tears. He
licked away those remnants and she opened her mouth to
him, deepening the kiss.

Melissa's head was spinning; her mind reeling with the feelings he created in her. She'd been so alone until he'd stepped out onto the balcony. Even before he'd touched her, she'd connected with him. Now here he was, kissing her again. She let herself enjoy the sensation of how right his kiss felt. Met his tongue with her own and pressed herself tight to him. Like some kind of genetic memory, she recalled every little nuance of his body's contours. Remembered his strength and caring as he'd made love to her. A surge of emotion ripped through her.

It was the tension and that transference thing again, she told herself.

She yanked away from him and brought her hand up to wipe the taste of him from her lips. "I'm sorry, Sebastian. We shouldn't be doing this."

He nodded slowly. "You're right. We probably shouldn't be doing this."

She felt disappointed, again, then something definitely short-circuited in her brain because she blurted out, "Why not?"

"Because I can't be your hero, Melissa. I'm not cut out for it." He took a step back toward the door and away from her.

She raised her chin slightly and with a trace of defiance in her voice said, "I'm a modern woman. I don't need to be saved."

Sebastian gave a soft little laugh and smiled sadly. "Everyone needs to be saved eventually, Melissa."

She moved until she was standing barely an inch from him. His shaky exhalation washed over her face. It reminded her of that wonderfully sweet and enticing kiss. Up this close, it was impossible to avoid the full impact of his presence. Strong and capable. Sexy. Way too sexy.

She cupped his cheek and he didn't pull away. *That was good. But not enough.* Gently she brushed her thumb across his skin, which was rough with the start of an evening beard. The whirl of emotions in his gaze touched her. In some ways, they were very similar creatures.

She saw his fear. Determination. Loneliness. Yearning. The last made something inside of her clench tightly, for she knew what it was like to want that much. She whispered, "Do *you* need to be saved?"

In the second before he turned and strode away, she thought she saw his answer—that he didn't think himself worthy of salvation.

She wanted to go after him but she didn't know how to run toward something, only how to run away. She'd been doing it her whole life. First from the hurt caused by parents who couldn't love her. Then from the impossibility of a normal existence, given her role in Ryder's undead life. It had been easier to run than to face reality with all its problems.

But now Sebastian made her feel something she'd never felt before. Something that dared her to rethink what her life was supposed to be. It was only by accepting this challenge that she could find out what was meant to be…or not meant to be.

Chapter 5

Given that he didn't think of himself as hero material, Melissa was prepared for Sebastian to cut and run when Diana asked, "Are you with us on this?"

Sebastian stood by the table, his arms crossed against his chest. A defiant edge to his stance. "If you're in it, Diana, I'm in it."

Feelings of unworthiness rose sharply again, but Melissa ignored them. "You and Sebastian don't have to be involved. Ryder and I can handle it."

Diana laid her hand over Melissa's in a comforting gesture. "You don't have to be alone anymore. Plus, it may take the right connections to get the information we want."

"Meaning?" Ryder asked.

Diana looked across the table at her lover, but refrained from reaching out to him. "The locals might be a little concerned with a Fed like me asking any more questions. I may need someone else to do the asking."

"But that's one more person in the loop who might become aware of Ryder's secret. What if we just left this alone?" Melissa suggested, concerned that the inquiry into her parents' death might do more harm than good.

Sebastian surprised her by saying, "If these events are connected, whoever broke into your office may not be satisfied with what they got. They may come looking for more. You can't risk that."

"No, you can't," Diana said. "We're not really sure what happened with your parents yet, but if they were murdered—"

"Then whoever did it is willing to go to any lengths to get what they want," Ryder finished.

There was a moment of silence as Melissa considered all they had said.

"What if you had been in your office, Melissa?" Sebastian asked. "What if the intruder had found you there?"

Melissa was about to answer that she could take care of herself when Diana spoke up, "How'd they know you were gone? They timed the burglary perfectly. That would require knowledge of your whereabouts and that you had the journal with you." There was silence all around. "I need you to think about everyone who was at the hospital that night. Anyone who would have known where you were. What you were doing. Make a list of names so we can check them out."

Melissa thought back to the staff that had been present and those who had dropped by after the theft. It was easy enough to remember, but it was difficult for her to imagine that any of them might be responsible. Despite that, she said, "I can do that. But what about my parents? How will you get more info on the accident?"

Diana glanced at Ryder uneasily. "Peter Daly. He assisted me on the Williams case."

Melissa waited for Ryder's reaction, aware of his dislike for the handsome NYPD detective. His face hardened slightly and his gaze narrowed. "How do you know we can trust him? He and I are—"

"I know he had issues with you during the Williams investigation, but if I vouch for you—"

"He'll be your willing lapdog?" Ryder asked testily.

Melissa uneasily shifted her glance from Ryder to Diana, then to Sebastian as she said, "Detective Daly doesn't need to know much. Just that we want more details on the crash."

"We may not even need Daly," Sebastian added and wiggled his fingers as if he was busy typing on a keyboard. "Most records are electronic now. A little hack here, a little hack there—"

Diana angrily slashed her hand through the air. "*Hermanito*, don't even think about it."

Sebastian held his hands up in surrender. He knew his sister well enough to know she wasn't kidding. "We do it whatever way you want."

"Whatever way *I* want." Ryder slammed his hands flat on the table. "It's my secret—"

"But it's *my* parents who were possibly murdered," said Melissa as she jumped to her feet. "And it's my neck that's on the line if whoever took the journal wants more."

She looked from one person to the other, and finally to Sebastian. "So unless there's a risk that the good detective will nose around for info on Ryder, I don't see why we shouldn't ask him for help."

Melissa glanced at Ryder, but he just muttered, "I have no problems with Daly so long as he keeps out of my business."

Melissa coughed uneasily to draw attention back to herself after a too-long silence. "So we're done, right? Diana, you'll let us know when you have more news."

"And I'll get to work on the equipment and programs," Sebastian said, jumping out of his seat and grabbing Melissa's hand. "I think I owe you coffee and dessert."

* * *

Once out on the street, Sebastian took a deep breath. "It was getting a little—"

"Tense up there," Melissa said, buttoning up against the night chill and burying her hands in the deep pockets of her wool peacoat.

"Was it me, or was Ryder getting all alpha male?" Sebastian asked as they strolled westward.

Melissa rolled her eyes. "It was definitely getting run-with-the-wolves with him."

Sebastian chuckled and glanced at her out of the corner of his eye. "And you. That was pretty alpha to call the shots."

A broad smile erupted on Melissa's face. "It was, wasn't it?"

"Is Ryder generally so—"

"Jealous?" Melissa raised an eyebrow to underscore her query.

"*Sí.* Would he get, you know…all demony if Daly got in his face?" As he said it, Sebastian made a snarly face and curled his hands as if they were claws ready to scratch someone.

Melissa chuckled. "I've never seen Ryder get fangy except to feed."

"Was it weird? To see him… What's the right term? Change? Transform? Seems to me if I'm going to be dealing with this—"

"*You* don't have to deal with Ryder, Sebastian. That's my job." Clearly uncomfortable with the new direction of their conversation, she said, "You did mention dessert, didn't you?"

"I did, only I'm not really a sweets kind of guy."

She paused in her walk, forcing him to stop and face her. "That's a shame," she said.

Puzzled, he asked, "Why?"

"Because dessert is the best part of the meal. It's the reward after a hard day."

Sebastian eyed her up and down and shook his head. "No

offense, but it seems to me you don't pack away dessert all that often."

Melissa examined herself, beginning with the coat she wore. She realized for the first time that it hung loose on her. It had fit just right when she had bought it, but that had been before the death of her parents. Before her world had gone topsy-turvy. Meeting Sebastian's gaze, she said, "You're right. It's been a long time since I've had the leisure of getting dessert. Or being able to take long walks with nowhere to go."

He pointed at her. "Doc, don't ever let it be said you're not direct and to the point. So a mobile dessert is in order."

Melissa grabbed his finger and gave it a playful shake. "Around the block. There's a tiny coffee shop that has an awesome hot chocolate they drown with whipped cream and little drizzles of caramel."

Sebastian grinned and looped his arm through hers. "Sounds like a plan."

Sebastian was used to working alone. It went with the territory of being a computer programmer. Despite that, he had been a trifle uneasy as he set up the equipment in Ryder's office. What could he blame it on? Maybe the fact that he was alone in an apartment with a vampire?

Not that he wasn't used to working with night owls, being one himself. Only Ryder was...

A bloodsucking, possibly lethal night owl?

It was crazy, Sebastian told himself as he set up the computer and assorted peripherals so he could commence the scanning. His sister was involved with this thing and Melissa not only lived with him, but was obviously quite fond of him.

He'd wondered about Ryder for days as he worked in his apartment to create the program for saving the scanned images and made arrangements with friends to create a peer-to-peer network to securely hold all the data. He'd tried to concentrate on the technology, but in the back of his mind were questions about Ryder and his relationships with both Diana and Melissa.

Sebastian knew Diana could take care of herself, but Melissa…

Didn't need a hero, he reminded himself, recalling how capable she had been the other night.

As he kneeled beneath the desk to check the connection of the scanner to the USB port, he reminded himself that all Melissa wanted from him was his techno-knowledge. Nothing else.

"Need anything?"

Sebastian jumped up, banging his head on the bottom of the desktop. "Shit."

He eased from beneath the desk, rubbing his head as he glared at Ryder, who was standing almost on top of him. "Don't sneak up on me like that."

Ryder stepped away. "Not sneaking. I knocked. Repeatedly."

Sebastian crammed his hands into his jeans pockets and rocked back and forth on his heels. "Yeah, well. I didn't hear you."

Ryder narrowed his gaze. "You're uncomfortable around me, aren't you?"

Evasion was not one of Sebastian's traits. "You might say that."

Ryder gave an amused smile and sat down on the sofa at the far end of the room. "There's no need to worry. I don't bite humans."

"You bit my sister," Sebastian challenged. He leaned against the edge of the desk and tried to adopt a nonchalant stance.

"She told you about that?" There was a hint of surprise in Ryder's voice.

"We're close. Have been since before *Papi* was killed."

Ryder rubbed his index finger across his lip as he considered the young man across the room from him. He'd sensed something between Sebastian and Melissa and had worried about it.

Sebastian was too young, with a rebelliousness that normally boded ill. Despite that, he'd helped when called upon and Ryder had no doubt Diana strongly believed in her brother. Melissa also had clearly developed feelings for him. Feelings that could not only cause her a great deal of pain, but could place her in danger if she trusted this child to keep her safe.

Child. It was the only way Ryder could think of Sebastian, given the age difference between them and the differences in their life experiences.

"Melissa and I are close," Ryder said. He was unprepared for what came next.

Sebastian skewered Ryder with his gaze. "Do you love her?"

Ah, so he has feelings for Melissa, as well. "I do. As a friend. As a sister. As my companion."

"Your companion," Sebastian said with a strangled laugh. He walked across the room to stand directly before Ryder. "She's trapped by that and by the loyalty she feels toward you."

Ryder didn't need to be reminded. Melissa had confessed as much to him. It had come as a shock that she felt so differently from all the Danverses before her. Or maybe they had all felt the same, but lacked the courage to say it. He'd borne that guilt for months now and had told himself he was capable of dealing with it. Until now.

"She's free to go when she wants," he growled.

Sebastian surprised him again. He squared his shoulders and stood up to Ryder. "She won't go until you set her free."

They stood there nearly nose to nose for several seconds until Sebastian finally stepped away.

"I need to get some other equipment. I'll be back later." He walked out the door.

Ryder watched him go. There was no hint of his having tucked his tail and run. On the contrary, there was a swagger that said Sebastian had no problems with standing up for what he believed.

Ryder had to admire him for that. He also had to admit that he might be wrong about whether Sebastian was right for Melissa.

But Sebastian was definitely wrong about one thing. It wasn't Ryder who had to set Melissa free. That was something she had to do herself.

As Ryder left the room and returned to his floor of the duplex it occurred to him that Sebastian could provide the goading Melissa needed to do it.

Amazingly the thought didn't displease him the way he thought it would have.

Chapter 6

She'd made a list.

She'd checked it twice.

She didn't know who'd been naughty, only who'd been nice.

The problem was, those who'd been nice might have been the ones who'd been the most naughty.

Melissa hated having to second-guess everyone's motives. It wasn't in her nature to question what was behind someone's actions or whether she was misreading a glance or an errant look. With as much time as she spent in the hospital, having to wonder about each of her co-workers was creating quite a strain.

Tossing the list onto her desk, she closed her eyes and leaned back in her chair, once again going over the events of the night the journal was stolen. Where she had been and whom she had seen. How long she'd been in the E.R. and after, what she recalled from her walk back to her office and the discovery of the theft. As it had every other time, the same list of names came up. Number one on that hit parade was her friend Sara, the nurse in charge of her floor.

Sara had been on duty that night and free when Melissa had been called to the emergency room. She'd been on the floor when Melissa had returned from the E.R. and had come by immediately after the theft to offer her help. Had her offer been a smokescreen to throw Melissa off?

Although Melissa wasn't one to normally plug into the hospital grapevine, she'd done so the last few days and discovered a great deal. Gossip said that Sara had been working a ton of extra hours, but no one knew why. Only that Sara needed the money.

Tony, the muscle-bound security guard who had been with Melissa in her office, had supposedly been tossed out of some kind of competition for testing positive for steroids. Melissa knew little about Tony other than that he had always been unflaggingly polite and helpful. As for his purported steroid use, the grapevine hinted that he had passed the random drug tests done by the hospital. Nevertheless, the rumors made him a possible suspect. Who knew if he could trade the prescription medicines stolen from her office for the steroids he needed to bulk up?

There had been a few other orderlies and nurses there that night, along with her father's old friend, Dr. Edward Sloan, but overall, it was a rather short list. And she wanted to take her friend Sara off of it.

Sara came from a tough neighborhood on the Upper East Side and had risen from poverty the hard way by doing a stint in the Army that had taught her the basics of being an EMT, and later had helped pay for a nursing degree. Melissa knew Sara had been trying to move her family to a better area. Maybe that was why she needed cash.

Being her friend, Melissa could probably come right out and ask, only Sara was prideful about certain things, money being one of them. Melissa had it and Sara didn't. That was always a source of conflict between them. Was it enough of an issue that Sara would steal or deal drugs to balance the scales? And why would she take the journal?

It left a sour taste in her mouth as she scooped her list of names off her desk and stuffed it into her lab coat pocket. Taking a look at her watch, she realized it was time for her last rounds before going home.

To most people, home was a sanctuary where they could escape the grind of their daily lives. For Melissa, it just meant a different kind of grind except…

Sebastian might be there. He'd been around the last few days; busy wiring and setting up equipment. So far with her schedule, it had been easy to avoid him, but now that it was her turn for some midday shifts, they might finally run into one another. She was still conflicted about whether that might prove difficult…or decidedly interesting.

The door to the women's locker room was ajar.

Melissa caught sight of Sara, who looked around before stuffing something into a knapsack. The knapsack tipped over and two blood bags spilled onto the floor. Sara quickly scooped them up and jammed them back into her bag.

Melissa pushed through the door.

Sara whirled, a look of worry on her face that turned to a broad smile as she recognized her friend. "Whew, you scared the crap out of me."

"Worried?" Melissa asked, trying to appear nonchalant while angry that she'd now have to move Sara back to Number One on her list of suspects.

Determined to find out what was going on with her friend, Melissa entered the combination on her lock, but kept an eye on Sara to see if any other interesting things fell out of her knapsack. Like the stolen journal.

Sara nodded and turned back to her locker. "Just spooked since the other night."

Melissa took off her white coat and hung it up, pausing to slip the suspect list into her knapsack. She glanced at Sara, who was easing off her nurse's scrubs and tossing them into the laundry basket. Her friend seemed calm and no longer worried. Had she misread Sara's actions? Could there be some logical reason for her to be taking the blood?

Like the reason you do? an annoying voice in her head challenged.

"Were you on the floor when it happened?" Melissa asked as she, too, slipped off her hospital garb and pitched it into the hamper.

"I was with a patient. They'd buzzed me about some pain, so I had to call the resident," Sara began, part of her explanation muffled by the shirt she was putting on over her head. "You know, I thought I heard something, but it wasn't all that loud. And I didn't see anyone come down the hall from the elevator, so I guess they used the stairs."

Melissa reached for her oxford shirt. "Sounds like they had it all planned out."

Sara shook her head. "But we were around. We were sure to see them unless... Maybe they wouldn't have taken a chance if they saw someone on the floor. Maybe they would've just gone to another office."

"Or maybe they would have hurt someone? Is that why you were spooked before?" Melissa offered, hoping to find some reason for Sara's furtive actions.

"*Sí*," Sara answered and gripped the edge of her locker with one hand, facing Melissa. "I've been working a lot of hours. If I can't be safe here..."

"Is everything okay?"

"*Mami* hasn't been well." Sara's face grew hard and unreadable, her motions slightly flustered. "I'd rather not talk about it." As they both finished dressing, she remained silent.

As they walked out of the locker room together, Melissa didn't press, sensing Sara's unease. When they neared the elevator bank, Melissa laid her hand on Sara's arm and said, "If you need to talk, if there's anything I can do to help, just let me know."

Sara gave Melissa a tired smile. "Thanks for the offer, but you can't even begin to guess the half of it."

Melissa considered the possibility that she knew exactly what was up with Sara, but she said nothing else. It was safer to go to the source, for if there was one person sure to know more about other vampires and their keepers, it was Ryder.

The journal flew across the room and hit the wall with a dull, but satisfying, thud.

Useless. Totally useless.

The Danvers clan had apparently been guarding some kind of secret for a long time, only this journal hadn't provided any information on the nature of their clandestine duties or how those duties tied into Frederick Danvers's recent experiments.

Another lab rat had died. Just one more rat to go and there was still nothing to keep the cell strain going. Nothing to give a clue as to how to activate the frozen samples.

It was risky to try anything else right now. Security had been tightened at the hospital and the surveillance of Melissa's office had revealed nothing. If she had other journals, she wasn't endangering them by bringing them to the hospital.

Which meant she might have them at home. Only a home intrusion posed many increased risks, including injury to the inhabitants. Not that collateral damage of that kind was a problem, but if Melissa was the last Danvers with knowledge of the secret, the risk of losing her was too extreme. At least for now.

There was one lab rat and a fresh supply of human blood to inoculate with the cell strain. Maybe this time it would take.

Chapter 7

"Are you sure it was a blood bag?"

Melissa dragged a hand through her hair. "As sure as I could be without checking her knapsack." With an exasperated sigh, she continued, "Is she like me? A keeper? It would make sense, wouldn't it? As a nurse, she knows a lot of medical stuff. She could take care of needs like yours."

"Possibly." Ryder lowered his gaze as if further considering her question.

Diana, who was perusing the list Melissa had given her earlier, jumped in with, "Sara Martinez. It's a common name. Anything else you can give me? Birth date? Social Security Number?"

"We're both Virgos. I think she was born on August 27th."

"Virgos, huh? That makes you headstrong and intelligent. And would it be so bad if you had fellow-keeper company?" Sebastian asked.

Ignoring him, Melissa shot up off the sofa and paced a step

or two before facing Ryder and Diana. "So is it possible? Could Sara be a keeper like me?"

"I know there are other vampires, but I don't know who they are or where they are."

Melissa examined him, trying to figure out how he could be so damn complacent about this. But she saw that while his tone sounded relaxed, he tapped his closed fist against the arm of the sofa in a nervous gesture. "How could you *not* know?"

To stop the growing tension between Melissa and Ryder, Sebastian quipped, "It's not like there's some secret organization like VLAD, Melissa."

"VLAD?" She faced him, a confused look on her face.

"*Sí.* Vampires, Lycanthropes And Demons. Get it? VLAD. Like the Impaler." He made a staking motion with one hand.

It brought a small smile to Melissa's lips and dragged a strangled chuckle from Diana.

"Is it possible that your father knew somehow? Maybe he figured out what Sara was up to? Confronted her about it?" Ryder asked, completely ignoring Sebastian's attempt at humor.

Melissa seated herself on the arm of the sofa, so close Sebastian could smell her perfume, a scent with a hint of lilacs. So close he could detect the tightness of her body as she answered, "My father was kind of old-fashioned that way. He was a doctor. She was a nurse. There was no reason for him to get to know Sara."

"But maybe she knew about him," Ryder replied. "Maybe she wanted something from him."

"What?" Melissa pressed, her hands fluttering in the air with her distress.

"Information she obviously didn't get," Sebastian supplied. Then he asked Diana, "Are we sure someone killed Melissa's parents? There's no room for doubt about that?"

"None. The copies of the reports Peter Daly got for me show gross errors during the initial investigation." She turned her attention to Melissa. "Is there anything else you can think of—"

"Nothing, but maybe there's more in my father's journals. Maybe I should get started there instead of with the older ones."

"Not without some safeguards," Ryder advised and looked across the small distance to Sebastian, pinning him with his gaze. "Are you ready to get started?"

Sebastian sat up straighter and squared his shoulders, bracing himself for anything else Ryder might say. "I finished all the programming and setup this afternoon. We can scan tonight if you'd like."

"The sooner, the better," Ryder confirmed.

"I need a break and even though I'm not really hungry, I need some dinner. After that, Sebastian can get started. Once he's done with Father's first journal, I'll start reviewing it to see if I can make sense of what was going on."

Diana's stomach grumbled noisily and she placed a hand over her midsection to quiet the rumble. "My stomach seconds the dinner plan."

Some of the earlier tension dissipated as the talk turned to routine things.

Ryder offered, "Chinese? Now that it's dark, Diana and I can go pick up something while Sebastian scans."

"Sounds good. Make mine Kung Pao Chicken, very hot," Melissa said.

"Like it spicy, do you?" Sebastian teased, and a gleam entered his eye to let her know food was the last thing on his mind.

Business only, Melissa thought. Only something inside made her want to shock him. Grinning boldly, she answered, "The hotter, the better."

Sebastian worked as quickly and efficiently as one of his fancy computers, Melissa thought as she occasionally looked up from the older journal she was reading. There didn't appear to be a wasted action as he placed her father's first journal on the flatbed scanner and methodically digitized the pages. The first volume was a slim one and Sebastian was halfway through it by the time Diana and Ryder returned with dinner.

By tacit agreement, the conversation during the meal stayed away from their investigations. Anyone eavesdropping on their dinner would never have thought anything out of the ordinary was going on. It could have been a double date, without the fear of murder and mayhem looming over their heads.

After dinner Diana returned to her office to get some second opinions from her staff, and Ryder, sensing he was no longer needed or wanted, excused himself.

"Do you mind if I change into something more comfortable?" Melissa asked. When Sebastian grinned at her, she blushed hotly. "As in sweatshirt-and-pants kind of comfortable, and *does your mind always have to be in the gutter?*"

Sebastian raised his hands in surrender. "Sorry, but the cliché was too much to resist."

"Well, try. This is supposed to be business." Although she was having serious doubts about her own abilities to resist his charm and keep to the agreement.

"Yep, just business. So go get comfortable—" he did a Groucho Marx kind of eyebrow wiggle "—while I scan away."

Despite her better judgment, his actions dragged a laugh from her. She playfully jabbed him in the arm and retired to her bedroom to change.

Quickly slipping into sweatpants and a T-shirt, she returned to Ryder's office, where Sebastian was now three-quarters of the way through the journal. Melissa held up another diary—the next one by the second Danvers—and asked, "Mind if I keep reading this in here until you're done?"

Without shifting his gaze away from the monitor or breaking the rhythm of his work, Sebastian inclined his head in the direction of the couch in the office. "Make yourself at home."

Home. As she settled herself onto the leather couch and pulled a light throw over her legs, she did feel homey with Sebastian in the room.

What did he think of everything that was going on? Would he be glad to be done with his end of it? Would he volunteer for something else or go his own way, much as he seemed to do with everything in his life? It saddened her to think he would leave without a second thought.

As he lifted his gaze, it collided with hers. She guiltily shifted her attention back to the journal, telling herself to concentrate. She wasn't sure whether she'd read the page before, so she began again.

And again and again. She yawned, the dinner and comfort of the couch making her sleepy. She battled drowsiness, but it was a losing fight. Closing her eyes, she told herself it would only be a quick nap.

At the speed Sebastian was going, he'd soon be done with the first of her father's journals. She counted on him to wake her so she could get to work and find a cure for Ryder, or at least find out if she had some keeper company.

Chapter 8

Sebastian slipped the last pages of the journal onto the bed of the scanner. With a few keystrokes, he imported the image into his program, then named, encrypted and saved the document to a disk located at a remote server.

Done, he thought and looked in Melissa's direction to see if she was ready for the next journal.

She clearly was not.

He slowly rose from Ryder's chair and padded quietly across the room. Placing the journal he had just finished on the coffee table, he knelt by the edge of the sofa.

She looked younger while she slept, but there were still smudges of dark circles beneath her eyes, a testament to the fact that she had not been resting well. Who could? he thought and delayed waking her, content to sit there and observe her for a moment. He was feeling decidedly guilty about having to pull her from what was probably a well-deserved rest.

Her lips formed a smile. He itched to trace the edges of it, remembering another slumbery one the morning after their sole night together. Their amazing night together.

Down boy, he told himself. It was just business.

He was about to reach out and wake her when she chuckled, surprising herself out of sleep.

Her eyes, a deep midnight highlighted with brighter bits of aquamarine, slowly opened. When she saw him there, her smile grew wider. "I was a little tired," she said in soft husky tones.

Sebastian brushed back a lock of hair that had fallen onto her forehead. "You laughed in your sleep. Something funny?"

"VLAD."

He snatched his hand back, obviously surprised. "VLAD? As in—"

"Vampires, Lycanthropes And Demons." Melissa sat up and stretched. "I thought it was funny."

Sebastian tried his best not to notice how the soft fabric of her pastel pink T-shirt clung to her curves and rode up with her stretch to expose the taut muscles of her midriff. Get your mind elsewhere, he warned himself. "Ryder clearly didn't think so."

Melissa shrugged. "Ryder needs to lighten up. Lose that broody immortal act."

It was Sebastian's turn to chuckle. "Give Diana time. I'm sure she'll shake him up."

Melissa rested against the arm of the sofa. "I guess all I've seen is FBI Agent Diana. It's hard for me to see her as—"

"A wild and crazy kind of girl?" Sebastian glanced her way. "I'm sorry again. I know it couldn't have been easy to hear Diana tell you about your parents tonight."

Another shrug, only this time she wrapped her arms across her midsection, belying her unease. "Thanks. This may sound weird, but I wasn't feeling sad. It kind of made me angry."

Sebastian sat next to her on the couch. "Care to explain?"

"When they died the first time, I was angry. At myself for not calling the police right away. At the weather and God and even at my parents. Especially my parents."

Sebastian could understand the anger, having lived through it himself when his father died. "Unresolved issues."

A confused look crossed Melissa's face. "How—"

"My dad was killed in a drive-by shooting when I was eighteen. We hadn't really had a good relationship."

Melissa reached out and covered his hand. He was surprised by her actions, but when he faced her, her gaze was tender. "*I'm* sorry."

He smiled tightly. "So why the anger again?"

"Because whoever killed them robbed me of the chance to settle things between us. To maybe make things right," she admitted with no hint of evasion.

Another first. From her touch to her being open with him, this was something new. Something… He stopped there, because this something was supposed to be all about business. Only sitting here, holding her hand and talking with her was definitely about something more. He liked it and wanted to keep the conversation going. "I felt the same way. Like there was so much more I could have said to my dad. So much more I could have done to make him proud of me."

"He'd be proud of you now." Melissa gently squeezed his hand as if to reassure him.

When Sebastian met her gaze, Melissa realized he didn't agree with her assessment. It was almost a repeat of the other night when he'd left her on the balcony and she wondered what could have made Sebastian so uncertain of his worthiness.

As if you don't know, a little voice in her head challenged, reminding her of her own failed relationship with her father.

"You don't know me all that well, yet," he said, but there was a hint of both challenge and jest in his tone.

"Not yet," she replied. "But there's time."

"Definitely." He grinned and a deep dimple formed on one side of his face. "So this isn't business, but I like it."

So do I, Melissa thought, but couldn't admit it just yet.

"Well, people have friends at work. Friends they talk to about things. So why can't we be like those kind of friends?"

Sebastian narrowed his eyes. His grin grew broader as he pointed at her. "I've been a bad influence on you, haven't I? Admit it."

She grabbed his finger and gave it a teasing pull. "I'll admit it on one condition."

"Shoot. What do you want?"

"Why'd you cut your hair?"

A simple enough question, but with an answer too complex to explore right now, Sebastian thought. With a shrug he replied, "Remember those unresolved Dad issues? Just trying to look respectable."

Melissa reached out and ran her fingers through the longer strands at the top of his head. He smelled the clean scent of her, and desire jumped to life. He fought it down, but it wasn't easy.

"I liked it long and I liked the T-shirts and other stuff."

Sebastian glanced down at the neatly pressed dress shirt he wore, another concession to what he thought would be considered respectable. "Boring much?"

"Boring," she agreed with a small nod.

"So I can go back to being disreputable Sebastian."

"You can go back to being you."

"Me, huh?" Inside there was surprise, confusion and wait… What was that? Was it pride? Maybe even self-confidence and happiness? Grinning broadly so that it almost hurt, he said, "I kind of like this work-friends thing."

There was a slightly confused but happy expression on her face as she admitted, "So do I, only…I guess it's time I tackled that journal."

Leaning forward, Sebastian snagged the book from the coffee table where he had left it earlier and handed it to her. "Nap time's over."

She grabbed the book from him. "Slave driver."

Chuckling, he rose and glanced down at her. She looked good enough to kiss, only work friends didn't kiss, did they? So he forced himself to move away from the sofa and back to Ryder's desk to start the next book.

While he scanned, he battled the need to look her way. So she liked his longer hair and preferred his T-shirts? But thinking about all they had revealed to each other tonight was dangerous because…

Überanal Doctor Melissa didn't do bad boys. Only, she had already *done* him and liked it.

She *had* liked it, he thought with a grin, and while he scanned, he considered which T-shirt he might wear tomorrow. And how long it would take for his hair to grow out 'cause maybe Good Girl Melissa might consider a repeat performance with Bad Boy Sebastian.

Sebastian wasn't feeling quite as positive after three days of scanning with no sign of Melissa. Rumor had it that she was having an exceptionally rough time at the hospital, which slowed her review of the journals. So Ryder had taken over the task for the last few nights.

Sebastian, however, was wondering if Melissa had reconsidered her earlier decision to become work friends. Was that the reason for her absence?

When Ryder strode up to the desk, surprising him, Sebastian bolted upright in his chair. Glaring at the vampire, Sebastian said, "Can't you wear a bell or something?"

"Spooked?" Ryder challenged. "Ready to call out VLAD and have my membership yanked?"

"Or maybe upgraded, because you have been just way too lurking in the shadows lately." He tried to resume his scanning, only Ryder stilled Sebastian's hand as he moved the mouse.

"Diana has more news."

Sebastian swiveled around in the chair. "Bad, I guess."

Ryder nodded, but said nothing else.

"And the journals? Anything so far?" Sebastian asked.

"Nothing."

Sebastian had been hoping for something beyond a nod or monosyllabic answer, but it was apparently not forthcoming. Clasping his hands together and adopting what he hoped was a casual stance, Sebastian glanced up at Ryder looming over him. "How's Melissa?"

"Busy."

Anger surged through him. He was struggling to locate a snappy rebuke, when Ryder surprised him by saying, "She'll be home later tonight. We need to talk about things and I'm hoping you'll hang around for that."

When he met Ryder's gaze, he saw a different look there. He couldn't quite call it welcoming—there was still something about the whole vampire thing that threw off his radar— but it was at least more friendly than before.

Or maybe Ryder was just hungry and eyeballing a prospective snack. Regardless, Sebastian wouldn't miss seeing Melissa later that night.

"I'll be here."

Chapter 9

Quitting time.

Melissa was dead tired and counting the minutes until she arrived home. Granted, Ryder had called to say a big powwow was planned, but he'd also let her know that Sebastian would be there.

Which brought a smile to her lips.

The smile didn't last as she pushed through the door of the women's locker room and encountered Sara. Uneasiness crept through her, even though Sara was a friend and had never given Melissa cause to worry—blood bags and possible theft notwithstanding.

Sara was almost finished dressing. On the small bench was her knapsack.

Melissa wondered if it contained blood bags.

"*Hola*," her friend said as she noticed Melissa approaching.

"*Hola* to you," Melissa responded, opening her locker and eyeing Sara's bag.

Sara seemed as relaxed as always as she pulled on a shirt. Momentary inspiration seized Melissa. While Sara was distracted, Melissa grabbed her bag and swung it onto the bench. Right into Sara's knapsack.

Sara's bag tipped over, spilling its contents onto the floor. Both Sara and Melissa rushed to pick up the items.

"Sorry," Melissa said. Then she noticed the two blood bags on the floor along with Sara's other things.

Sara tossed them back into the bag quickly, but gazed up at Melissa to gauge her reaction. "They were expired and put out for destruction."

Melissa crossed her arms. "People might wonder what you're doing with them."

"Maybe the same thing you are," Sara responded with a tight edge to her voice.

Nailed, Melissa thought. She'd had more than a year to prepare her excuse. "Experiments? Is that what you're doing?"

With a harsh laugh, Sara sat down hard on the bench, cradling the knapsack to her midsection while shaking her head. "You might call it that only… My mom's been sick. Real sick."

"You've brought her here for treatment, right?" What could tie Sara's mom's illness to the blood?

Closing her eyes, Sara whispered, "She's terminal. That's what they said."

Having lived with her own mother's illness, Melissa understood what Sara was going through. She sat down on the bench next to her friend and wrapped an arm around Sara's shoulders. "I'm sorry. Is there anything I can do?"

Tears slipped down Sara's face, but she wiped them away. "No. Some women in the neighborhood were talking about a man they visit to cure their ills—a *santero*. They claimed he helped them get better."

"So you went to him? To a voodoo doctor?" Melissa was surprised that someone with Sara's training would fall for the antics of a charlatan.

"Not voodoo. *Santeria*," Sara explained as if that would make all the difference in the world. "The *santero* said helping my mother would take a big offering. That a normal sacrifice wouldn't do and he needed human blood."

For feeding? Melissa wondered if this *santero* was actually a vampire like Ryder. And if he was, Sara was in for a world of hurt when her mother's cure failed—or worse if his cure was to turn her mother. Melissa gave Sara a reassuring hug. "You know it may not work. Why don't you bring your mom back here? I can talk to her doctors. See what else—"

Sara pulled away from Melissa and rose, clutching the knapsack as if it were a lifeline. "I need to try this. Even if it fails. Just like you and your dad have to do your little experiments."

Her dad's experiments? Had he used the same ruse she had when caught taking blood for Ryder? "My father? What was he working on?"

Sara shrugged. "Don't know. One day during rounds, he made a mistake. Luckily I caught it, but he was totally distracted. Said your mother was really sick again and he had to finish up his work so he could help her."

"When was this?"

Sara slipped one strap of the bag over her shoulder as she considered Melissa's question. "I'm not really sure, but I'd say a few months before the accident."

Melissa sat down heavily on the bench. Those last few months had she noticed anything different about her father? She came up blank.

"You okay?"

Sara's concern was evident on her face. Melissa had no doubt it was genuine; she could take Sara off the list of suspects. Rising, Melissa hugged the other woman. "Promise me that if your *santero* turns out to be a quack, you'll bring your mom in to see me."

"Promise," Sara replied. Then she walked out of the room,

leaving Melissa to wonder just what her father had been up to and whether it had anything to do with Ryder.

Melissa's head ached from all the assorted facts and questions Diana had raised during their little briefing. "So bottomline it," she said curtly, eager to add the information she had gleaned today from her friend.

"There's a gap of a few hours between when your parents gassed up the car an hour from home and when they died. Where were they?" Diana tossed the question out for consideration to everyone as they sat around the kitchen table once more.

"Dinner?" Sebastian leaned his arm across the back of Melissa's chair. Surprisingly there was something comforting about that gesture, Melissa thought.

"No credit card receipts, although they could have paid cash. Only, they had taken a break for lunch right before they stopped for gas. We were able to trace that credit card charge," Diana explained.

"A friend's house?" Ryder said, and glanced at Melissa.

"They didn't mention stopping anywhere and as for friends, there are a few in the area."

"I'll need the names," Diana said, and passed her pad and pen to Melissa.

Rubbing her forehead, Melissa asked, "What about the other names?"

Diana shook her head. "Nothing really, except Edward Sloan has something funny in his history. I have one of my people checking it out further."

As Melissa wrote down the names of her parents' friends, she wondered what could be so odd about Edward's past. Her father and Sloan had known each for as long as Melissa could remember. Since the deaths of her parents, Edward had been a mentor of sorts. He had been one of the first people by her office after the break-in.

Diana sneaked a peek at the names Melissa had written before continuing, "All new people, so no possible connection with those at the hospital. Seems like we're running into a bunch of dead ends here."

"Not really," Melissa blurted out.

Everyone looked at her and she told them about her discussion with Sara. About the possibility that her father had been conducting experiments of some sort in an effort to help her mother.

Sebastian rubbed her back in a comforting gesture and Melissa shot him a grateful smile before her gaze settled on Ryder. "Anything in the—"

"Nothing in the journals so far. Although I think you should read them for yourself. Maybe there's something there that I'm missing."

"Or maybe the information is in a later journal. Maybe Melissa should take a look at one of those," Sebastian suggested.

Ryder nodded and Diana echoed his agreement. "That makes the most sense. If your dad was conducting experiments of some kind, maybe they had something to do with his murder."

"But why kill my mother, too?" The pitch of Melissa's voice rose with her agitation. "Why her? Or was it just a case of being in the wrong place at the wrong time?"

Sebastian laid his hand over hers and continued to rub her back. "We'll know soon, Melissa. And whoever did it will pay for what they did."

Melissa didn't feel quite as confident. The killer had managed to hide his original crime for more than a year. They were only a little closer today to finding out who it was than they had been days ago. Dejection threatened to overwhelm her. The stress of not knowing was taking its toll. Physically and mentally.

She had to do more. She rose from the table and said, "So what do we do next?"

Sebastian watched as Diana and Ryder exchanged an uneasy glance. Finally Diana said, "We keep investigating. Eventually we'll get a break."

"Right," Melissa replied, and Sebastian suspected she

wasn't convinced by his sister's optimism. "I guess I should tackle the more recent journals. I'm going to dig them out so Sebastian can scan them first."

She hurried from the kitchen, which in the past week had become command central. After she had gone, Sebastian said, "How long before we get a break? It doesn't seem like she can take much more."

"She can handle it as long as she has us," Ryder said. "As long as she knows she's not alone in this."

Diana placed her hand on Ryder's shoulder. "It's a lot for her to deal with."

Ryder twined his fingers with hers. "She'll deal."

He surprised Sebastian by looking his way and asking, "Right?"

Again Sebastian didn't know quite what to think of Ryder's words. Were they a challenge to or an acceptance of Sebastian's role in all that was happening? Squaring his shoulders, he replied, "She'll deal with us beside her."

"Then it's settled," Ryder said.

Diana kissed Sebastian's cheek then whispered in tones low enough so only he could hear, "*Hermanito*, be sure of what you're doing."

He knew she was concerned and meant well, but her comment made him wonder. Did his sister worry he was not up for the task? Perhaps she thought he might not be strong enough to face the coming adversity, much as *Papi* might have doubted him.

Shaking his head to drive away those thoughts, Sebastian waited for his sister and her vampire lover to leave the room. How did she deal with it? With Ryder and what he was? With the risk that went with it?

The answer nagged him as he walked out of the kitchen and back to Ryder's office.

She can deal with it because she's a better man than you.

Chapter 10

"Rest," he said, easing the journal out of Melissa's hands.

"Ryder said—"

Sebastian laid a finger on her lips to silence her. "It makes sense to read the later journals, which you've been so kind as to identify and leave for me to scan. So I'll scan and you rest."

A small smile spread beneath his index finger before Melissa eased back into the cushions of the sofa. "You can be very demanding at times."

It took all his willpower not to lean over and kiss her smile away. Put those luscious lips to better use. Fighting back a groan, he said, "I'll wake you when I'm done."

"You'll wake me in an hour whether or not you're done." She snuggled deeper into the cushions of the sofa and pulled a throw over her legs.

"Now who's being demanding?" he said with a smile.

He liked the way she seemed able to let loose with him. As he had a few nights ago, he turned his attentions to safeguarding the journals while keeping an eye on Melissa. As she had a few nights ago, she fell asleep within minutes.

He wondered if it was some trick they taught you in medical school. After all, residents worked wickedly crazy hours and any free time for sleep was precious and not to be wasted.

Time being a finite thing for most people, unlike it was for Ryder....

Sebastian wondered about Ryder's existence before Diana had come into the picture. Had his life been fulfilling with only the Danvers family as his support? Sebastian didn't doubt Melissa's affection for Ryder. Even if she hadn't made it clear to him, he'd seen firsthand how committed she was to the vampire and how even before the deaths of her parents, she had viewed him as part of her family.

Which made him wonder about the kind of man Frederick Danvers had been. Especially considering he had ignored a daughter as beautiful and intelligent and loving as Melissa. Could he have been as distant and intolerant as his own father, or possibly worse?

As Sebastian looked over at Melissa, he pitied the child who hadn't been loved and the young woman who'd had her life stolen from her. But Melissa wouldn't want his pity, and as for his love...

Despite what had recently happened between them, Melissa had made it clear that her life had no place for love or for a normal man like him.

That was a shame, he told himself as he reached for the journal, eager to be finished with his task. The quicker he was done, the quicker he could get her out of his mind—or find a way to convince her that she was wrong. Maybe there was a place for him.

And if there was, could he be strong enough for her? If not, he had to gracefully extricate himself from her life. He refused to consider that it would be much a much harder job to yank her out of his heart.

* * *

The hallway was long and narrow. Dimly lit by bare bulbs in industrial-style sconces on the walls.

She inched along slowly, keeping one hand on the rough concrete surface of the walls as if to keep touch with reality.

The sound of her own breathing was rough, bouncing off the corridor and echoing loudly. Her foot caught on something, and the sound of her slipper was a loud zip that stopped her in her tracks.

Melissa's heart beat so loudly in her head that she couldn't hear anything else. She waited for her father to open the door to the lab at the end of the hallway, but the door remained closed. Taking a deep breath, she moved onward, farther into the main wing of the house.

She crept forward until she was almost to the door, but then paused as something dark and slick slid from beneath the edge of the wood. It looked too much like blood, only there was so much of it. It ran around the edges of her pale pink slippers with the little yellow flowers that Uncle Ryder had bought her.

The door flew open, revealing her father in a bloodied lab coat, his normally precise hair in disarray. He held his hands over something on a table. Something that shifted for a moment before opening and sending a torrent of blood onto the floor toward her.

She began to scream....

Sebastian grabbed her gently as she bolted upright on the sofa, breathing hard, the remnant of her scream still ringing in the air.

The door to the office flew open.

Ryder stood in the doorway, naked except for a pair of boxers, his hands clenched at his sides. "Melissa, are you okay?"

His question was followed by the sound of hurried footsteps. Diana came to the doorway in a robe that had been hastily tossed on and her Glock drawn for defense. She glanced uneasily at Ryder. "How'd you do that? One second you were there and the next…"

Ryder shrugged. "I don't know. I just heard Melissa and reacted."

"Like The Flash?" Sebastian prompted, but didn't wait for Ryder's reply. He gentled his hold on Melissa, slipping his arms around her shoulders.

Melissa shot him a grateful smile. "Thanks, but I'm okay. It was just a nightmare. A weird one."

Ryder took a step into the room. "Do you need—"

Diana laid a hand on his arm and prevented him from going any farther. "I think things are under control here. On the other hand, you and I need to discuss your little disappearing act."

"But—"

"*Now*, Ryder. *Por favor.*"

Sebastian could tell Ryder was uneasy about leaving them, but acquiesced to Diana's request. Of course, not before shooting Sebastian a warning glare.

Once the door to the room closed, Sebastian reluctantly released her. "Are you sure you're fine? That was one hell of a scream."

Sighing, Melissa dragged her hands through her hair and leaned back. "I'm fine. I guess all this tension led up to the nightmare."

"Want to talk about it?" He sat next to her and draped his arm across the back of the sofa. As Melissa settled into his side, he hesitated before moving his arm down and wrapping it around her.

Melissa took a moment to appreciate so many things: the warmth of his body close to hers; the smell of him, still fresh after a long day; the comfort of his embrace. The last still confused her, and for a moment she pondered whether to tell him about the dream. Maybe doing so would lessen the fear factor and keep it from coming back.

In soft and sometimes hesitant tones, she gave him the details of the nightmare. He patiently listened, not interrupting her until she got to the end. "I never really had nightmares as a child. After finding out about Ryder…" She hesitated. "Nothing like this one."

"Maybe the business about your parents' deaths and the journals made it happen."

"Maybe," was all she said and snuggled deeper into his side.

He was quiet for a little while, but then he asked, "Do you think it was something real that happened? Something that scared you as a child?"

She tried to remember. Her father had once had a small lab at home. He'd spend long hours down there. Especially when her mother was going through one of her "bad spells," as the household staff used to call them.

As a child, Melissa hadn't understood the toll her mother's anemia took on her family. All she'd known was that during those times she was supposed to play quietly and stay away from her mother so she could rest.

As a doctor, Melissa had learned how anemia could rob a person of strength and cause debilitating pain. But even with that knowledge, it hadn't made it easier to understand her mother's remoteness and absences, which lingered well after her mother was over one of her spells. And as for her father…

"Whenever Mother was really ill, Father would go into his lab. By the time I was older, we'd moved and Father would work in his lab at the college. I don't remember anything out of the ordinary."

Sebastian squeezed her arm reassuringly. "Was your mother always sick?"

"My father met her when he was a resident. She'd come for treatments. The beautiful but dying patient fell in love with the brilliant young doctor, like in one of those grand love stories."

The pain in her words was impossible to ignore, Sebastian thought. For Melissa there had been nothing grand, and apparently very little love from two people self-absorbed with

each other and with the illness that had brought them together. Sebastian even suspected Ryder had had little to do
with the Danvers family except for his obvious involvement
with Melissa. "I'm sorry," he said.

She yanked away from him and shifted to the far end of
the sofa. "Don't you dare pity me, Sebastian Reyes. That's the
last thing I want from you."

Sebastian shook his head and sighed harshly. "Melissa.
Querida. I can never figure out what you want from me. First,
it's just business. Then, it's just friends. And now—"

She shut him up by kissing him. Her brain at that moment
wasn't working very fast and she couldn't think of any other
way to counter everything she was feeling right now. Of avoiding that she needed some from-the-soul admission from him.
She only knew that if she didn't kiss him at that moment…

And, dear Lord, was she thankful she did.

He brought his arms around her back, reached up and dug
one hand into her hair to keep her mouth tight to his as the
kiss went on and on. The kiss intensified as she met his mouth
over and over again, managing to draw a breath every now and
then to counter the dizzying effect.

When he slipped down to lie on the couch, she went with
him, settling her body against the length of his. She joined him
in the deepest and slowest of kisses until her body was shaking and just kissing him wasn't enough.

She broke away, her breath ragged as she glanced down at
him. "Touch me, Sebastian."

Chapter 11

He grinned and in his unpredictable and unrepentant way, said, "I'd thought you'd never ask."

He grasped her waist with his hands, tenderly urged her to straddle him, then covered her breasts with his hands.

There was nothing playful about the way he looked at her. Touched her. He cupped her until her nipples peaked against the soft cotton of her T-shirt. Grasping each hardening tip between his thumb and forefinger, he applied gentle pressure until she moaned and had to move against him to satisfy the ache growing inside.

"Sebastian?" she asked, although she wasn't quite sure what she wanted except more of him. More of his hands and his mouth and…

He must have known what she wanted. He slipped his hands beneath the hem of her shirt, slowly eased it up and even before it hit the ground, he brought his mouth to one breast, suckled it gently while continuing to tease the other with his fingers.

Melissa moaned. She cupped the back of his head and shifted her hips, drawing herself along the hard ridge of his erection. The ache and dampness between her legs intensified as he loved her with his mouth and hands.

Her taste was so sweet in his mouth and the soft cries coming from her only made him want more. But Sebastian knew she was vulnerable right now and it wasn't just because of the nightmare. In the past week, she'd been on a roller-coaster ride of emotions and while he wanted nothing more than to make love to her, Melissa might regret anything they did tonight.

And what about you? he asked himself even as he eased off her sweats and turned their bodies until they were both on their sides, Melissa's back against the cushions of the sofa.

The honorable thing to do would be to stop, but he had to take one more taste of her nipples. It was impossible they were so delicious or that their hardness against his lips was so irresistible.

He was still telling himself one more taste when he kissed his way down her body to the juncture of her thighs. As he parted them and she shifted to lie on her back, Sebastian lost what little restraint he had left.

He only knew that he wanted to show her just how special she was. She'd had so little of that in her life.

Bending, he brought his mouth to the center of her and found the nub buried beneath the dark blond curls. With his tongue he caressed her, and as her soft cries grew louder, Sebastian sucked her swollen clitoris until Melissa raised her hips to his mouth, needing more.

Sebastian gave it to her. He slowly eased his fingers into her.

She was wet and oh so hot. He licked her as he moved his fingers in and out. Her taste was rich. The smell of her musky and enticing.

His erection tightened to the point of pain inside his jeans, and he groaned against her center as his control fled.

"Sebastian." Her insides tightened against his fingers.

"Sshh, *querida*," he said tenderly, and continued moving inside of her, drawing her closer and closer to the edge.

She moved her hands down to his shoulders and entreated him to join with her, but in soft tones he urged, "Just let go, Melissa. Enjoy it, *amor mio.*"

He pressed his thumb upward into her clitoris and as his mouth sucked at her, she lost it. Clutching the hard muscles of his shoulders, she cried out her completion, shaking with the force of it.

While her body slowly relaxed, Sebastian eased up the length of her. With tenderness, he urged her to her side, cupped her breast and rode his thumb over the still hard tip of her.

Even with the remnants of her climax still washing over her, Melissa needed more. She slipped her hands down his body to the fly of his jeans, but he hurriedly stopped her. "Not yet, Melissa. Not until—"

"We know what we want? Besides sex?" she interrupted, a little confused by his sudden streak of virtue. "Then why this? Why—"

He kissed her and she could taste herself on his mouth. It was both unnerving and satisfying in a way she couldn't quite define. Just as, intelligent woman that she was, she couldn't quite define him or what was going on between them—or wasn't going on.

As he ended the kiss and eased away from her, she met his gaze. As before, there was a wealth of conflicting emotions there. They matched her own. "Thank you," she said, grateful that he somehow had a better sense of control than she did.

Funny really, since he was the rebel and she was supposed to be the one able to govern her emotions.

"You can thank me by closing your eyes and trying to get some sleep." He drew her close, wrapping one arm around her bare back while with the other he drew a throw over her naked body.

She could have argued, but she was too tired, both emotionally and physically. And it felt too right to lie beside him. Except for one thing. He had way too many clothes on.

She closed her eyes and embraced him.

Diana snuggled into Ryder's side, but the only warmth there was that of her own body. It was still one of the things she was getting used to even after months of being his lover. But his earlier disappearing act that night…"How did you do it?"

Now in the quiet aftermath of their lovemaking, she hoped he'd provide an answer. Instead, all she got was the slight tightening of his body next to hers.

"I don't know. Although I'm certain that isn't what you want to hear."

Diana cradled her head with the arm she propped on the bed. She gazed down at her lover. Her vampire lover. Raising her free hand, she laid it over the center of his chest, directly above his heart. There was a beat there. A steady beat that grew intense with their loving. A gentle and tender heart, she knew, for he loved her and cared deeply for Melissa.

But he didn't care for himself. It was the reason he knew so little about himself and others like him. "It's unfair of you to not find out, Ryder," she said. "To yourself and to Melissa."

His tension grew. It was evident in the increasing stiffness of his body beneath her hand. She wasn't surprised when he pulled away from her and slipped from the bed.

She watched as he dressed. "Where are you going?"

"To find vampire friends. That isn't going to happen during the daytime. Isn't that what you want? What you think Melissa needs? So she'll be free—"

Diana jumped out of bed. She knew his anger wasn't just about Melissa. "Ryder, I *am* free. And I've already made my choice, *mi amor.*" She raised herself on tiptoe and kissed him.

He was unyielding against her, so she deepened the pressure of her kiss and wrapped her arms around him. Slowly his tension ebbed and when it did, he said against her lips, "I wish I knew more. About myself and others. I know there are others."

It was impossible to miss the heartfelt wish in the tone of his voice. "In time, Ryder, you need to find out more. For yourself and for Melissa."

Ryder brought his arms beneath her legs and picked her up, taking her back to bed. Laying her on the dark maroon-colored sheets, he paused to admire her physical beauty, only a small part of what made him love her. "And what about for you, darlin'? Shouldn't I know it for you?"

Her smile was knowing and determined. "You know all you need to know for me, Ryder."

"And that is?" he asked as he pressed her down into the mattress.

"That I love you."

He cared for her, Sebastian thought as he held Melissa and observed her sleeping. Of course, his emotions were all wrapped up in the protectiveness he felt toward her and his fear for her safety.

Funny, he'd never thought of himself as a protector kind of guy. But that *was* what he was feeling. Not good. What if he couldn't handle the danger?

He would never be able to forgive himself if he failed her.

Better to get out now, Sebastian told himself. Before he lost his heart to her. Before her feelings for him became more than physical. He knew Melissa had suffered too much rejection in her life and he didn't want to be the cause of more.

Armed with that knowledge, he slowly moved from her side, which wasn't easy since one arm had fallen asleep beneath the slight weight of her body. She barely moved, but the throw shifted, revealing one breast, the nipple relaxed without his caresses. Full and soft, just waiting for him to…

He groaned and with a shaky hand pulled the throw over her shoulders. He would finish this night's job and leave.

Before it was too late.

Which it might be already, he realized as with every set of pages scanned he found himself looking her way and wishing things could be different. That he could be the kind of man she needed.

And not what he was.

The slight shift of his weight and the sudden chill the absence of his body brought alerted her to the fact he was leaving. She wanted to protest, but knew it was better this way. She was still too confused about all that had gone on.

As she watched him through barely opened eyes, she saw his bewilderment. Saw his longing, which tugged at her heart.

Only Melissa knew his longing was ephemeral. When all was done, his emotions might be no more than a passing fancy brought about by the weird circumstances into which they'd both been thrown. Like the last time. When Sebastian was faced with the reality that her daily existence revolved around Ryder—as it had to, she reminded herself—Sebastian would be gone.

He'd already warned her that he wasn't cut out to be a hero.

She'd already had a taste of what it was to be with him then have him leave. Their one night together had left her wondering and wishing for things that couldn't be. Tonight had her wanting even more, and she knew it would be more difficult to deal with his exiting her life once again.

And he *would* go. She didn't have whatever it took for long-term emotional involvements.

Her parents had taught her that.

So she pretended to be asleep until he was done with his work. When he came to her side to let her know he was done, she pretended that he had just woken her.

"I have to go."

She sat up, the throw tucked tight against her chest to hide her nakedness. "I know," she replied, awkwardly taking the journals he handed her in one hand while clutching the blanket with the other.

There was an uncomfortable moment when he seemed about to bend down to kiss her, but he didn't. Instead, he stood before her, ill at ease, and then gave her a curt nod. "See you tomorrow?"

"Sure," she answered readily. Too readily.

He seemed to recognize it for the lie it was. He gave her a tight smile and quickly left the room.

Melissa hugged the journals to her, telling herself that they were what was important in her life right now. Something in them might hold information about her parents' murders. Might even help her find a way to deal with Ryder's condition.

But the vague possibilities of those thoughts lacked the appeal of the very solid warmth of Sebastian's reality.

Chapter 12

The inoculation of a new rat with the unusual cell strain from the remaining Danvers rat had been a bust. Within an hour of being infected, the rat had developed high fevers that could not be controlled. Convulsions had followed and barely three hours had gone by when the new subject died from uncontrolled hemorrhaging.

Confusing, given the apparent healing properties and seeming longevity the cell strain had bestowed on the earlier subjects. Taken directly, the strain was virulent and deadly, which might prove useful in other applications.

But not now.

The current interest was in discovering how it could heal. Healing being the most imperative demand at this moment. With the failure of every other avenue of vaccination, and the final rat literally on its last legs, there were no choices left.

Unfortunately, if Melissa had other journals, she was

guarding them closely. Surveillance had shown her doing nothing other than routine hospital work.

It was time for a personal visit to see what she was up to.

The news Diana had for Melissa the next day was a mixed bag.

First, the anomaly in Sloan's history was due to a stint he had done with the National Security Agency. His records were sealed and open only to those with the highest of security credentials, leaving Diana with no way of obtaining additional information for the moment.

Second, Diana's detective friend, Peter Daly, had been able to pry from the Burglary Division the fact that they had a possible suspect in the hospital break-in. An APB had been sent out for the man and the Burglary Division would let Daly know more about him as soon as they had collared the suspect.

Last, and most important as far as Melissa was concerned, Diana had nosed around Sara's neighborhood and confirmed Sara's story about the *santero* and her mother. While the *santero*'s request for human blood was a little odd, *Santeria* was a recognized religion. Unless he violated a law, there was little they could do about him.

"So you think we can rule Sara out?" Melissa asked, gripping the phone tightly while she waited for an answer.

"There's nothing to connect Sara to this possible burglary suspect, but I would still be cautious around her."

Melissa held her breath for a moment before asking her final question. "How do we get more info on Edward? If his record is sealed—"

"Let's discuss that tonight." There was a pause and Melissa heard someone in the background, as if they had just walked into Diana's office. A second later Diana came back on the line. "I have to run. I should be at Ryder's by nine. Is that good for you?"

Melissa confirmed that it was. She'd just hung up the phone when a knock came at the door.

"Come in."

Dr. Edward Sloan stepped in, wearing a navy blue Brooks Brothers suit, starchy white shirt, and a blue-and-red striped tie. Raising one bushy gray eyebrow, he said, "I see things are back to normal after the burglary. I hope I'm not interrupting anything right now."

Melissa shrugged, uncertain of the reason for Edward's visit. "You were a great comfort that night, Edward. And it's always good to see you," she said even though the last thing she wanted was his company until she knew more.

Edward's blue eyes were alert and assessing as he sat in one of her guest chairs. "You seem worried. Was anything important taken?"

Suddenly facing the possibility that Edward had something to do not only with the missing journal, but with her parents' deaths sent a shiver of fear through Melissa. She fought down panic and forced a smile. "Turns out the only things missing were my scrip pad and some spare change for the soda machine."

"Are you sure?" His concern seemed real enough. For a moment, Melissa took comfort in it, recalling how his presence had been a balm since the crash that had killed her parents. And then she remembered that Edward was a suspect in their deaths.

"Luckily, nothing else." She grabbed a pile of papers and shuffled them, trying not to tip him off to the fact that she was unsure about him.

Edward rubbed his hands together, seemingly reassured. "Well, that's wonderful then. In the meantime, you know where to reach me."

Edward had assumed Frederick Danvers's position as chief of hematology at the hospital. In that capacity, Edward had made a point of trying to help his old colleague's daughter. In fact, he had become a mentor of sorts, guiding her through the maze of hospital politics and acting as a sounding board on some of her more complicated cases. But with doubt about Edward looming large in her mind, there was nothing her father's old friend could provide at the moment. "I know where to reach you. I just need to do a few more things so I can get some rest before being on call again."

He nodded as he rose from the chair. His movements were stiff and almost a little tenuous. "Am I glad these old bones don't have to worry about that anymore." As he turned and walked toward the door, he tossed over his shoulder, "Let me know if you need anything."

Wanting to make it seem as if nothing was out of the ordinary between them, she said, "Maybe later this afternoon you can take a look at one of my cases. I could use your help with it."

Edward favored her with a small smile. Melissa told herself it was her imagination that made it seem like a snake's sibilant smirk. "I'll be back later, then."

It was unusual for Melissa to leave the hospital for her break, but occasionally she and Sara grabbed a quick lunch together at a nearby restaurant. Sara had actually surprised her today by suggesting they go out for a bite. The outing would give Melissa time to talk with Sara away from prying eyes.

At lunch they left the hospital together and walked a few blocks to a small Mexican restaurant they both loved. After the waiter left their nachos and promised to return with their meals, Melissa mustered the courage to begin the conversation.

"How's your mom?"

"The same," Sara replied in a flat tone.

"The other day you mentioned—"

"The *santero*?" Sara shrugged and grabbed a tortilla chip loaded with cheese from the platter. "I dropped off the blood and he promised me he'd see *Mami* in a few days."

"Did you pay him anything?" If Sara had, maybe Diana's friend could investigate the man for possible fraud charges.

"He doesn't ask for any money. If you're happy with what he does, you're free to leave what you can. Money. Food. Alcohol."

Chewing on a chip thoughtfully, Melissa wondered just what kind of con the *santero* was running. Or maybe she was being cynical. Maybe he really had some kind of healing ability. Modern science occasionally failed where other kinds of alternative methods succeeded.

Her father would have tried anything to help her mother. He would have moved the earth and the sky. Although nothing in the journals suggested it, maybe her father had resorted to means as drastic as Sara's *santero*.

"You okay?" Sara laid her hand over Melissa's as if sensing Melissa's upset.

"You said my father was doing experiments. How did you know that?"

"I ran into him in the hallway once. I had a rack filled with blood samples ready to go to the lab."

"Ran into—"

"As in literally ran into." Sara made two fists with her hands and banged them together to emphasize what had happened. "My rack hit the floor along with the one your father had in his hands. Luckily none of the tubes broke, but he made a big fuss about having his samples. Said it was something he was working on and couldn't be mixed in with the patients' samples."

A sick knot formed in Melissa's stomach. There was a very short list for what might have been in those test tubes.

"Are you sure you're okay 'cause you are looking exceptionally pale."

Melissa snapped out of it, not wanting to alarm Sara. "I know what it's like to be desperate to make someone better."

"Your *mami* was sick for a long time, *verdad?*"

Melissa was about to answer when the waiter moved the almost-full plate of nachos aside and deposited their orders. The tone of the conversation had stolen her appetite, but at the enticing smells coming from the plate of quesadillas in front of her, hunger returned with a vengeance.

She picked up her fork and motioned to Sara's plate. "Eat. My mother had been sick since she was a child. She met my father when she went to the hospital for treatments. Some said it was a miracle she was alive as long as she was."

"Or that she had you. The doctors must have warned her against it," Sara interjected around her mouthful of taco.

Melissa had never considered it before, but given the severity of her mother's anemia, having a child would have been an issue. Most people would have guessed her mother had gone to the extra effort because she really wanted children, but Melissa couldn't accept that. Her mother had never had much interest in her child. And her father's attentions had always been elsewhere. Melissa had been a very distant third, or possibly fourth, considering how much time her father had given to his patients and students.

"Earth to Melissa. Come in, Melissa," Sara teased.

Melissa shook her head in self-chastisement. "It was a risk, although I never thought about it. We weren't close."

"*Mami* and me…" A wistful tone crept into Sara's voice. "It's like having a big sister. She always has time for me. Makes me laugh. Keeps me on the straight and narrow."

"That must be great. I can understand why you're willing to try anything, only… Do you think my father's experiments had anything to do with my mother?"

"Definitely. It wasn't for the hospital or his classes."

"No, not his classes." Melissa had helped her father with those labs, which all consisted of preprepared histological samples for review.

"You know, Sloan might be able to help you out," Sara said. "He and your father were tight. If there's something to know, he's the one."

Although Edward and her father had been friends, Melissa hadn't gotten the sense that they'd shared much in the months before her parents' deaths. On the contrary, at the hospital gala just a month before the crash, she'd detected almost a chill between the two men, but had written it off as due to the competitive battling that sometimes went on in hospital politics.

Since her parents' deaths, Edward had been the soul of propriety and helpfulness. "I'll see if he knows anything," she said, although with the information Diana had given her earlier that day, she wasn't sure how she'd approach her father's old friend.

It was a dumb move to visit her at the hospital, Sebastian thought. It would accomplish nothing good. But after scanning what Melissa had said was her father's last journal and tackling some of the earlier ones, he'd had enough of working and not enough of seeing Melissa.

On the short walk from Ryder's apartment, he debated the wisdom of what he was about to do. Reminded himself that the most logical thing would be to go home. His work was almost done, and after that there would be nothing else to keep him close to Melissa.

Except that since he'd left her last night, Melissa was the only thing he'd been able to think about. The realist in him said it was because of the almost painful physical condition their encounter had left him in. The romantic in him fancied the thought that they could be happy together.

To which the realist replied that all he could do was hurt her because he could never be the kind of man she needed. Melissa was a complicated woman with even more complicated needs. Needs beyond his capabilities.

To which the rebel in him said—Fuck you. Sebastian told himself the voice of the realist was just his father talking, failing to see what Sebastian was truly capable of.

Right now, with all the arguments in his head Sebastian was certain of only one thing—if he could make Melissa happy for just one moment, that was enough. Armed with that knowledge, he pulled his black leather duster tighter around him and continued his walk to the hospital.

He paused at the door for security to check him out and then strode to the hospital directory. There was a moment of pride at seeing her name posted at this prestigious hospital, where only the cream of the crop practiced.

At the nurses' station where he stopped to ask the way to Melissa's office, an attractive Latina raised her head from the chart, gave him a smile. "May I help you?"

Sebastian peered at her name tag. Sara Martinez. *The* Sara Martinez, he realized, recalling her name. "I'm looking for Dr. Danvers."

"Are you a friend?" she asked.

Was he? "Maybe more," he answered with a grin.

She responded with a broad welcoming smile of her own. "That's good. Melissa could use more friends." She leaned toward him until she could see over the top of the nurses' station. Pointing down the hall, she said, "Right at the end of that hallway. It's the first door to your left."

"Thanks."

He arrived at Melissa's office to find she wasn't alone. She was sitting on the sofa with an older man, having some kind of discussion. They failed to notice his arrival, so he tapped softly on the open door to announce himself.

There was a moment of confusion on Melissa's face, followed by a smile so warm and inviting, it sent a blast of heat through him.

"Sebastian." Melissa rose and motioned for him to enter.

The older man slowly got up from the low-lying couch. When the gentleman was standing, he held out his hand to Sebastian. "Dr. Edward Sloan. And you are?"

Ah, Sloan. The one with the missing time in his life. If that wasn't enough to give Sebastian pause, there was the man's restrained air, which bordered on hostile. He shook the doctor's hand. "Sebastian Reyes. I'm Melissa's friend."

"A friend?" Sloan questioned. He raised one gray and rather bushy eyebrow and glanced at Melissa. "This is something new, isn't it?"

Definitely hostile. Sebastian waited, almost expectantly, for Melissa's reaction.

She didn't fail him. Slipping her hand into his, she smiled at the older man. "Yes, Edward. It is. We've known each other for several months now." Melissa glanced up at Sebastian and continued, "Edward is an old friend of my father's."

He strove for the right tone. Respectful. Courteous. Even though the look the man was giving him was anything but either of those. "It's nice to meet you, sir. I'm sorry I never got to know Melissa's dad."

"So young man. What do you do?" The question was accompanied by another dose of the hairy eyeball.

"Edward," Melissa warned, but failed to dissuade the older man.

"My dear. With your parents no longer with us, I somehow feel as if—"

"It's okay, Melissa," Sebastian said and gently squeezed her hand. "I'm in computers. Security and programming, to be exact."

"Hmm. My stockbroker tells me that's a rather volatile sector right now."

Melissa stepped between the two men and motioned Edward to the door. "If you don't mind, Edward. I didn't realize how late it is. Sebastian and I need to go, and I have a few things to finish up before I leave."

With a polite incline of his head, Edward left and Melissa quickly closed the office door behind him. She faced Sebastian, a pained look on her face. "I'm sorry."

Sebastian waved off her apology. "It's okay. In a way, the old guy is right."

Melissa strode to her desk, where she shuffled a few files. "He's got no say in my personal life."

Her personal life, huh? Sebastian stood behind her, watching over her shoulder while she nervously made her piles of papers and files. "Is it personal now?"

She whirled to face him. "Don't you think? Considering how we left it."

Sebastian tucked a stray lock of hair behind her ear. "How *did* we leave it?"

"Unfinished?" She brought her hands up to nervously grip the edges of his leather jacket.

"Really? And why would you say that?" He took a step closer, forcing her to lean against the edge of her desk.

"Because as I recall, the pleasure was all mine." There was a strong stain of color on her cheeks, and he rubbed the back of his hand against that flush.

His skin was cold against her cheek, which was a good thing considering how hot she felt from his nearness. When he took yet another step closer, she was forced to sit on the edge of the desk with her legs straddling his hips. "Sebastian?"

"What do you suppose we should do about last night?" He rested both his hands along the outer slope of her thighs.

Locking her gaze with his, she said, "We take the next most logical step."

Sebastian laughed, but there was a tinge of hardness to it. "The next most logical step being sex, right? Because for good girls like you, a romp with a guy like me—"

"That's not the way it is," she said quickly.

He arched one dark brow and forced himself even tighter into the gap between her legs. For good measure, he grasped her buttocks and drew her close.

"Isn't it?" he asked at her sharp gasp of pleasure.

Chapter 13

This was truly getting interesting.

From the way this man had his hands all over her, he was quite a friend.

Or at least that's the way it appeared from the camera in the picture—the one of Melissa and her parents snapped during a hospital gala—which sat in the middle of her desk. It was in a frame like dozens of others the hospital had purchased and given out to the various attendees. Those pictures sat scattered throughout the building, gathering dust, unlike Melissa's photo, which rested in a place of honor. It was one of the few pictures of the Danvers family all together.

Swiping one of the other less-cherished photos had been easy. Inserting a fiber optic camera and then switching the frames had been a little harder. Monitoring her for nearly two months had been unbearably boring, until finally he'd stolen another journal.

And now this very fascinating development.

Melissa's friend shifted his hands back and forth along the edges of her skirt. He slipped one hand beneath its hem and moved inward while his other hand shot upward, out of camera range. It didn't take a rocket scientist to figure out the destination of that hand.

Surprising. Melissa hadn't seemed like the kind of girl to engage in a quick nooner at her desk. Or was it better to say on her desk?

Either way, this new friendship might present either fresh opportunities or additional problems.

Only time would tell. For the moment, it was time to observe. And enjoy.

Melissa clasped her legs together as Sebastian shifted his hand upward. "Please, Sebastian. Don't do this."

He stopped and cupped the side of her face with his free hand. "Why? So you can be the good girl? Say you didn't really know what you wanted?"

"Because I care, damn it. Because I want to be right with you." She pulled away from him, skirting back on the desktop.

"Right with me." Sebastian ground out the words and turned away from her, every line of his body tight with anger, but not at her. At himself. He hadn't meant it to go this way.

Facing her once more, fists clenched at his side, he said, "Would your parents have approved of me?"

"It doesn't matter what anyone thinks besides me."

She caressed his cheek. "I'm as afraid as you are, maybe more. I don't know about having a normal life. I don't know if I even can."

Covering her hand with his, he asked, "What if *I* can't?"

"Can't try?"

"Can't give you whatever you need," he answered honestly.

"Afraid I can't handle it? Well, I can," Melissa responded, even though in her heart, she wasn't sure she really could. Still, she wanted to try.

Sebastian met her gaze. Her eyes blazed bright blue with determination. Her chin tilted upward in stubborn defiance. He remembered that look well. He'd seen it the night she'd found out that her parents might have been murdered. It was her Girl Power look—the one that said, I don't need you to save me.

But he suspected that she did need him as much as he maybe needed her.

"Well?" Melissa prompted at his prolonged silence.

He liked the spunk that seemed to flare to life only around him. She needed more of that, so he said, "I can deal," and kissed her.

Sebastian picked up the picture of Melissa and her parents. Melissa had been called out of her office for a last-minute consultation, and he'd been intrigued by the photo since he'd sat down in her chair to wait for her return. He examined it carefully, wondering about the people the photographer had captured.

There was no doubting the connection between the three individuals. Frederick Danvers was in the center, with the two petite women standing before him. Most would have said Danvers looked distinguished. But there was a hint of strain evident in the furrow along his brow and in the tight set of his mouth.

Not so with the two women, who wore nearly identical smiles.

It was obvious where Melissa had gotten her good looks. Even with the stamp of illness on her persona, Elizabeth Danvers had been a beautiful woman. If not for the pallor and the frailty visible in the nearly birdlike bones of her shoulders, she would have been as stunning as her daughter.

Melissa.

Her name slipped from his mouth on a sigh, confirming to him just how bad he had it.

She was gorgeous in the photo, in a gown whose blue was

as deep as a midnight sky. It matched the jewel-like gleam of her eyes and clung lovingly to her curves. Curves more ample than she had now.

She'd lost weight in the year since the picture had been taken. The photo just confirmed the toll her parents' deaths had inflicted on her. A surge of protectiveness welled up in him again, only this time he didn't battle it. He'd made his decision to give it a go with her, in spite of his misgivings, and he wasn't going to hold back on whatever he was feeling.

As he went to return the photo, something glinted from the edge of the frame, grabbing his attention and dragging something loose from his memory. Using guarded motions so as not to tip anyone off in the event his guess was on the money, he pretended to examine the picture once more. He ran his fingers across the surface of the glass as if in a caress while tilting the frame to catch the light.

Again there came the telltale glint from one corner where the carved black wood met a chrome accent piece surrounding the inner edge. Faking a smile, he placed the frame back on the desk and rose from the chair as if he didn't have a care in the world.

Walking out into the hallway to wait for Melissa, he closed the door behind him. He glanced at his watch. Only ten minutes had gone by.

Leaning against the smooth wall, he slipped his hands into his pockets. Was he just being paranoid, or was there a fiber-optic camera worked into the frame? If he was right, what had he and Melissa mentioned during their talk? What had Melissa discussed with Diana or Ryder from her office?

He was so lost in his thoughts, that he didn't realize Melissa had returned until she stood directly in front of him, waving a hand in his face.

"Hello! Thinking much?" she teased. She was about to enter her office when he took hold of her arm and gently eased her close to him.

"I think you're being bugged," he whispered. "Just get your things so we can go home."

Melissa narrowed her eyes, silently questioning him. When she realized it was no joke, she nodded. "I'll be right back."

True to her word, she was in and out of the office in less than a minute.

Once they were on the street, Melissa asked, "What makes you think someone was spying on me?"

"I thought I saw something in the frame on your desk. The one holding the picture of you and your parents."

Melissa made a face. "I've had that frame for nearly a year. Do you mean to tell me—"

"He could have broken into your office. Or—it's a common type of frame—it would be easy to swap it out without you noticing." Sebastian realized that his long-legged stride was making Melissa have to nearly run to keep up with him so he slowed his pace.

"It would explain how they knew about the journal. Is there any way of making sure?"

Sebastian nodded and paused at the corner as traffic moved past them on First Avenue. "I can bring in my laptop and try to tap into the wireless signal."

"Why is this happening?" Shaking her head, Melissa let out a resigned, tired sigh. "What next, I wonder? Could something I'm carrying be bugged?"

He wanted to call himself a fool a thousand times over for not thinking beyond the frame in her office. "Yes. Anything new? Anything someone gave you?"

Melissa slung her knapsack from her shoulder and gave its exterior a cursory once-over. Nothing appeared to be on its surface or in the straps. Quickly rifling through it, she confirmed that it held only those things she had placed inside. "Nothing."

"Good." The light turned and they resumed their walk. "We'll talk to Diana and Ryder about this later tonight. Hungry?"

"Not really. I ate a big lunch with a friend. Mexican."

"Your friend's Mexican?" Sebastian teased.

Melissa laughed as he'd intended and playfully jabbed him in the arm. "No, the food. But of course, you knew that."

He grinned. "*Sí*, but I like seeing you smile."

"So are *you* hungry?" Melissa asked and slipped her hand into his as they ambled back to her apartment.

Sebastian glanced down at their intertwined hands and his grin broadened. "Always, but I can wait until later. Maybe you'll be hungry by then and we can grab a bite."

"It sounds like a plan."

"It definitely does."

Chapter 14

The door shut with a resounding slam that reverberated through the large open space of the living room.

Ryder stood with his back to them, arms braced on his hips as he stared at the door where Diana had just stormed out.

Melissa tossed a quick glance at Sebastian before saying, "Where do we go from here?"

Ryder whirled to face them. "We do what we had planned—"

"Up until the hacking part," Melissa finished for him.

"Diana will have a hemorrhage if we do the hacking part," Sebastian added.

Ryder glanced over his shoulder at the door. "I think she already did."

"Naw, that was just Diana working up a righteous anger," Sebastian clarified and gave a small wave with his hand. "I'm surprised you haven't seen it before."

Ryder surprised her by grinning and rubbing his ribs as if

they were sore. "Let's just say we work out her anger in a different way. Slightly painful, but more effective."

Melissa shot a glance at Sebastian, wondering what it would take to push him that far and how he would react when pushed. Would he react physically like his sister? That thought led her to images of getting physical while making up. Heat raced through her, but she fought it back. She should be thinking about the investigation.

"So if we stick to the plan—except for the hacking part that is—Sebastian will come with me to the hospital to see if I'm being bugged and try to track down the signal," Melissa said.

"And Melissa will read the entries in the last journal," Sebastian added. "Maybe there will finally be something worthwhile in that one."

Melissa nodded and finished with, "Then we can decide what to do about getting more information about Sloan."

Ryder let out a frustrated sigh and dragged a hand through his hair. "And your grand plan is for me to sit and do nothing. Day after day, I'm goddamned trapped in here. And Diana…"

"Is out there. In the dark," Sebastian said. "*Dark* being the operative word if you're a vampire, right?"

"Subtle, Sebastian. Very subtle." Ryder glanced at the door with longing. "Seems to me it *is* dark outside. Just the right time of day for a little ol' bloodsucker like me."

"I think you know where she lives."

"And works," Melissa added.

Ryder smiled. "Seems you two have everything worked out. Don't wait up."

In a blur of motion, he was out the door.

Sebastian was a little unnerved and he realized Melissa was, as well. "Not used to seeing that?"

"Not sure he's even used to it. Ever since he was hurt, it's almost like he's regressing. Like he's becoming more of a vampire."

"Why's that do you think?"

Melissa shrugged. "His life has become more isolated, for one. He's still too weak to go out except when the sun is almost totally gone. He's needed more feeding—"

"And you accomplish that how?" Sebastian was alternately intrigued and repulsed by the concept of vampire dinners, possibly even angry at the knowledge that his sister had been a snack on at least one occasion.

Melissa held her hands up to stop him from going further. "Not personally. I get expired blood bags or pick up blood from a butcher downtown."

Sebastian rubbed at one eyebrow with his index finger. "Speaking of expired blood bags. Have we eliminated Nurse Sara from the list of suspects?"

"What do you think?" Melissa leaned toward him on the sofa. She had made herself "comfortable" again, this time in charcoal-gray yoga pants and an oversize maroon T-shirt.

Shifting closer to her on the sofa, he cradled her cheek. "I think suspect *numero uno*, and possibly only, is your Doctor Sloan."

Melissa's brow furrowed as she considered his comment. He soothed the lines there with a finger. "No more thinking, Melissa. It's time for a little R & R."

"Rest and relaxation?" she asked with a smile.

"Actually, I was thinking Ryderless." He slipped his arm behind her neck and applied gentle pressure until she shifted on the couch and sat on his lap.

Once she was settled there comfortably, Melissa smiled and ran her fingers through his hair. "So that's one *R*. What's the other one?"

He closed his eyes. "Hmm, I like that."

She increased the pressure of her fingers on his scalp and turned in his lap to straddle him. "How about the other *R* is for rubbing?"

Shooting her a half glance, he cupped her breasts and, with

the barest of pressure, moved his fingers along the tips. "Rubbing, like this?"

Her breathy "Yes," confirmed that they were on the same track.

As seductions went, it was a slow one. Which was good. Exceptionally good. With the softest of caresses, her nipples hardened into tight peaks. As she skimmed her hands to his shoulders and kneaded the muscles there, he grasped the tips of her breasts and rotated them tightly between his thumb and forefinger.

She let out a soft, almost pained gasp and he paused. "Too rough?"

"Could we add another *R*?"

His erection nearly burst through the denim of his jeans, especially when, without waiting for his reply, she rubbed her center along the length of it. He knew then, like the other night, there would be no stopping.

Somehow he worked his wallet out of his pants, as well as the condom he kept there. In a blur as fast as that of Ryder's disappearing act, Melissa's pants were somewhere on the floor, along with his jeans, and he was sheathed in the condom.

He met her gaze as she poised herself directly above him, and there was no doubt about what would happen next. They'd waited too long already.

Grasping the naked flare of her hips, he gently glided her down onto him, as deep as he could go. When she would have moved, he applied slightly more pressure to keep her still and said, "Not rough. Not yet."

Melissa's breath was trapped somewhere in the middle of her chest. Her heart seemed to stop beating until he ripped her T-shirt off her body, baring her to the heat of his gaze.

She looked down at him. At the angles of his face made sharper by the light from the lamps at each end of the couch. At his eyes so dark with passion, the brown of them had seemingly melded with the black of his pupils.

She groaned and clasped his head to her. His lips encircled

the sensitive peak of her right breast and suckled it, drawing it deeply into his mouth. She moaned again and tried to move on him to ease the growing tension between her legs, but he swept one arm down, held her in place.

"Not yet, *amor*. You're so hard against my lips." He shifted his mouth to the pale skin of her breast. "So sensitive."

His words undid her. "Sebastian," she said and a little mew of pleasure escaped her as he took her other breast into his mouth.

"Sweet," he whispered in soft tones before he teethed her hardened nipple. She ground herself down on him, needing more.

"Tell me what you feel," he urged as he sat up to suck at the sensitive spot between her neck and shoulder.

She bent and kissed the side of his face. "Shaky," she replied, her breath uneven then gone as he sucked harder, to the point of pain.

Sebastian ripped himself from her and gulped in a breath. He'd left a mark. "Sorry."

She gave him an unsteady smile. "I liked it."

He had to close his eyes and muster what little restraint he had to keep from coming right that moment. She wasn't the only one who was shaky, he thought, his body trembling from his battle for control. She soothed him by running her hands along his shoulders, but it wasn't enough. His shirt still separated his skin from hers.

Sebastian didn't know if he said it, or if she just sensed it.

Melissa reached down, grabbed the hem of his T-shirt and pulled it off. When her eyes deepened to a midnight blue, he knew that she was pleased with what she saw. When she eased close, brushed her breasts against him, it was the end of his restraint.

He rose, still buried deep inside of her, and she wrapped her legs around his back.

The action forced her onto him even farther, surrounding

him with a heat he could feel even through the skin of the condom. She shifted on him, nearly pulling out, then slipped down deep. It made him want… "I wish I could feel the wet of you, Melissa."

He took a step and then another until he was at the door of her room.

"Tell me what else you want." She moved on him again.

His climax was building, low in his belly, and gathering force. His breath exploded from his chest; his arms and legs trembled so badly, Sebastian knew they weren't going to make it to the bed. At least not yet.

He turned until her back was braced against the wall. Gripping her sides with his hands, he drove into her, relented to her request. "I want to be buried so deep I don't know where I end and you begin."

His voice was uneven as he said it. Rough with his longing. Rough like his movements as he increased the force of his penetration, driving her against the wall. She welcomed it, wrapping her arms around his head as he suckled her breasts. Tightening the embrace of her legs and meeting his movements with the shift of her hips.

Melissa gulped an uneven breath and kissed the top of his head. After, he raised his face and took her lips in a kiss that seared her with its demand. She opened her mouth to him and lost all sense of herself. All sense of everything except the way their bodies were joined. Everything except the heat and the musky smell of sex and Sebastian.

One rough thrust ripped a moan from her but she welcomed it, whispering her need against his mouth. Pleading with him to finish. To take them over the edge by releasing the climax that had built inside her, twisting her insides into a tight knot of need.

With another harsh drive, it happened. His breath caught and his muscles rippled beneath her hands. There was the sudden swell of him inside, releasing an answering surge from deep within her.

Melissa cried out his name, closed her eyes and threw her head back as pleasure rushed through every part of her body. But she didn't release her grip on him, nor did he withdraw from her.

As the tide of their climax ebbed, Sebastian tenderly eased her from the wall and cradled her in his arms.

Melissa held on to him as if he were a lifeline, her arms and legs wrapped around him as he took the dozen or so steps necessary to get to her bed.

When he slipped with her onto the sheets, he was still joined with her and to her surprise, growing hard once more.

At her questioning look, he shrugged and gave her an almost apologetic smile.

She was lying there, exposed to him, her legs dangling over the edge of the bed, Sebastian tucked inside her. She should have felt sated, but somehow, even with the remnants of her climax lingering, she didn't.

Melissa couldn't get enough of him, and as Sebastian slowly began to move, his actions tender and gentle compared to moments before, she realized he couldn't get enough, either.

Chapter 15

Ryder lingered in the night air, savoring the crisp chill of the coming winter. Enjoying the freedom the darkness gave him from the four walls of his apartment. Dreading the visit to Diana.

He'd walked for blocks and blocks until he'd reached the buildings along the avenue in the midthirties. As he stopped at one corner, listening to the sounds of jazz filter from the open door of a restaurant on one of the side streets, the urge Ryder had been battling rose up, stronger than before.

He slipped from the avenue into a small alley. With a single leap, he landed noiselessly on the first level of the fire escape. A second jump, followed by a third and he was up on the roof, staring upward at a full vanilla-colored moon.

He outstretched his arms, let the beast loose, knowing he had to tire it out before he got to Diana.

Diana. He growled at the thought of her. At her anger and her passion. Heat built within him and his fangs slowly slipped down.

Taking a deep breath, he jumped from one rooftop to the next until he neared the ledge closest to the street. Gathering speed, he raced toward the gap and launched himself across the breach.

His landing was not as smooth this time. Ryder had never become sure of his vampire footing. He'd battled hard to hang on to his humanity. In the last few months, however, his enforced confinement during the day and his increased need for the blood that healed him had upset the balance he'd developed.

The surprising thing was, Ryder had found that giving in to the animal within him every now and then had brought with it an invigorating sense of power. An alluring and altogether dangerous sense of power.

Energized by the animal, he continued his flight along the rooftops, drawing closer and closer to Diana. His need grew until he arrived at her building.

Bracing himself on the granite ledge of her roof, he took a step and let himself plummet downward.

Jab. Jab. Punch. Jab. Jab. Roundhouse.

Diana repeated the routine over and over, striking the heavy bag with speed and precision. Alternating occasionally with a dropkick. Uppercut substituted for the jab-punch combo.

Her arms were growing weary, but she kept at it. The workout helped to release the anger and frustration from earlier that night. Finally, she couldn't go on anymore. With one last series of blows, she lost her footing and had to grab the bag to keep from falling. As she held on to the leather and took a deep bracing breath, the hackles on the back of her neck rose.

Easing away from the bag, she turned to look out her bedroom window. That was when she saw a silhouette on her fire escape. *His* silhouette. There was a slight movement as he realized he'd been seen, yet he remained outside where he was.

Fine, she thought. She undid the Velcro on her boxing gloves and pulled them off. Tossing them to lie at the foot of the heavy bag, Diana unwound the wraps around her wrists and hands, and flung them onto the floor, as well.

He still didn't make a move and the anger from earlier that night flared to life once again. Wanting to exact some kind of punishment, she stared straight ahead and reached for the draw-string of her sweatpants. With a quick tug, she loosened the ties and eased the pants down her legs, kicked them aside. She grabbed the hem of her T-shirt and dispensed with it, as well.

Diana stood there in nothing but her string bikini panties and sports bra. Slipping one finger beneath the miniscule band of her panties, she began to draw them down.

It was then she finally got a reaction.

He was through the window and standing before her so quickly, all she had seen was a blur. He placed his hand on her hip to stop her.

When she met his gaze, she experienced a little fear, followed by fascination and longing. With one finger, she traced the edge of his brows above his electric gaze. Then she allowed herself to cup his cheek and run her thumb across the hard edge of his lips and the slight hint of fang protruding beyond their fullness.

"Into the whole creature-of-the-night routine lately, aren't you?" she said in challenge, but didn't stop moving her thumb across his lips. The fangs grew slightly longer and more pronounced.

"Does it bother you?" His voice was a low, almost rumbling growl.

As she shifted her thumb across his lips again, he grabbed it with his teeth, bit down on it just a little. Not enough to draw blood. Yet.

Heat twisted her insides into a knot of need. Bending her head to one side, she bared her neck to him. Daring him.

She was trembling with a combination of fear and anticipation as he wrapped an arm around her waist and brought her close. He grazed the side of her neck with his fangs. The pressure of his teeth increased and for a moment, Diana thought she'd pushed him too far.

Ryder pressed his fangs against the pulse beating thickly beneath them. He remembered the sweetness of her. How her blood had tasted on his lips, rich with their passion. The animal in him wanted to sample her again. Wanted to be buried deep within her as he savored her lifeblood, spiced with the flavor of their lovemaking.

Somehow he reined in the animal and let the human resume control again. The heat that signalled his transformation ebbed from his body as his fangs receded. Instead of the vampire's bite, he placed a gentle kiss on the spot she had offered up so readily, then released her.

"I came to talk. To try and convince you—"

"To break the law?" She stepped away from him. With a quick stride, she was at her dresser, slipping off her damp bra and panties before putting on a fresh pair of pajamas.

He approached her as he pleaded his case. "What if we can't get any more information on Sloan? Are you willing to risk someone getting injured—"

"Instead of hacking into the NSA computers? I'm supposed to uphold the law, Ryder."

He grabbed her arm as she walked past him toward her bed. "Things are never that simple, Diana."

She glanced down at his hand, her face hard and unyielding. "Sometimes they are, Ryder. I've built my entire life around doing the right thing."

He released her and dragged a hand through his hair. "And what of my life? Or should I say, my lack of life? Tell me what's right about it, Diana? Tell me what I did wrong to merit the life I have?"

Diana's heart ached with his pain. She embraced him and held him close for long seconds. Cradling his head to her, she said, "Did you ever think the reason you're here now—that you're the way you are—is because you were good?"

A harsh laugh escaped his lips. "And this," he said, transforming into vampire mode, "is my reward?"

Standing on tiptoe, she brought her lips to his and cupped the back of his head to keep him there when he would have pulled away. "If not for this, we'd never have met."

He answered her with a kiss so demanding, she wasn't sure whether it was the vampire or human in control. Frankly, at that moment, she didn't care.

Chapter 16

She'd woken up in a man's arms exactly three times in her life. Including this morning, two of those times had been with Sebastian.

The first had been with Ryder the night her parents had been killed. He'd arrived at what had then been the apartment she shared with her parents, about half a dozen blocks away. She'd managed to hold it all together until he'd arrived. After though, the floodgates had opened wide, and when she'd fallen apart, Ryder had held her in his arms until she'd calmed, and after, while she slept.

Melissa much preferred waking with Sebastian.

She was tucked into his side, his arm slung loosely around her back, her thigh draped casually over his legs. Heat bathed her body from the contact with his body. She shifted slightly and winced at the soreness between her legs.

At her movement, small as it was, he roused and turned onto his side to face her. "Mornin'," he said, the tone of his voice low and slightly raspy.

There was a smile on his lips as she kissed him. "Good morning."

He slipped his hand onto her waist and eased over until their bodies came into full contact. At that touch, every nerve ending in her body flared to life. Although she hadn't thought it possible, desire rose to the forefront once again.

Sebastian didn't want to rush. Every minute with her might be his last. Whatever was happening between them… Even with her in his arms, he feared so much. Most of all, failing her.

And so because of that, and mindful of how they had passed the night, his actions were gentle and oh-so-languorous. The passion that came because of it reached deep, brought them to a level more intense than before.'

He stroked her with his hands, mindful of what she liked. He needed her hands on him, stroking and caressing. Urging him on until he rolled her beneath him and gently entered her.

As he cradled her in his arms afterward, both their bodies shaking and unsteady, he realized he didn't know what he'd do without her in his life, and swore he'd do what he could to keep her there.

He just hoped it would be enough.

Melissa sat at her desk going through her typical routine. She sorted through all her mail, tossing aside the junk, putting magazines to the side and grouping everything that needed attention. As she did so, she shot a quick glance at Sebastian. A too-quick glance. She didn't want to tip off whoever was watching to the fact that she was aware of their surveillance.

Sebastian was typing away on his laptop. He'd explained that wireless devices had a limited number of frequencies and that he could tap into the signal, even if someone had taken the time to activate encryption of the transmission. With a grin, he'd said it would only take a little bit longer if it was encrypted.

He loved the challenge of it, she realized. Even with only an occasional peek, it was obvious he was totally absorbed in what he was doing. With a wave of his hand and an even broader grin, he motioned that he had picked up a signal. His concern that she was being spied upon hadn't been off the mark.

Reaching into his pocket, he pulled out his cell phone and dialed her number. Her phone rang and rang, but she didn't pick it up. Once he hung up, he said out loud, "It's only a video signal. No audio."

Melissa rose from her desk and grabbed one of the magazines, trying to make it appear as if she was just going somewhere else to read. But once next to Sebastian on the sofa, she glanced at the screen on the laptop. There was her desk in grainy black and white. Inspecting the rest of the room, she wondered aloud, "Could there be other cameras?"

Sebastian quickly looked around. "Possibly, only the more there are, the greater the risk of discovery. And if he—or she, for that matter—only wanted to monitor you, the one in the frame was probably enough."

"And if there's more?"

Sebastian shrugged. "Then they'll know we're on to them and maybe do something more drastic. Something that will draw them into the open."

"You're sounding very law enforcement-like," she teased.

Sebastian chuckled and paused in his typing. "One of the hazards of being related to too many cops."

No sooner had Sebastian said that, then he was back to his typing.

"What are you doing now?" Window after window was popping up on his laptop. Too fast for her to follow.

"I've jacked into the hospital network. Whoever is spying needs to send that signal somehow. The most likely way is through the network." His fingers flew over the keys.

He paused for only a moment as he said, "I'm in."

He resumed his typing and she watched as he began scrolling through a list. Melissa craned her neck to see.

Users. Files open. As he moved downward, she immediately saw her user name with an entry. She'd logged in that morning to look at her mail and access some patient information. Farther down the screen, she noticed a familiar user name. Gesturing to the entry, she said, "That's Sara."

"How do you know?" he began, then held up his hand. "Wait, don't tell me. You and Sara know each other's info in case of—"

"An emergency," she finished.

"At least you don't have your password on a Post-it note on your monitor, right? Please tell me that."

"No, I don't." She had it neatly written in her daily planner, which she kept in her top desk drawer where anyone could see it whenever she wasn't in her office.

Returning her attention to Sebastian, she saw that he'd shifted to another set of entries, apparently to confirm Sara's user name. "How did you do that?"

"Used a back door. System sees me as the administrator. That means I can see whoever is on, what files they're using. Sara's in the same network files you are."

With a few key strokes, Sebastian moved down the list. The user names were a combination of portions of the users' names and random numbers. That made it easy to locate Sloan's user name, but according to the system, Sloan had no files open.

Turning to Melissa, he asked, "Is Sloan in the hospital right now?"

"He should be," Melissa answered quickly. "Why?"

Sebastian turned his laptop so she could see it more clearly. "You and Sara have similar files open."

"Probably the mail system and patient records."

Nodding, Sebastian continued. "If Sloan is in, he's not logged on to the system. Or he is and is hiding it somehow."

Melissa shook her head. "People Sloan's age aren't usually computer-savvy."

"NSA, remember? Sloan's not what he seems." He powered down the laptop and closed its case. "We won't get any more info here, Melissa. What about the journals?"

With a tired sigh, Melissa relaxed into the cushions of the sofa. "I'm starting the last one. The one before didn't give me much to work with. Just the kind of stuff I keep track of—anything unusual with Ryder that day. What I did to help him."

Sebastian sensed there was something else. Something she wasn't telling him. He cupped her cheek and applied gentle pressure until her gaze met his. "What else, Melissa?"

She looked away and in barely a whisper said, "Comments about my mother. Treatments that had been working before were no longer effective. She was dying."

Sebastian embraced her. She was a little stiff at first, but then she relaxed and grabbed hold of him. Definitely progress. And possibly even more rewarding than sex.

He battled his natural inclination to say something, especially something witty or funny. He just held her, providing comfort. He had sensed from all their encounters that she'd had little of that in her life.

He intended to change that.

Melissa's eyes were riveted to a section in her father's journal.

> I know what I am going to do is wrong. It violates all the duties with which I have been entrusted, but I cannot bear to lose Elizabeth. She and Melissa are my life. Melissa. I know I have failed her in so many ways but if this experiment succeeds, Melissa may be free from the burdens I have had to bear. From the duty I must otherwise pass to her to honor.

"Melissa?" Sebastian said, jarring her from her father's memoir.

She handed Sebastian the journal and motioned to the entry.

He was silent long after he had finished. Finally he turned to her. "The only way he would violate his duty is if—"

"His experiments had to do with Ryder. If something my father planned to do to help my mother involved Ryder." She took the book back from Sebastian. Running her hands over the neatly written words, she wondered at what her father had intended. What Ryder had that—

"Ryder's immortal," she said. "He can't die the way we can. The way my mother was dying." With a quick look at Sebastian, she pressed onward. "Maybe my father thought that if my mother was like Ryder, she'd be cured."

With a shrug, he asked, "So why not just let Ryder turn her?"

"Because he wasn't sure what she'd become," Ryder said.

He stood in the doorway, his body rigid with tension. Diana was by his side.

"How long have you been there?" Melissa asked.

"Long enough." He strode into the room and held his hand out until Melissa gave him the book.

She stood, and just as Diana came to stand beside Ryder, Sebastian rose and took his place at Melissa's side. If lines were to be drawn, it was clear who would be with whom.

Ryder thumbed through the pages, too quickly for a human to read. But Ryder wasn't human. "Anything?" Sebastian asked.

"Nothing I can understand, but maybe Melissa can." He took a step toward Melissa, his stance almost menacing.

When he spoke again, his voice was lower, with an odd rumble to it, like that of a big jungle cat. Sebastian was transfixed by it and by the gradual transformation that was taking place. "Maybe you can figure out what your father did."

Ryder thrust the diary out at her and by now his eyes were glowing with a strange light, and sharp, bright white fangs protruded from beneath his upper lip. "How he betrayed me. Endangered both of us."

"Ryder, it isn't that simple," Melissa pleaded, which only

made him angrier and way scarier. Sebastian took a step to place himself between Ryder and Melissa, and his sister did the same.

"Ryder." Diana laid a hand on his chest. "This won't accomplish anything."

He spoke in low tones. "Frederick Danvers knew what his duty was. He knew the dangers of revealing what I am to others."

"His wife was dying. He wanted to help her," Diana said.

"Keep it simple, Diana. Remember?"

Sebastian sensed it would only get uglier if it went any further. He cared too much about both Melissa and his sister to let it continue. "We could go around on this all day, but isn't the most important thing to find out exactly what Melissa's father did and how Sloan found out about it?"

Ryder turned his glowing gaze on Sebastian. Ever so slowly, he returned to normal. It was only when his human side resumed control that he spoke again. "So your short list of suspects is down to one? On what basis?"

Sebastian quickly rattled off what he had been able to determine that afternoon in Melissa's office. It had been clear both from the network administrator's screen and a surreptitious visit to Sara's station that she was not the one receiving the video from Melissa's office.

"And so that makes Sloan our guy?" Ryder interjected.

Sebastian counted off each reason on his fingers. "He has sufficient knowledge to understand what Frederick Danvers was doing. He had access to Danvers on almost a daily basis. He may have known Melissa's mom's condition had become serious. Then there's this whole NSA gig."

"So shadowy government types are always guilty of something? Am I hearing you right?" Diana said in challenge.

Melissa'd had enough. Taking a step past Sebastian, she pleaded her case, "If it isn't Edward, who is it? We have no other suspects. No other leads."

"But no motive. Why would he want your parents dead?" Diana countered.

Melissa had no answers. *Not yet.* She turned her father's journal over and over. Holding it up, she said, "There may be something in here, but then again, there may be something in Edward's NSA file."

With an exasperated sigh, Diana said, "I can't access his file. I'm not sure I have anyone who can—"

"Except me," Sebastian said. "I can—"

"No, you can't. Not ever, *hermanito,* because if you did, I wouldn't hesitate to lock you up," Diana repeated the warning she'd issued the other night before storming out of the apartment.

Melissa glanced from brother to sister. Sebastian's defiant brown gaze was locked with his sister's determined green one, but in both gazes there was regret, as well. Sebastian would be as hard-pressed to ignore his sister's request as Diana would be to enforce her threat.

Melissa only hoped that neither would be necessary.

Chapter 17

"You may not want to hear what I've got to say," Diana told Melissa the next day over the phone.

Melissa leaned back in her office chair to listen to Diana's report. "Please go on."

"Our hospital break-in suspect turned up in the morgue. Possible drug overdose."

She closed her eyes and sighed. Diana had been right when she said Melissa wouldn't like the news. "Truly a dead end."

"Not really."

Sitting back up with a snap, she said, "There's something that can help us?"

"My detective friend told me the suspect died of an overdose of an unusually potent synthetic heroin. Not very common, which is why the M.E. decided to call in Homicide. And guess what the good detective found?"

"Another overdose like this one?" Melissa guessed.

"Exactly like this one. Plus, that overdose occurred just

after the crash that killed your parents. Two dead bodies within days of incidents connected to the Danvers family means something, both to me and Detective Daly," Diana replied.

Melissa released a tired sigh. "But I still haven't confirmed what my father discovered that someone was willing to kill for."

"Four bodies adds up to something very valuable."

Valuable? Ryder wouldn't consider his state one of value, but since reading the short but damning excerpt from one of her father's last entries, Melissa knew her father had seen something in Ryder's vampirism that could help her mother. She had little doubt he'd acted upon that belief and she was just waiting for something else in the journal that would confirm her suspicions.

"Whoever did this… It may make sense just to let this lie for a little while."

"Telling me to back off on this, Melissa? We haven't known each other very long, but I didn't think that was like you."

"Please be careful, Diana. I just want a little more time with the journals so I can give you more to work with."

"Both victims are ex-cons with long records, so it may be possible for my contact to stonewall for a few days. But only for a few days. In the meantime, I'm going to visit the M.E. to talk over the toxicology report. Hear what he has to say that he can't put in writing."

For a moment, Melissa wished there was more that she could do. More that would help Diana with the investigation, but for now, there was nothing. "Thanks for all that you're doing. And if you need me for anything—"

"I know I can count on you, Melissa. As soon as there's anything else, I'll let you know." Diana hung up.

Melissa replaced the phone in its cradle and headed to the sofa, out of camera range. It was time to get back to her father's journal and try to discover what could be so important that someone would have killed for it.

It was harder than I had thought and not just because guilt made me reconsider what I had done. Putting the

patient down was not easy. With his sense of taste, I
didn't dare put anything in his food. I did the only thing
I could think of—I delayed one of his feedings, hoping
his hunger would be so strong that he wouldn't notice the
taste of the sedative. Watching the patient feed has always
been difficult for me, but it was even harder this time
knowing that I would violate first his trust, then his body.

Melissa kept on reading, carefully making mental notes of all
her father had done. Waiting for the moment when he would explain why he'd needed Ryder's blood. What her father had hoped
to find once he'd examined the specimen. It was slow going as
she kept vigilant for clues as to what her father may have learned
and whom he might have trusted with the knowledge.

An hour passed. A knock came at the door to her office.
Melissa hastily marked her spot, closed the book and tucked
it into the large pocket in the front of her lab jacket. Her father had favored small slim journals that could be carried eas-
ily. "Come in," she called out, and grabbed the copy of *The
New England Journal of Medicine* from her coffee table.

The door opened a crack and Sara poked her head in. "You
okay in here? I buzzed you about the patient in 420, but you
didn't answer."

Melissa glanced at her phone. The red message light was
blinking off and on. "Sorry, I must have been so engrossed in
this," she said, waving the magazine in the air, "that I didn't
hear it."

Tossing the magazine onto the coffee table, she followed
Sara down to the patient's room. The young man had been di-
agnosed with leukemia five years earlier, but had gone into
remission after only a minimal round of treatments. That had
lasted for about two years before the disease had returned. Another round of treatments, longer and more intense, had again
forced remission of the disease for a couple of years, but now

The Silhouette Reader Service™ — Here's how it works:

Accepting your 2 free books and mystery gift places you under no obligation to buy anything. You may keep the books and gift and return the shipping statement marked "cancel." If you do not cancel, about a month later we'll send you 4 additional books and bill you just $4.24 each in the U.S., or $4.99 each in Canada, plus 25¢ shipping & handling per book and applicable taxes if any.* That's the complete price and — compared to cover prices of $4.99 each in the U.S. and $5.99 each in Canada — it's quite a bargain! You may cancel at any time, but if you choose to continue, every month we'll send you 4 more books, which you may either purchase at the discount price or return to us and cancel your subscription.

*Terms and prices subject to change without notice. Sales tax applicable in N.Y. Canadian residents will be charged applicable provincial taxes and GST. Credit or Debit balances in a customer's account(s) may be offset by any other outstanding balance owed by or to the customer.

NO POSTAGE
NECESSARY
IF MAILED
IN THE
UNITED STATES

BUSINESS REPLY MAIL

FIRST-CLASS MAIL   PERMIT NO. 717-003   BUFFALO, NY

POSTAGE WILL BE PAID BY ADDRESSEE

SILHOUETTE READER SERVICE
3010 WALDEN AVE
PO BOX 1867
BUFFALO NY 14240-9952

If offer card is missing write to: Silhouette Reader Service, 3010 Walden Ave., P.O. Box 1867, Buffalo NY 14240-1867

the young man was back in the hospital. So far, the treatments were not helping.

"He's complaining of pain in the abdominal area," Sara explained. "It seems distended, as well."

Melissa conducted a brief examination that confirmed Sara's observations. She turned to her friend. "Afraid the spleen's been compromised?"

"That's why I called you," Sara said.

Melissa calmly asked the patient a few questions, extended her examination a little further to better pinpoint the source of his pain. When she was done, she said, "Don't worry, Billy. We're going to run some tests and in the meantime, I'll have Sara give you something for the pain."

She was just finishing up with her notations on the young man's chart when Edward Sloan came by.

"Problems, Dr. Danvers?" He glanced from one woman to the other. "Nurse Martinez?" Ice dripped from his voice as he addressed Sara.

"On the contrary, Edward. Sara made some keen observations about Billy Preston. Unfortunately, I think he's having problems with his spleen. After the tests—"

"You'll let me see the results. We'll decide whether or not surgery is warranted," Edward instructed, his tone so paternal it bordered on insulting.

"Certainly, Dr. Sloan. If you have a moment, may I speak with you in my office?" Melissa asked. When the older man nodded and walked away down the hall, Melissa finished up with Sara.

As she turned to meet Edward, Sara laid a hand on her arm. "Don't let that ol' snake do a number on you."

"I gather you two don't get along." Melissa wondered why she hadn't noticed it before.

"He got in my business a couple of times. Got in your father's face, as well, if I recall." Sara moved to walk away. This time, it was Melissa who stopped her in her tracks.

"When?"

Sara looked upward as she seemed to search for an answer. Finally she said, "A few weeks before your dad died. I heard them arguing about something in your father's office when I went to drop off a chart your father had requested."

"Do you know what it was about?"

Sara shook her head. "Not really. Something about a new treatment, I think."

Maybe the treatment her father had planned on trying on her mother. Melissa took a step closer to Sara and in tones soft enough so that only Sara could hear, said, "Don't mention that again to anyone. Especially Sloan."

There was a confused look on Sara's face. "What's up, Melissa?"

"Something bad, Sara. You need to keep quiet about that conversation and anything else you might remember about my father and Sloan. Trust me on this," Melissa urged.

Sara nodded. "You know I trust you, girl. If I remember anything else, you'll be the first to know."

Melissa watched her go, then returned to her office. Inside, Edward had made himself comfortable at her desk and was busy looking at the photo of her and her parents. "Ah, the good ol' days," he said, and held the photo out to her.

It was almost as if he was testing her. Without a moment's pause, she grabbed the frame, examined the photo and faked a smile. "It was a wonderful night. My mother and father were in such good spirits. Even my mother—"

"Looked beautiful, just like her daughter," Edward said.

There was an unusual tone in his voice. A wistful one she'd never heard before. She handed the photo back and he glanced at it one more time, almost longingly, before he returned the frame to its spot on her desk. His actions brought a round of doubt, which she needed to dispel. "My father was hopeful about the treatments she was taking."

Edward's face hardened immediately. "You knew about them?"

"Not really. He only mentioned them in passing that night, when I commented on how well mother looked." She was surprised at how smoothly she'd lied. Prevarication was a not a trait of which she'd thought herself capable.

"Oh," was all he said.

"Did you know about them?" she pressed.

"Frederick mentioned them to me in passing, as well. Quite frankly, your mother's condition was so severe that I wrote it off to Frederick being unable to deal with reality." As he spoke, Edward looked back to the photo. "She was dying, you know."

Melissa laid a comforting hand on his shoulder. "I didn't know, Edward. My parents and I were never very close."

There was a ripple in his body. One of shock, it appeared to her. When he met her gaze, his was inquisitive and disbelieving. "You expect me to believe that your father didn't tell you her condition was that grave. That he didn't tell you he was trying something new in an effort to cure her."

"Believe what you will, Edward. The truth is, I knew little about their lives." The sad part of that statement was that it was the truth.

Because of that, doubt left his gaze. "If your father kept any papers, you should look through them. See what he was doing."

"I don't think there are any," she lied.

"He was a marvelous researcher in addition to being a fine doctor. I find it hard to believe—"

"Again, believe it, Edward. And if there were papers, why would he leave them to me? I haven't seen the inside of a lab since med school," she said, trying to throw him off the scent.

"A shame, with a mind like yours. Plus in a teaching hospital such as this one, it's only a matter of time before you'll have to consider some kind of research."

Melissa hadn't forgotten that eventually she'd have to do more in order to move up the line. But for now, the only experiments she was interested in were her father's. "I'm glad you think I have a fine mind, Edward, although it didn't seem that way in the hall a few minutes ago," she said, trying to turn the conversation away from additional questions about her father.

"I'm sorry about pulling rank on you out there in the hallway. Most of my anger was with Nurse Martinez. She's a meddling sort, isn't she?" Edward's disdain for her friend was clear. Not to mention worrisome if he had any suspicions about Sara and her father. She only hoped Sara would take to heart her earlier admonitions.

"Apology accepted. As for Sara, she means well. However, seeing that you're concerned, I will speak to her about her involvement with the patients."

Edward nodded, seemingly satisfied with Melissa's concession. He rose from the desk with stiff and almost lethargic movements. "Are you okay, Edward?"

"Just a touch of age, my dear. No need to worry." With a dismissive wave of his hand, he continued to the door, but paused for a moment before leaving. "If you ever decide to resume your father's work, I'd be delighted to assist."

Melissa forced a smile to her lips. "If I find anything about it, I'll be sure to let you know. As for working together, it would be a delight."

Edward's clear blue-eyed gaze was assessing for a moment. Then he stepped from her office, closing the door behind him.

Shifting to the side of her desk, Melissa picked up the phone and dialed Ryder. When he answered, she said, "We need to talk tonight."

"Diana isn't available."

"I know. She's meeting the M.E.—"

"And Detective Daly about the suspect in your break-in."

There was that hint of anger in Ryder's voice again at the mention of the NYPD officer. She worried about whatever was going on between Diana and the detective that troubled Ryder so much. But she was even more worried that what she was about to suggest to Ryder would violate Diana's trust in her.

I can count on you, Diana had said earlier that night. But Diana would probably not approve of what Melissa thought they had to do next. "Diana's being absent might be for the better, Ryder," Melissa said and waited anxiously for his reply.

"Just remember that whatever we decide is something we're all going to have to live with. In my case, for a very long time."

"I know, Ryder, and believe me, I wouldn't be thinking about this if it wasn't necessary."

His tired and almost defeated sigh came across the line. "I hope you're right."

Chapter 18

Lying, meddling bitch.

She knew more about her father's experiments than she was letting on.

The last lab rat was near the end of its life. Its red blood count was well beyond acceptable limits, literally choking all the blood vessels and organs with the imbalance. Destroying the necessary white blood cells and platelets that kept a body running. Soon the hemorrhaging would begin, followed by a slow and likely painful death.

Nothing had stopped the relentless onslaught of the red blood cells, which had been altered by the Danvers cell strain. Yet Danvers himself had been able to control the multiplication of the cells. Well, at least early on.

One set of rats had almost supernatural healing powers and strength beyond that of their uninoculated counterparts. And they'd lived long beyond the span of regular rats and of the rats stolen from Danvers's lab. Rats that Danvers had likely been using as control samples.

A step was missing—the process Danvers had used to maintain the superrat specimens. Whatever it was had not been revealed in the journal stolen from Danvers's lab nor in the incredibly boring memoir taken from Melissa's office.

Judging from her unconvincing act this afternoon, Melissa was well aware that she had important information about her father's experiments and the source of the cell strain.

There would be no more waiting now. No time to dawdle. Otherwise, the illness would be too far along to allow for a possible cure. The Danvers cell strain could only do so much and maybe there had been too much delay already.

Action had to be taken immediately.

"The toxicology reports on both the overdose victims confirms that it was heroin, but synthetic and very potent. Very designer." Diana paced back and forth in the kitchen, obviously unnerved by her earlier visit to the morgue.

"How designer?" Ryder asked.

"M.E. wouldn't put it in writing, but as far as he's concerned, this heroin wasn't designed to be sold on the street. It was intended to kill. There's only a handful of black ops organizations who'd do that," she answered.

"Like the NSA?" Sebastian asked, raising one eyebrow to emphasize his point.

Diana shrugged. "Possibly. Could be a rogue, as well."

Melissa finally piped in. "It seems careless to get rid of two people so close together both in time and location. It was bound to raise suspicions."

"If Peter hadn't asked around, no one would have looked for another body. The first case was in Westchester and not within the NYPD's jurisdiction," Diana explained.

Melissa shot Sebastian an uneasy look. "So does this help us at all?"

Diana's full lips thinned into a tight line and she let out an exasperated sigh. "There's no other forensics to tie the murders together. Although the tox reports should be enough. The only other thing— Sloan worked for the NSA from sometime in 1999 to September of 2003."

Ryder leaned forward. "That's just one month before Melissa's parents were killed."

"Too close for coincidence," Sebastian said with a nod.

"But we have nothing from Forensics for probable cause—"

"Which means what? That we sit around and wait for another body to turn up? Maybe one of us?" Melissa asked angrily. She strode to the kitchen island, where she gripped the edges of the counter tightly. Her shoulders rose as she took in a deep breath.

"We have to do something. We can't just wait for something else to happen."

Sebastian watched as Diana walked over to Melissa and laid a hand on her shoulder. "I've asked Peter to go out on a limb for me— He's agreed to put a tail on Sloan. See what he's up to and where he goes."

"If Sloan finds out he's being tailed—" Ryder said.

"Your detective friend could be in a lot of trouble. Sloan's a respected department head at one of New York's premier hospitals and if he's the killer…" Sebastian's voice trailed off.

"But it's all we have right now, isn't it?" Melissa said sharply. "And it's not much." Dejection colored her tones, and Sebastian could understand why. Her parents and two others were dead and she was still not remotely close to finding out whether Sloan was responsible.

"We'll have something soon." Ryder glanced at Diana, who added, "I have someone trying to get more information on Sloan. It may take just a little more time."

A little more time being a luxury Sebastian didn't think they had.

Sebastian gripped the metal railing of the balcony, his knuckles white. He had a hell of a choice to make—betray his sister or fail the woman who was coming to mean so much to him.

A soft footfall from behind alerted him that he was no longer alone.

"Sebastian?" Melissa asked, her voice low and hesitant.

"This is not a good time, Melissa." Definitely not a good time, he thought. His father would have expected him to crawl away and hide when faced with a tough decision. Maybe his father had been right to say that Sebastian's games and computers were an escape from the harsh realities of life. In his games, Sebastian could control everything and always make it end the way he wanted.

But this wasn't a game. It was real life and no matter what he decided, nothing would ever be right again.

"I just wanted to say…" There was a long and tremulous sigh as she paused.

Sebastian turned to face her. He had no doubt she was as troubled as he. The strain showed on her face, paler than usual. Her blue eyes were that stormy gray of turbulence. "What can you say that will make whatever I decide right?"

She flinched, almost as if he had struck her. "I just wanted to say that no matter what you decide, I will understand."

Sebastian looked away and expelled a harsh laugh. In his entire life, no one had ever understood. Not his mother. Definitely not his father. And as for the sister he loved and admired almost more than anyone else—she would never understand.

"If I say no—"

She took a step closer and laid the tips of her fingers on his lips. "We'll find some other way of getting the information about Sloan."

He examined her face, searching it carefully but could find nothing that contradicted what she was saying. Her understanding brought a mixture of relief and sorrow. The one person who seemingly could accept what he did, he might have to disillusion.

"What if we can't? What then?"

She shrugged. "I don't know. Maybe we can draw him out somehow."

"No way, no how. If Sloan's the man, he's killed at least twice. If Diana confirms that these other two deaths are related, there's no way I'm willing to let you take that risk."

"I'm a big girl, Sebastian. I can deal."

Laughing curtly, he said, "You can deal with a multiple murderer? He's one of the men in black. The bogeymen that make people go away without anyone knowing about it." He emphasized that point by moving his hands like a magician doing a trick.

"I have Ryder to watch my back, and you."

He realized she was totally serious. She had unquestioned faith in him. Which scared the shit out of him.

Closing the distance between them, he embraced her tightly, but what could he say?

"Will you stay tonight?" she asked, the side of her face buried against the spot directly above his heart.

Did she hear the way the beat stopped, then started once more, faster than before? Did she know that with those few words, she had made him hers?

"Yes," he answered.

She stepped away from him. She was smiling broadly and her eyes had turned a rich blue with bits of aquamarine. Her happy eyes. He took her hand when she offered it and followed her into the apartment.

Chapter 19

Sebastian doubted there was anything better in life than sleeping in late with a beautiful woman. Possibly the night they had spent together. Being with Melissa had been an amazing experience.

But last night had been about more.

After leaving the balcony, they'd gone to her room where she'd locked the door and slowly undressed him. When he would have done the same for her, she said, "Not this time. This time, I want the pleasure to be all yours."

She explored his body and found those spots that made him shake. Brought him to the edge with her lips and hands, taking him into her mouth and making him so hard it almost hurt.

The pleasure that had followed had been even better. She'd undressed for him, urged him on with her soft cries and the words of love she murmured as they came together.

Afterward, he'd held her and they'd fallen asleep, but during the night they'd roused, made love again. He'd been able to see the first streaks of sun coming through the window that faced the East River. He'd forced himself to get some rest then, knowing that they only had a few more hours to sleep.

He'd have to call a friend to help him crack the NSA as soon as they were out of bed. He only hoped what information he got would be worth Diana's justifiable wrath. She'd made her position quite clear.

Unfortunately, he had no choice but to ignore it.

"Where are we going?" Melissa asked as she glanced around at the run-down buildings that lined the cobblestoned street on Manhattan's Lower East Side.

"To see a friend," was all Sebastian said until they reached one multicolored and partially rusted steel door in what appeared to be an abandoned warehouse. Then he cupped her cheek and said, "Just go with the flow. He's a little odd. Thinks he's unearthed some kind of conspiracy and that the government is out to get him."

Sebastian banged on the door's dented metal surface. There was a sudden crackle of noise and a tinny voice spewed from a weather-scarred intercom on the inside frame of the door. "Reyes. What are you doing bringing a narc with you?"

Sebastian glanced over his shoulder at her and rolled his eyes. Turning back to the door, he pulled his black leather duster tight around him. "She's not a narc. She's a friend. Are you going to open the door or are you going to let the Feds keep on snapping my picture while I freeze my ass off out here?"

The door opened, but just enough for her and Sebastian to ease through. It was dark inside and before her eyes had adjusted to the dim light, the door slammed behind her, followed by the snick of multiple locks closing.

Someone stepped away from the door and stood before them. Short and stout, with thin, shoulder-length hair that could have been either dirty blond or light brown. It was so lank with grease that it would take a washing or two to determine its true color. His eyes were a bright hazel and inquisitive. He scrutinized everything about her until he finally addressed Sebastian. "She's uptight, but a true believer. Hot. Is she yours?"

She figured his analysis could have been worse, and yet his attitude annoyed her. "No one owns me, little man."

"Spunk, too. You're a lucky man, Reyes," he said, as if she wasn't even standing there.

About to say something else, she stopped when Sebastian slipped his arm around her waist and squeezed gently, reminding her that they needed this little gnome's assistance. She kept quiet.

"Lenny, I need to get into the NSA," Sebastian said.

"Dude! Why not ask for the keys to Fort Knox." The man paced in front of them as he rambled out loud. "That's a tough one, but we can do it. We'll have to use the multihomed unit with the spoofed addresses. Relay through a bunch of different other PCs that I've cracked, also spoofed. Can't stay on too long."

"Understood."

Melissa was glad he understood because she was totally lost in the technobabble. Not to mention immensely grateful that Sebastian had graduated from the school of personal hygiene, unlike his little friend.

"Let's have at it, then." Lenny motioned for Sebastian to follow him.

Melissa trailed behind the two men, passing shelves filled with what looked like cast-off computer equipment and miles of assorted cables and wires. It was dark, forcing her to stay close to Sebastian to avoid getting lost in what she could only describe as a warren.

Toward the back of the maze of shelves and equipment, there was finally an opening and some light. Four tables sat in the midst of the clearing, each bearing at least two or three monitors and a few printers.

Multicolored cables trailed from the equipment down to the ground where a number of computers rested. Little green and yellow-orange lights blinked on each of the machines, and at every monitor there was a different kind of activity going on.

The two men went to one table and Sebastian motioned for her to take a seat. She found what was left of a disreputable-looking black leather executive chair. It was a little lopsided and dull yellow foam rubber peeked out of holes in the leather. She wheeled the chair over and sat on it daintily, not trusting it to remain upright. She leaned forward and watched what the two men were doing.

Seeing that Melissa was settled comfortably, Sebastian twined his fingers together, then flexed them. To make sure he was in sync with his friend, he asked, "We get to their site. Do a port scan followed by—"

"That might not be necessary." Lenny peered around the dark room, as if to make sure no one could see him. He then pulled a small black binder from amongst a slew of computer manuals and papers located between the two computers. He opened the binder, flipped about halfway through and motioned to the printed results on the paper. "Here's the server address, open ports and some user names." With a shrug, he continued, "Got bored one night."

Clapping him on the back, Sebastian said, "Len, you should get a life, but then again, you just made mine a hell of a lot easier."

Sebastian wondered if Melissa should remain. He was sure that would make her a conspirator somehow, but as his gaze met hers, he detected the determined glint of steel there and knew better than to ask her to leave.

Typing in the address, he made his way through one of the open ports to a log-in screen. He picked one of the names on the list that didn't have a check next to it, assuming the others had already been used by Len. "Do you prefer CAIN or Cracker Jack?"

"Neither, man. Got my own little password cracker." Len motioned to the one icon titled Cheese on the PC Sebastian was using. "Get it? Crackers and cheese," Len said with a little snort and a phlegmy laugh.

"Lame, Len. You definitely need to get out more." Sebastian executed the program, which quickly began running through the millions of possible password permutations. Len kept time on his watch while also monitoring the relays he had set up. Still waiting for the program, Sebastian shot a glance at Melissa, who now sat anxiously on the edge of her chair.

"Remember, the clock is ticking. If we're not getting a result in the next minute or so—"

"We'll abort and try with the next user." Sebastian kept a close eye on his own watch as seconds turned to minutes. He was about to abort the program when the dialogue box on the screen indicated he was being logged on.

"Don't waste time. In and out fast," Len reminded him. Sebastian double-clicked the icon for what appeared to be a database. The opening window confirmed that it was, but the program was password protected again. First he tried the one for the network log-in. When that failed, he once again executed Len's Cheese program. He kept an eye on his watch, knowing time was growing short.

When Len motioned for him to disconnect, he aborted the session. "No," he muttered under his breath, but before moving on to the next user name, he and Len changed the IP addresses on his computer and Sebastian studied the network passwords.

At first, it seemed like a random pattern of numbers and characters, but soon he thought he detected some kind of order in the first few characters. He narrowed down what he needed to know to the last four characters.

He accessed the remote computer again and plugged the first characters into the password cracker program. It took a fraction of the time to log on to the network. Once he was there, he searched out some files on the local drive and hit pay dirt in a file for one of the mail programs. Despite warnings, users often used the same password for various programs. Hopefully, this user had done just that and kept the same password across all his connections.

Entry into the database was almost instantaneous, confirming Sebastian's suspicions about the password, but that didn't stop Len from warning him again. "Find whatever it is that you need and find it fast."

Sebastian worked the keys like a concert pianist, locating the database table that held information on NSA operatives. Again there was another password and he cursed beneath his breath.

"Problem?" Melissa asked, but he ignored her, wishing that the user of this password had high enough security clearance, but he didn't.

Again he logged off, frustrated with his failure.

"Maybe we should just wait—"

"Third time's the charm." He examined the list of user names and properties that Len had obtained. There were a few administrators, typical of an organization of this size. And there were a couple of users with higher network security than others. One of those higher security users might also have sufficient clearance for the database.

The third time was a charm as he logged in and accessed the operatives database. He entered the password and held his breath. A second later, a search screen came up.

After typing in Sloan's name, he executed the search and got to the first entry in the file. Rather than waste time, or risk that a download would be detected, he copied the text from each screen and pasted it into a file saved on Len's PC. He was near the end of the history screen when Len said, "Time to end it."

The links on the database form indicated there were still a number of other screens, but Sloan's status and history were primary and he already had most of that. Another thirty seconds and he'd finished with the screens he wanted and terminated his session.

Leaning back in his chair, he breathed a sigh of relief and tried to control the shaking of his hands.

"You okay? You look a little flushed." Melissa inched closer and laid a hand on his cheek. Her hand felt cool and dry. He finally realized he was damp with sweat.

"Just an adrenaline rush." Glancing expectantly at Len, he asked, "Any problems?"

Len examined his monitor and typed in a few commands. When he turned to look at them, he had a broad but gaptoothed smile on his face. "Clean. Didn't detect anyone trying to trace the address back."

"Cool." Sebastian printed the information he had saved. For good measure, he copied the file on to a thumb disk he'd brought along and deleted the file from both the hard drive and the recycle bin. Motioning to the PC, he said, "You'll do a better cleaning later, right?"

Len nodded his head emphatically. "You bet. Can't risk anyone finding it."

"Thank you, Len," Melissa said and gave the man an impromptu hug. Sebastian chuckled when Len blushed a rather blotchy shade of red.

"Maybe you'll visit again?" Lenny asked, almost hopefully.

Sebastian clapped his friend on the back and said, "Why don't we take you to dinner once this is all done. In a few weeks?"

Len nodded eagerly and led them to the door where he undid the numerous locks. Glancing out the peephole, seemingly to satisfy himself that there was no one there, he eased the door open a crack. Melissa and Sebastian slipped out and onto the street.

Once the door slammed closed behind them and the multiple locks clicked into place, Melissa turned to him. There was sorrow on her face. "I feel bad for him."

Sebastian cupped her cheek. "Not everyone is lucky enough to find someone to share their lives with."

The dismay in her eyes instantly vanished, replaced by contentment. "No, they're not." She gave his hand a reassuring squeeze. "Maybe when this is all over, we should invite him over."

Something swelled in his chest. It might have been his heart expanding like the Grinch's. She was thinking there was a them beyond whatever was happening. A them that could be normal.

"That would be great."

Chapter 20

The initial results were promising until the hemorrhaging began. Something essential is missing, and yet the red blood cells from the rats are identical to those from the frozen samples of the patient's blood. I need a fresh sample, but fear risking it again. If the patient discovers my interest I don't know how he would react. But my Elizabeth is fading quickly. I don't know if she has a few months or only weeks, so I have no choice.

Melissa read on, aware that she was almost at the end of the journal. If she could finish in the next hour or so, she could fill the others in on what she had learned once she was back at the apartment.

She was shocked as her father described not only drugging Ryder once more, but deciding that the missing element might be in Ryder's bite. With Ryder still in vamp mode after sucking down the tainted blood, her father had milked his fangs

like a snake keeper might his pet cobra. Armed now with
samples of both Ryder's blood and the excretion from his
fangs, her father had continued his experiments.

Experiments that had, within a few short weeks, yielded
results. Normal rats inoculated with a combination of Ryder's
blood and the fang serum exhibited increased strength and
healing. Rats riddled with cancer underwent almost instantaneous remissions.

More importantly, none of the treated rats exhibited any
signs of other vampiric tendencies.

That seemed to puzzle her father.

The results are more than I could have hoped for in so
short a time. The scientist in me says to be patient and
do more tests. But this is no longer about science. It's
personal and with Elizabeth so weak, I cannot wait any
longer.

Fascinated, Melissa read on. Although it wasn't stated out-
right in the journal that her father had infected her mother
with Ryder's cells, she had no doubt that was what her father
had done.

But there was something else. Something that didn't make
sense. Beyond a short mention of her mother's improvement
at the end of the journal, there was nothing else about the
experiment.

Not like her very precise father, who, in the papers she had
already perused, meticulously detailed everything that went
on with both Ryder and her mother, and occasionally even
Melissa.

Those few entries about her had been jarring. They had revealed a side of her father she hadn't known existed. He'd clearly
been proud of her. Respected all that she had accomplished and,
dare she say it, some of the entries were even affectionate.

She went back to the beginning of the journal and the first

entry. It was undated like all the others, and if not for Melissa's knowledge of the situation, cryptic when it referred to Ryder. She flipped through a few more pages and ran across an entry making reference to a short trip her father had taken to a conference.

She recalled that trip, about five months before his death.

Continuing onward, Melissa kept looking for clues that would date the entries. Occasionally she pinpointed an event or other occasion. Finally, toward the last few pages of the journal, something jarred her memory.

Melissa has been offered a permanent position at the hospital. Elizabeth and I are so proud of her and all that she has accomplished, but we are worried, as well. She is so alone. I know we are to blame. We have never been able to treat her like a regular child with so much else in the way. Maybe this upcoming appointment to the staff will make her reflect on her life. Make her consider starting a family of her own. With Elizabeth getting better, we can even think of being grandparents, something we could not think about before. Maybe we can show Melissa's children the love we couldn't show her. Maybe…

As she had the first time, she battled back tears. So many maybes that would never come to fruition. And a family? With her life the way it was now? *Impossible.*

She drove that negative thought away. With Sebastian in her life, she'd actually started to believe that normal could happen. Maybe it could. Maybe her parents' wish for her—for a family and love—could come to pass.

Keeping that close to her heart, she flipped to the final pages and finally realized this couldn't be her father's last journal.

She'd been offered the position at the hospital nearly three months before the hospital gala. The gala had been a month before her parents' deaths.

Four missing months. Four months during which her mother had seemingly been cured of the illness that had stolen so much of her life. Four months that had hopefully given her mother the same joy and optimism apparent in her father's last entry.

His last entry. Her father would not have gone four long months without writing in the journal. Especially not when he thought he'd discovered something that had cured her mother. Something that might possibly be used to heal others.

Her father's last journal must be missing, and after reading the information that Sebastian had downloaded from the NSA, Melissa had no doubt that it was Edward Sloan who had it and Edward Sloan who had probably killed her parents.

Now it was time to decide what to do about it.

After one last round to check on all her patients, Melissa returned to her office to pack up her things. She was just taking the journal from her lab jacket pocket and stuffing it into her knapsack when there was a knock on the door.

Quickly zipping the bag, she called out, "Come in."

She was pleasantly surprised to see Sebastian. He was in his customary uniform: jeans and T-shirt, a *Simpsons* one this time. Over his clothes, he wore the long black leather duster he had worn that morning in deference to the winter chill.

"What are you doing here?" She slipped one strap of the knapsack over her shoulder and dropped a kiss on his cheek where the cold still lingered.

He grinned at her and took hold of her hand. "Came to walk my girl home." Apparently unsatisfied with her quick peck, he eased his arm around her waist, drew her close and gave her a slow lingering kiss.

Wrapping her arms around him, she answered the pull of his kiss, opening her mouth to his, meeting his tongue with hers. It went on and on until she wanted more and told him, butting her hips against his, moaning at the hardness of his erection. She broke away from him, slightly breathless. She leaned her forehead against his chest and asked, "It's six in the morning. What are you doing up?"

In answer, he shifted his hips against hers, but said, "Figured I'd get all the scanning finished last night so that when you came home, we could get some sleep." He shifted his head down, found the sensitive spot between her neck and shoulder and bit gently before he kissed it better.

"Seems to me sleep is not what you had in mind." Despite her teasing words, she shifted her hips back and forth against his. She was definitely in a similar frame of mind.

He pulled away from her, his dark eyes glittering with humor and a sexy glint. "Not to start with, but after. The deep exhausted sleep of the immensely satisfied. Are you game?"

"Definitely."

They walked out of her office with their arms wrapped around each other. They strolled past the nurses' station where Sara was just finishing up. As she saw them, she smiled and called out, "Have a good day."

Smiling, Melissa said, "I think we will."

Sara chuckled, clearly aware of what was up with her friend. Surprisingly Melissa felt no shame. Or doubt. Something new. With her parents, doubt about their feelings for her had been the buzzword. With Sebastian...

She glanced at him occasionally as they walked to her apartment. He cared for her, but with that thought came the realization that she couldn't be sure if those emotions would last. If they got through the current problem, there'd be another. Melissa was certain of that. Everyday life with Ryder demanded certain things and his involvement with Diana had seemed to make those things even more complicated.

Even if Ryder wasn't in the picture, there was her life as a doctor. Especially at a hospital like hers. Edward had been right when he said that in addition to the clinical work she was doing, they'd eventually require more research from her. In and of itself, being a doctor at this particular hospital was a difficult life, sometimes with long and erratic hours.

She wondered if Sebastian could handle it. Granted, his nontraditional life gave him a lot of freedom. Freedom to do what he wanted when he wanted, which was the total antithesis of her strictly disciplined life.

Would he grow tired of the restraints on his freedom? Was his free spirit unsuited to any long-term relationship? She hated that doubt had suddenly arisen.

Sebastian sensed a change in her from the stiffening of her body. "You okay?"

She shrugged. "Sure. Why?"

Sebastian stopped and turned to look at her more closely. "You just seem distant all of a sudden."

"I'm fine." She gave another shrug and started walking again, almost as if running from him.

Sebastian was tempted to walk away. He suspected that was what she wanted him to do and he could guess at the reasons for it. Primary reason number one—she was suddenly unsure of him. Still uncertain he was capable of the long haul. But he wasn't about to give her ammunition to bolster that doubt. So he fell into step beside her, but said nothing, sensing she needed the space.

Silence reigned as they reached her building. When they entered her apartment, they both stopped short. Diana was sitting in the living room. It shouldn't have surprised him. She'd dropped by Ryder's the night before when she'd come in after her meeting with Daly. They'd spoken briefly. Too briefly. He'd gotten the sense that Diana suspected something was up with him. She hadn't pressed, however, wrongly believing that it was something personal rather than criminal.

He should have realized she'd spend the night with Ryder. That's what two people who were involved with one another did, wasn't it? It was what he'd wanted to do with Melissa until she'd suddenly gone all Ice Queen on him.

"Buenos dias, hermanita." He gave her a hug.

"Hermanito. You're up early, or should I say, up late?" As she looked from him to Melissa, she arched an eyebrow in question, something tipping her off to a possible problem.

"Late. I finished scanning her father's journals early this morning and decided to meet Melissa." In what was getting to be habit, he slipped his hand into Melissa's. He was pleasantly surprised when she gripped back.

Diana didn't fail to miss the action and was about to say something when Ryder descended the stairs. "Hail, hail the gang's all here. Did you say you had finished scanning?"

"I did."

"And I completed my father's last journal, only it isn't," Melissa chimed in.

Ryder strode over until he stood behind Diana. "It isn't what?"

"His last journal," Melissa explained. "It ends just about four months before his death. Up until then, there were meticulous entries about everything. About the experiments."

Diana quickly said, "Tell us about the experiments."

Tension immediately erupted in Melissa's body. Sebastian could tell from the way her hand tightened on his, as if she needed an anchor. "Maybe we should sit. It's a long story."

A long painful story, especially since at the end of Melissa's account, they'd have to add the information they'd obtained on Sloan. Diana would know then what he'd done.

He offered Melissa what comfort he could as she recounted the details of her father's betrayal. It might have been easier had Ryder responded with anger, as he had the last time. Instead he remained quiet, but his face grew harder as each incident was revealed. When Melissa finished, he rose, his back turned to them. It was obvious, from the tight set of his body to the long rough breath he exhaled, what he was feeling.

Sebastian met his sister's gaze and knew she shared her lover's pain. She laid a hand on Ryder's back, soothing him although not a word passed between them. After what seemed like hours, Ryder finally faced Melissa once more, his anguish apparent. "I know Frederick did it for a good cause. I can understand wanting to protect the one you love."

Diana slipped her hand into Ryder's and the vampire dropped a kiss on her forehead as she leaned into him. The simplicity of the action, the freedom with which it came, bespoke of their love for one another. Sebastian hoped it would one day be that way with him and Melissa.

When Melissa's gaze met his, it was guarded, as if she got the direction of his thoughts, but couldn't reciprocate. She pulled her hand from his grasp and gripped her thighs as she continued.

"He meant well, but what he did… I'm sorry, Ryder."

Ryder shook his head vehemently. "You have nothing to apologize for. And no matter what your father intended, he clearly must have been careless enough to let someone else become aware of what he was doing."

"Edward Sloan knew. The NSA let him go over concerns about his mental stability," Sebastian said, girding himself for his sister's reaction.

"And you know this *how?*"

Sebastian met Diana's gaze directly. "We couldn't wait anymore, *hermanita*. We were getting nowhere and every day that passed—"

"Daly's watching Sloan as we speak. All we need is one little misstep and we have sufficient probable cause."

"For what? His little voyeur act? In the meantime, Sloan's managed to kill four people and not leave a trace."

"Please tell me you didn't break into his files," Diana asked, her voice tight with exasperation.

Sebastian continued as if his sister hadn't asked her question. "His handler at the NSA thought Sloan had lost it. Sloan was ranting about some kind of cells that he thought could be used to create a unit of 'supersoldiers.' Ones with superior strength, highly developed senses and the ability to heal quickly when wounded."

"Which was why Sloan was terminated roughly one month before the Danvers's crash," Diana finished, surprising him. At his reaction, she went on. "You're not the only one with information, *hermanito*. The difference is, I got it legally late last night from a reliable source."

Diana turned to Ryder. "Did you authorize this? Did you know what he was doing?"

Ryder placed his arms across his chest, clearly on the defensive. "I didn't, but I'm not sure I would have stopped him if I had known. Every day that Sloan is free is a day we're all at risk."

"And if Sebastian's break-in was noted and traced?" she argued.

"It wasn't. Len was—"

"Another person in the loop?" Ryder asked, his tone harsh.

Melissa quickly jumped in. "Len only knew we wanted to get information. He didn't know why and we didn't say."

Diana faced the other woman. "We? You mean you were in on this? You made yourself a knowing conspirator to a felony?"

It was clear from Diana's tone and the look she shot Sebastian just what she was thinking. He'd seen that particular look more than once on his father's face. He shot off the sofa and stood nose to nose with his sister. "Why don't you just say what you really mean? That you expected better of Melissa, but knew I'd eventually do something wrong because I'm a screwup."

"You're not a screwup, but what you did *was* wrong," she said calmly, although her hands were balled into fists by her side.

"It was important to get the information. I got the information."

"So did I. And I didn't risk us all to do it."

Ryder stepped up behind her and laid a hand on her shoulder. "He says he wasn't detected."

His sister whirled and directed her anger at her lover. "So what if he wasn't? It doesn't change the fact that he broke the law. A law I'm supposed to enforce. Do you expect me to turn a blind eye because it's my brother. Because it helps you?"

"Yes," was all he said.

Sebastian expected Diana to explode. He waited for the additional censure. Instead she stalked to the door of the apartment and walked out. The door closed behind her not with a slam, but with a quiet click that was even more telling.

"I'm sorry, Ryder, but I had to do it," Sebastian finally said.

Ryder was silent, but there was an angry tic along the side of his face. Sebastian expected him to vamp out as he had the last time he'd gotten angry, but he didn't. If anything, his calm as he spoke was unnerving. "Whatever you do affects me and mine. Don't do it again."

Melissa jumped to his defense. "Sebastian only did it because—"

"You asked? Don't betray me the way your father did, Melissa. You and I…" He paused, clearly distressed. Looking away for a moment, he dragged a hand through his hair, then scrubbed his face with his hands before proceeding. "You're not just my companion. You're my family. I will do whatever it takes to keep you safe. But don't go behind my back again."

He pointed a finger at Sebastian. "And you. Don't give me reason to dislike you."

Ryder was gone with a speed that Sebastian wasn't sure he'd ever get used to. Which left him in the large and altogether too-quiet living room with Melissa. "Maybe it's time that I left."

He'd been waiting… No, correction. He'd been *hoping* she'd contradict him.

"I think that would be best," Melissa said, shattering his illusions.

"Right." He rocked back and forth on his heels, delaying

in the hopes of a reprieve, but it was not forthcoming. He paused at the door. "Will I see you later?"

She met his gaze directly, but tried to school her emotions. "Maybe."

Sebastian had suffered so much rejection in his life that he should have been immune to Melissa's. Somehow he wasn't. It burned like a knife going into his gut because he'd wished for so much more from her. For so much more for them.

Only he'd been mistaken. Again. His father would have said that was typical of him—chasing after pipe dreams instead of reality. Melissa was a pipe dream. The sooner he accepted that, the quicker the pain in his heart would heal.

Chapter 21

Melissa lay in bed, staring up at the eggshell-white of the ceiling.

She was fully dressed. After Sebastian left, she couldn't muster the energy to change. And despite how tired she was, her mind was a Tilt-A-Whirl of emotions. Foremost among them, disgust at how she had behaved toward him. She'd driven him away and, in doing so, hurt him. Sebastian's face was like an open book and at her *maybe*, the only emotion there had been pain. All-consuming pain.

She of all people could understand distress of that kind. The anguish that came from being rejected by those you cared about. Those who you wanted to love you back.

For as long as she could remember, she had wanted love like that from her parents. She'd been a good little soldier and done everything they'd wanted in the hopes that they'd acknowledge her.

It had never happened. Nothing she'd ever done, including conforming to what she thought they considered the perfect little daughter, had ever been enough. Well, at least she hadn't thought it had.

Her father's memoirs had given her hope that the situation had been otherwise. That her parents had some affection for her. Sad that the crime responsible for taking them away had finally given her something she'd been lacking all her life—their affection and an understanding of why it had seemed to be absent.

Until Sebastian, who'd given her his affection and more. Knowing all that she was and all that she might not ever be, he'd trusted her. Pain of an almost physical kind rose up in her. She laid her hand on her midsection and pressed down, trying to make the ache go away, but it didn't.

She knew there was only one thing that would ease her misery.

Racing from her bedroom, she ran into Ryder as he passed by the door to her room. "Sorry." He grabbed her to keep her from falling after the impact of their collision.

"Going somewhere?"

"Listen, I know you don't like Sebastian, but—"

"I asked him not to give me reason to dislike him. Surprisingly, I find him refreshing," Ryder admitted.

"Refreshing? Mouthwash is refreshing. So is toothpaste and Altoids and—"

"You love him."

Faced with that plainly worded statement, there was little to say except, "I just might."

Ryder surprised her by smiling. "So what are you going to do about it?"

"What do you think?"

Melissa didn't wait for his response. She snagged her purse from where it rested on the table by the couch and raced out the door.

* * *

Sebastian walked for blocks, not really seeing or hearing anything around him. His mind was fraught with how the promise of the morning had been replaced by so many harsh words. With Diana. With Melissa.

He had no doubt Diana felt strongly about what he had done. How strongly remained to be seen, but no matter his sister's decision, he'd abide by it. Even if it meant going to jail. He was man enough to be responsible for his actions, even if his sister doubted that he was.

Just as Melissa doubted. It was hard for him to understand why she had turned from him. He'd always been up-front with her. Been totally open with his growing feelings. He'd even put his concern for her emotions and safety above his own personal freedom and his relationship with his sister.

He had hoped for more from Melissa. His disappointment was so sharp, it became corrosive, eating at him. Keeping him warm inside despite the chill of the bleak winter day.

Eventually, the long night and tension-filled morning took its toll, making his legs and feet feel leaden. At the corner he checked out the street sign and realized he was just a few blocks from home. Quickening his pace, he took the most direct route, wanting to drop into bed and let sleep erase what memories it could.

As he turned onto his block, he noticed something on the stoop of his building. Once he was closer, he recognized the back of Melissa's head and the dark blue peacoat she favored. He stopped directly in front of her, but couldn't find his voice.

It was hard to say how long he stood there before she raised her head. Her eyes were shining as if she'd been crying, and even with his anger, the sight of her tears touched him. Swallowing hard, he said, "What are you doing here?"

She laughed harshly. "Besides freezing?"

An unexpected answer. He pulled his keys from his pocket and motioned to the door of his building. "I'm going in. You're welcome to join me, or," he said as he spread his arms wide, "you can stay here and keep freezing your ass off."

Melissa wished she had a witty rejoinder, but she was too tired and too cold. Plus, she had to save her mental reserves for what was sure to follow their entrance into his apartment.

She followed him inside, trekking up the three flights of stairs to the walk-up he shared with Diana. His sister would hopefully be at work and not at home. Maybe she was a chicken, but Melissa couldn't deal with Diana again. Not just yet.

Once inside, he stripped off his leather duster and negligently tossed it on the couch. Without looking at her, he headed to another room and called out, "Would you like something warm to drink?"

How polite and impersonal. How ridiculous, given what had gone down between them barely a couple of hours earlier. "Tea would be fine. Chamomile if you have it."

Melissa slipped off her peacoat, tossed it beside Sebastian's, and joined him in the kitchen. He was busy puttering around, filling a teakettle. He placed it on the gas range and lit the burner. Once the kettle was warming, he turned and faced her, his hands on the edge of the stove. "No need to wait here. I'll bring it in—"

"Somehow I didn't expect that the next time we spoke, it would be about tea."

He brought his arms across his chest and adopted a stance that was somewhere between insolent and carefree. "Really? So sorry to disappoint you, but then again, that's par for the course."

Melissa took the few steps necessary to stand directly before him. "Don't."

"Don't what? Betray my sister? Piss off a vampire who could suck me dry if I annoyed him too much?" His face was hard and unyielding.

"Don't buy into what your father thought of you. You're nothing like that." Melissa's urging only earned a bleak sigh from Sebastian.

She laid a hand on his arm, but he pulled away from her touch. "Sebastian."

"What do you want, Melissa? What are you doing here?" He refused to meet her gaze.

"I'm here because I know that I hurt you. You deserve more. I'm sorry."

Sebastian couldn't believe she wanted more between them. "Apology accepted. So once you're done with your tea—"

"Don't shut me out. My whole life I've been shut out and damn it, I won't let you do it." With each word, her voice escalated not just in volume, but in distress.

Sebastian came as close to her as he could without touching her, because if he touched her... "You said that I shouldn't buy into what my father thought about me. I thought I hadn't, until this morning."

He shook his head and took a deep breath. Shoving his hands into his pockets, he continued, "I knew I had disappointed my sister, but when I saw the same doubt in your eyes—"

"I'd be lying if I said I was sure of you right then. Of how you felt about what was going on with your sister. Whether what you felt for me was strong enough to last."

She stopped short and bit her lower lip. In softer tones, she said, "I'm not sure about *me*, Sebastian. That you could still care for me."

Two such wounded creatures. He finally gave into his need and cupped her cheek. It was still chilled from the cold. The hiss of the teakettle became a whistling screech. Without looking, he reached back and shut off the burner. Tea was the last thing on his mind.

"Whatever is going on between us is complex. Definitely uncertain. I'd be a liar if I said that I didn't worry." He brushed his hand through the thick silk of her blond hair.

Meeting her gaze so that she'd have no doubts, he continued, "About me and whether I'm strong enough to handle the kind of life you lead. About whether you can believe that what's going on between us is real."

Melissa looked away and in a voice so faint he had to strain to hear, she said, "It is, but this morning… I hate that I've complicated your life. That you've risked so much for me."

Sebastian gently urged her to look at him. "Because you doubt yourself, *mi amor.*"

His brightness and warmth spread to her and she found herself smiling. "So can we rewind? Go back to this morning and all the plans we had?"

Sebastian wrapped his arms around her and brought her close. Laying his face alongside hers, he whispered in her ear, "Like a long nap. Waking together. Maybe sharing lunch?"

She cupped the back of his head and dropped a kiss on the side of his face. "I was actually thinking of something else first."

"Breakfast?" he teased.

She nipped his earlobe playfully. "Are you playing hard to get?"

He pulled away, his dark eyes glittering with both merriment and desire. "Maybe."

She chuckled and shook her head. "You enjoy this way too much."

Sebastian laid a finger on the line of her cheekbone. "I do. I enjoy making you blush." He trailed his finger down to her lips and traced the edges of her mouth. "The way you smile and how those lips warm next to mine."

As if to emphasize his desire, he gave her the barest whisper of a kiss. As he pulled away, she found herself leaning toward him, wanting more. He gave it to her, but not in the way she had expected.

He ran his finger down the open neckline of her oxford shirt, then swept it to the center of one breast, where with a mere flick of that finger, he brought her nipple to a tight bud. "I enjoy the blush on your breasts when I kiss them." He replaced his finger with his mouth.

Even with the barrier of the fabric, the heat and wet of his mouth rocked her to the core. She clasped his head to her and he urged her backward until her backside was leaning on the edge of the kitchen table. But that wasn't enough and she lay down on it and urged him into the vee formed by her legs.

Sebastian braced an arm on the kitchen table and glanced down at her. Her cheeks were flushed. Her eyes, wide and dilated with passion, followed his every move as he worked free the buttons of her shirt and opened it wide to display the delicate lace bra she wore. He touched her breasts, tugging at her nipples with his fingers until they peaked. She wrapped her legs around his hips until he was pressed tight to the center of her.

He knew then there was no stopping.

Chapter 22

He undid the front clasp of her bra and her breasts spilled free, her nipples a sweet caramel color against the paler vanilla of her skin. He cupped them and she sucked in a breath. When he moved his fingers to play with their hardness, she moaned and closed her eyes against what she was feeling.

"Open your eyes, Melissa." He kissed her lips, then worked his way down to her breasts.

He risked a quick glance upward and was pleased to see she had responded to his request. Her eyes, blazing bright blue with her desire, were glued to his every move. It made him swell tighter against the fabric of his jeans. Made him want to bury himself inside her and watch those marvelous eyes darken even more with passion.

Somehow he controlled the urge to rush. He took her nipple into his mouth. She was warm and so sweet. She urged him on with her soft cries and the shift of her hips against his body.

He repeated his caress for the other breast, and slowly

moved his way downward, trailing kisses along her midsection, pausing at her navel to dip his tongue into the sweet indentation and thank whoever had invented low-rise jeans.

Moving a little farther, he encountered the waistband of those jeans and quickly undid them. Then he stayed away from her only long enough to peel her jeans and panties from her body. He paused for a moment to examine all that he had revealed.

Her skin was flushed and glistening. The curls at the juncture of her thighs were a slightly darker blonde and soft, he thought as he passed his hand over them.

When he looked up, she was still watching him. As his gaze locked with hers, she seemed to experience a moment of shyness. She covered his hand as it rested against her most intimate spot.

Without breaking eye contact, Sebastian reversed the position of their hands and gently urged her hand downward. He joined his fingers with hers at the center of her. Exhorted her to move them.

There was shock in her eyes, followed by the deepest of pleasure as he slipped a finger within her, and she did, as well. Slowly they stroked together, building her passion. Building his as he imagined replacing those fingers with his erection. Feeling the same heat and wet surround him. Drawing him into the center of her.

Sebastian groaned and withdrew his hand. He fumbled with the buttons on his jeans. Grasping her hips, he positioned himself to enter her, then cursed. He was about to move away for protection when she wrapped her legs around him to keep him there.

"I need to get something," he said.

The smile that came to her lips was shyly seductive. "I'm protected now. And I'm safe."

He nearly came then and there at her admission. At the latent request in her statement.

He managed to control himself. He tightened his hold on her hips and shifted her a little bit closer to him on the table. Slowly he eased into her, his eyes trained on her face. His heart focused on the wonder of being inside her, sharing his body and his passion.

She'd thought it couldn't get any better than it had been the other night and yet it was. Grabbing his shoulders, she tilted her hips upward, increasing the depth of his penetration. The slide of him built a friction inside, generating heat and even more wetness until a quickening began within her, gripping him to her. It spread throughout her body until she was holding him with her arms and legs. Pleading with him to drive harder and take her over the edge.

He pleasured one breast while he drove into her. He bit the tip of it, which released the tension that had taken over her body. Sobbing, she let it wash over her.

Sebastian heard her cries, took a deep breath and stilled within her, wanting to feel the rush of her climax. As she clasped him tight, he moved again, fighting against the tide of her passion, feeling his own answering swell that pushed him ever closer to his own release.

She surprised him by leaning upward and running her tongue around the edge of his nipple, teething it, which caused a pull deep in his groin. The sensation new and intensely satisfying, he continued to move in her until it was finally too much. With a groan, he gave one final shift of his hips, grinding himself into her as deeply as he could get. Spilling himself into the wet warmth encircling him.

His arms were shaky, his breath rough as he lay down on her, their bodies awkwardly draped on the table. When he finally withdrew, he scooped her up into his arms.

At her questioning glance, he said, "Time for some rest." His legs had a faint tremble as he walked to his bedroom, where he let her slip down to the ground.

When she tumbled into his bed, he paused a moment to

capture the moment in his mind. It was the first time she'd been here.

He vowed it wouldn't be the last.

She didn't know what woke her. Possibly the hard press of Sebastian against her belly, although when she looked at him through half-open eyes, she realized he was still asleep.

Melissa hoped it was dreams of her that had him hard and with just the barest hint of a smile on his lips. Because there was a spot inside her that seemed empty without him, she shifted and drew her thigh up over the flare of his hips. Reaching down, she guided him into her.

He roused with a start, but quickly recovered. "I thought it was just a dream." He smiled sleepily, the dimple on the side of his face deep with his pleasure.

Melissa tracked her finger across his lips where he nipped at it playfully. "I was missing you."

Sebastian slipped an arm beneath her head, pillowing it. His other arm he draped across her waist. "I'm here, *amor.*"

"Hmm," was all she said because the moment was too perfect to spoil with words. Instead she brought her lips to his, slowly exploring the contours of his mouth. Over and over, savoring each kiss until they finally broke apart, slightly breathless.

"That was nice," she said, and cupped the defined muscles of his chest.

"Very," he responded, his voice slightly husky. He mimicked the motion of her hand by bringing his up to caress her breast.

She watched the reaction of his body, felt it within her as he swelled. He, too, was watching, his gaze riveted to her breast, and Melissa looked down. The skin of his hand was dark against hers. The pads of his fingers slightly rough to the sensitive peak as he brushed them lazily across her. She liked when he touched her like that. Wanted him to do more.

Much as he had done last night, she covered his hand to still his motion. Feeling a daring she hadn't before, Melissa showed him just what she wanted and he eagerly complied. She let out a little gasp of pleasure and shifted her hips against his.

Sebastian bit back his own groan, pleased by her candor and by her need. He realized that what she was giving him, the sharing they had just reached together, was something totally new. Rewarding, but scary. It went beyond the joining of their bodies and he wanted it to be perfect. He wanted her to know he was hers.

He gripped the flare of her waist with one hand, slowly guiding her as he rolled onto his back and gave her total possession of his body. She took it, and gave more back.

As they lay together afterward, Sebastian held her close and silently prayed that this newfound love could survive the challenges that seemed to be a part of their lives lately.

He only hoped that when danger called, he'd be strong enough to face it.

Chapter 23

The coward's way would have been to wait for Diana to address his hacking. In retrospect, it was the pattern they'd fallen into during much of their childhood. Diana had been the problem solver and mediator between Sebastian and their dad.

But after walking Melissa to the hospital for her shift and armed with a new sense of resolve, Sebastian realized he couldn't wait for Diana. This was something *he* needed to address.

He took the subway down to her building and, after clearing security, rode the elevator to her office. He had been announced, so his sister wasn't surprised when he appeared at her door.

She asked her partner, David, if he wouldn't mind giving them a minute.

David glanced between the two siblings and excused himself quickly, but not before warning Sebastian, "Be careful there, bro. She's got a thorn in her paw that's making her mighty ornery."

"David." The threat in Diana's voice was clear.

With a wave, David left, closing the door behind him.

"I'm surprised you came," Diana said, obviously not about to mince words.

"You could warn me a thousand times not to do what I did, but if I had to do it all again—"

"I'd hope that you'd ask me," she interjected.

"You would never agree to—"

"We won't ever find that out because you didn't bother to ask."

To say that he was shocked would have been an understatement. "You made your position obvious. I thought there was no room for discussion."

"Maybe you're right. Maybe there wasn't in this case. Mainly because we hadn't yet gotten to a point where such extreme measures were required." She sat behind her desk and, without waiting for his reply, she shuffled a few files around, located one and handed it to him.

Sebastian opened it up to reveal a history of Edward Sloan that detailed all the time before and after his employment at the NSA. He skimmed the information quickly and a few pages down found a tersely worded statement he recognized from his break-in. Closing the file, he held it up and asked, "How did you get this?"

"Through legitimate channels and some favors." She tilted back in her chair, leaned her elbows on its arms and steepled her fingers before her. "Not that any of that helps. Even with Daly tracking Sloan, we haven't managed to put together enough for probable cause."

Sebastian glanced through the file again and this time something else caught his eye. "Not even the fact that at one time Sloan was a research chemist working on a synthetic morphine product?"

Diana shook her head. "Gives him the ability to make the heroin, but doesn't establish motive or opportunity."

Anger flared in him. Even with all the information they had, it still wasn't enough. "I just love it when you get all official-sounding."

She lurched forward and snagged the file from his hand. "This isn't some game, Sebastian. It's life or death."

"Don't you think I know that? Melissa's parents are dead. So are two ex-cons. Any one of us—Ryder excluded—could be next."

"I want you out of this, Sebastian."

He laughed harshly and looked away. After a moment, he faced her directly. "Afraid I can't handle it. Afraid that—"

"I'll lose you. I couldn't bear to see you hurt or worse, *hermanito*. And I'm not so sure I can handle Sloan."

He searched his sister's face. Her anguish was transparent and he recognized just how hard that admission had been for her. Special Agent Reyes was supposed to be able to control everything. "I can take care of myself," he reassured her.

"And Melissa? Can you take care of her?"

Sebastian considered what he and Melissa had shared that morning, the promise of it latent with all the inherent risks. "Melissa would be the first to say she doesn't need a hero, but if need be, I can try."

With a harsh breath, Diana replied, "Try? There is no *try*, Sebastian. It's not a game where you can reboot if you don't like the outcome. It's either do or fail."

Her words stung, reminiscent, as they always were, of his father. "Is that what you really think of me? I'm not the little boy who needed to hide behind your coattails. I'm my own man now. I can take care of what I have to."

Diana was taken aback for a moment. There was steel behind his words that she hadn't heard before. A stiffening of his spine and a glint in his eye that confirmed his belief in his words. Pride filled her at the strong man sitting before her. But fear crept in as well. "Do you love her enough to risk your life? To become involved with someone who can never have a normal existence?"

His gaze was steady as it locked with hers. "Did you have a choice when you fell in love with Ryder?"

Her answer was immediate. "No."

Sebastian shrugged. "She believes in me and because of that, I believe in myself. I can't fail her."

Diana rose and laid a hand on his shoulder. "I believe you're a good man, Sebastian, one who's caught up in something much bigger than real life. Something very confusing."

"I'm not—"

"Confused? Then you're a better person than I am. I was confused as hell. Am still confused. Even when Ryder revealed to me what he was and I wanted to kick his ass so that the pain would go away, I couldn't stop loving him."

Sebastian pulled back a little at his sister's admission. He'd never imagined her not knowing what she wanted. "I know you love him. And I think you know how much I worry that he'll break your heart."

Diana nodded. "Just as I worry that being involved with Melissa will risk yours, *hermanito.*"

He was silent as he pondered her statement, then he gave a quick chuckle. "Seems to me that we have to trust each other's instincts."

She opened her arms. He stepped into her embrace and hugged her tightly. "Then trust me next time, Sebastian."

"I will, but in the meantime, what do we do?" he asked.

"It's time to flush our snake out of hiding."

The news was not good.

A visit to the specialist that day had revealed the cancer was spreading fast. Soon it would become even more debilitating.

All that was needed to make a difference was some of the refined cell strain Frederick Danvers had somehow perfected. Those cells had seemed to work magic on Elizabeth. Dear sweet Elizabeth.

Killing her had been difficult, especially when it seemed

as if she would finally be able to live a normal life. Had she been a different kind of woman, she might have opted for life with him rather than death with her freshly departed husband. But she hadn't, a testament to her strength of mind and her love for Frederick Danvers.

Danvers had been a lucky man to have all that he could ever have wanted—a beautiful adoring wife, an equally wonderful daughter, success in a career such as few could envision.

All things which might someday have been his.

There was suddenly something of interest on the monitor. With a smile, it was obvious someday might have just arrived.

The medical journal lay in the middle of her desk, the highlighting prominent. Various sections were tagged with sticky notes. Beside it were her own handwritten comments, as well as copies from some of her patients' charts, again with sticky notes and highlighting. It would appear clear to anyone that she was intent on duplicating an experiment and comparing it to the results she had achieved with her own patients.

Risking but a half glance at the frame on her desk, she wondered what her voyeur could see. Just another day at work, or something to pique his or her interest? In time, she hoped to draw out the killer. He would see her new experiments as a smoke screen for setting up a lab where she would repeat her father's experiments.

Melissa was a little queasy as she made the first call. She had assumed they had eliminated Sara as a possible suspect, but with only two people on the list, Diana believed they should at least offer Sara the bait.

Ringing the nurses' station, Melissa prepared herself for deceiving her friend and hoped she was not wrong to believe that Sara was innocent. When Sara answered, Melissa said, "I have a favor to ask. Do you think you could come by when you have a moment?"

"Hold on a sec." There was the metallic clank of charts and

ringing before the Muzak from the hospital's phone system clicked on. "Sorry. There was a bit of a rush right then. What can I do?"

"I'm thinking of doing some experiments and—"

"Like your dad did?"

Shit and double shit. "No, not at all. If you come down when you're free, I'll show you what I'd like to research."

Was it her imagination that it took just a little too long for Sara to respond? "Sure. Do you mind if I ask your advice about something?"

A little relief returned. "Of course not. Unless I'm called to the E.R. or doing rounds, I'll be in my office."

The sounds of activity surged forward on the line once again before Sara reacted. "This is a crazy night, but I'll try to break away in about fifteen minutes."

"Sounds good," Melissa said. After putting the phone down, she took a breath and braced herself for the next call.

Nervous energy crackled through her as Edward's voice mail answered. She hated to leave a message, so she hung up and tried his home number. Again, it rang and rang until the answering machine picked up. With a sigh, she replaced the telephone receiver in its cradle. She would try again a little later.

Returning to the journal and papers before her, Melissa reviewed the article and her own information. She skimmed through the papers one last time and was in the process of making a few new notes when a knock came at the door. "Come in," she called out, expecting Sara.

Surprise came in the form of Edward Sloan.

"Well, hello, Edward. I just tried reaching you." Melissa sensed something was off, but she was unable to pinpoint what. As always, he was impeccably dressed and perfectly groomed. His gait was a little slower than usual, but that was to be expected from a man who was nearing his midseventies.

"I was just on my way out," he said, motioning with his

hand to the door. "I wanted to make sure everything was fine after our little misunderstanding the other day."

"I am fine with everything, Edward. No hard feelings. Actually…" She grabbed the medical journal and all her notes and met Edward by the door. "If you have the time, I'd like to run something by you."

He smiled. A shark's smile or was it her imagination running rampant? Could they be wrong about him? Could the real killer still be undetected? "Of course, my dear. Anything to help you."

Once they were both settled on her couch, Melissa spread the papers out on the coffee table. Gesturing to the article, she said, "You were right the other day, Edward, when you said that in time I'd have to do more if I wanted to advance here. So as I was doing some reading, I came across this." She explained how the results in the journal matched those she had gotten with her patients, but how she was uncertain as to whether the mechanisms described in the article fit the patterns she had observed in her practice.

"You'll pardon me if I'm a little confused. These experiments—"

"Will help me establish my own reputation here. One not built upon what my father did."

Edward appeared taken aback. After impatiently examining the papers, he eased back onto the sofa cushions, wincing as he did so.

"Are you okay?" she asked.

"Just a touch of arthritis. Happens to the best of us, I'm afraid." His smile was forced and pain lingered in his eyes.

Once she was certain he had recovered, Melissa said, "I was wondering if you could help me set up a lab. I know my father—"

"Had one over in the university building. It may still be available, but are you certain this new experiment is the way to go? Your father's research was quite impressive." In that moment, whatever lingering doubts she might have had vanished. She finally saw him for what he was—Edward the Deceiver. Edward the Manipulator. Edward the Murderer.

Because of that, she carefully chose what she would say next. "I'm sure it was, although I must confess to knowing nothing about it. Still, once I'm more comfortable around the lab, maybe you can help with what you know—"

"Or you can check your father's things. Frederick was always the kind of scientist who kept meticulous notes."

Somehow, she schooled her emotions. Her voice, when she responded, was calm, with not a hint of either the anger or discomfort she was feeling. "You're probably right, Edward. After all, my father and you knew each other for how long?"

"Almost thirty years. But unfortunately, I know as little as you do about his last work." He patted her leg in a fatherly kind of way.

Melissa fought back a shiver of revulsion. "That's a long time to be friends." But apparently not long enough if he could sacrifice both her father and mother for his own gain.

"Ah, friends. Yes, we were friends. Your father and I. Your mother. She was quite a woman." There was a mix of emotions in his tone. He'd obviously cared for her mother, possibly more than he should have. Had that been one of his reasons for getting rid of her father? She decided to push him just a little to see if he pushed back.

"I never really knew Mother. She was always distant, except in the last few months when she was doing so much better. She and my father seemed so in love. Had you noticed?"

"Who could fail to see their affection for one another?" His voice was gruff. He moved his hands nervously on his legs, then stilled them suddenly. "They lived only for each other."

His response gave her the perfect opportunity. "And never for me. It must have been difficult for you, as well, being their friend and all. But Mother seemed so much better toward the end. I've wondered if it was because of what my father was working on?"

Edward again shifted his hands anxiously. "I understood the way they were. After all, your mother was very sick, but she *was* better at the end. I suspect that your father had—"

"Are you ready for me?" Sara asked. She barrelled into Melissa's office, but stopped short at the sight of Melissa and Edward sitting together on the sofa. "Sorry. I didn't know anyone was in here. Evening, Dr. Sloan."

"Nurse Martinez," he said with an imperious tone and haughty nod. "Is it your habit to barge into private offices?"

"I'm sorry, Dr. Sloan, only—"

Melissa stepped up to Sara's defense, rising from the couch to stand next to her friend. "It's okay, Edward. I had asked Sara to come in just before you visited."

Edward grunted and slowly eased himself to the edge of the sofa. Once there, he used the coffee table for leverage to stand. His movements were again slow and clearly painful. Melissa wondered why she hadn't noticed before.

"I need to be going anyway. Just remember I'm here to help you should you find any information," he said.

Melissa faked a smile and escorted the older man to the door. "I'll see if there's anything I've overlooked amongst my father's things and give you a call. In the meantime, maybe you can put me in touch with who I can contact about a lab room?"

Edward paused as he entered the hallway. "Yes. Yes, of course I will. I'll have a name for you in the morning."

Melissa closed the door behind him.

"And again I say he's a weird bird. What's he want this time?" Sara asked as she plopped down on the couch.

"He seems to think I have information about my father's experiments," Melissa replied without hesitation.

"But you don't. Right?"

"Right. So I was thinking of asking you if you knew where my father had his samples and things. Notes, stuff like that."

"Actually, no. I assume he kept them close by on account

of running into him with those tubes. You normally wouldn't be going far with samples."

Examining her friend as she spoke, Melissa decided that Sara was either a very good liar or totally innocent. Melissa held to the belief that it was the latter. "What's up with you? You said you had a favor to ask?"

"My mom…" Sara paused as her voice cracked. Tears shimmered in her eyes, but the odd thing was, they didn't seem like tears of sadness.

Melissa sat on the edge of the coffee table and laid a hand on Sara's scrub-covered knee. "She's not worse, is she?"

"That's why I need a favor. I can't take *Mami* to her oncologists. They'd just start poking and prodding if they thought she'd suddenly gotten way better." Sara motioned to her. "But you know there are things that happen that don't have explanations."

Confused by her friend's statement, she asked, "Why's that?"

"Your *mami*. The way she was all of a sudden not so sick anymore. I know you always wished she'd be better. Maybe you got your wish."

She'd wished her mother and father had loved her more, but that wish hadn't materialized until it was too late. The old adage of be careful what you wish for came to mind. "I think my father had a new treatment for her, but I'm not sure what it was."

"I so totally understand," Sara said with a wave of her hand. "This *santero* did his little *brujeria* on *Mami*. Three times she went over there with the blood he wanted."

"Why so many?" Melissa questioned, wondering what scam he'd been running.

"He said he could only heal so much at a time. He also said he wouldn't be able to do anything else for now. That we needed to wait and see what happened." Sara let out a frustrated sigh and brushed the long strands of her caramel-colored hair from her face.

"Do you think it's a con to get you to offer him money?" Melissa asked.

Sara shook her head. "I don't know. All I do know is that *Mami* seems better. But maybe he just cast some spell—"

"Come on, Sara. You don't really believe in that mumbo jumbo crap," Melissa admonished.

"Your problem is that you're too skeptical, Melissa. Too by the book. There's all kinds of things out there that you won't let yourself believe in, but that doesn't change the fact that they're still there."

Didn't she know it. Who believed in vampires? Which suddenly had her wondering if maybe there was more to this *santero* than he was letting on. "He didn't bite your mom, did he?"

When Sara spoke, it was nearly a screech before she calmed down a little. "Are you crazy, *chica?* He only laid his hands on her. Told her if her faith was strong enough, it would help her heal. Not much different than what you see on Sunday morning television, huh?"

Melissa nodded. "Faith is faith. You either believe or you don't. So you want me to run some tests? See if she really is better?"

"And if she is, I want to leave it at that, Melissa. No needles or other tests to see why."

Melissa understood completely. Sara wanted her mother to enjoy what time she had left. Melissa only hoped that this *santero* hadn't been faking. She didn't want to be the one to disappoint her friend with any bad news.

Giving Sara's hand a gentle squeeze, she said, "I promise. Nothing else. You can trust me."

"I know I can, same as you can trust me, *amiga.*"

And in that moment, just as she had known she couldn't believe Edward, Melissa knew she could trust Sara with her life.

Chapter 24

The lab her father had used was no longer available, but there was another one, smaller, which required a bit of organization and cleaning. Given that her purpose in needing the space was only a ruse, it was just right.

Although very messy, she thought as she walked in through the door, Sebastian trailing behind her. "Could use a *Mission: Big Sweep*, couldn't it?"

Sebastian arched a brow as he stood in the small free space in the center of the room and examined the three tables littered with a variety of beakers, columns and tubes. "Possibly even a bulldozer. Do you need all this?" he asked as he walked to one table and ran his finger over a thick layer of dust on one beaker.

Melissa laid her files on another less cluttered table and took stock of the equipment the previous occupant had left behind. Definitely more than she needed for the experiment from the medical journal or even for an experiment similar to her father's. From what she deduced from her father's notes, his needs had been minimal, mostly the laboratory rats and their requirements. "We can return what we don't need to the equipment room. I've already put in an order for some lab rats."

Sebastian leaned against the table and smiled. "I don't remember the article in the medical journal mentioning any animals."

She gave the edges of his black leather duster a playful tug. "No, it didn't. If Edward is the one, he'll know it, too."

He wrapped his arms around her waist and pulled her close. "How secure is this place?"

"Unless you have a key card to get in, there's the basic security check at the main door. Video in the hallways and elevators. Plain old lock and key for this room. That's it."

Pursing his lips, he replied, "Then I'm on you like beans on rice. When do we get started?"

Melissa ran her hand through the strands of his dark brown hair. Then with a puzzled look, she touched the slight stubble coming in around his lips and his chin. "What's this?"

He rubbed the fuzz across the side of her face before kissing the edges of her lips. "You said you liked disreputable."

She could deny it, but it would be a huge lie. For days he'd been back to the old Sebastian. He was dressed again in a T-shirt and black jeans, and had slipped his silver hoop back in one ear. As he'd helped her slip on her own jacket, she'd noticed the thumb ring and silver bracelet on one hand. Sexy, she'd thought, wondering what it was about his whole bad-boy thing that appealed to her.

"Hmm," she replied, rubbing her lips over the fuzz, liking the feel of the newborn goatee. She moved her face a fraction of an inch and slipped her lips over his. "Nice."

Sebastian opened his mouth against hers. "Very, very nice."

She returned the kiss, leaning into him. He brought his hand between their bodies and was moving it upward when a loud cough at the door jolted them apart.

Hot color flooded her cheeks as she whirled toward the sound. Edward stood at the door, an amused look on his face.

"I knocked, but no one heard. I'm sorry."

"No, not at all, Edward. You know Sebastian." She motioned to Sebastian, his arm still around her waist as if to announce his intentions.

"Yes. I believe we've met before." Edward strolled into the lab and made a face of annoyance as he ran a finger across the grime on the surface of one table. "This is quite a mess."

"Sebastian and I were just going to tackle it," she said.

Again Edward made a face to show his displeasure, but this time it was directed exclusively at Sebastian. "Yes, well. If you need someone who knows their way around a lab, let me know."

Sebastian stiffened. Giving him a reassuring squeeze, Melissa shook her head. "Sebastian and I can handle things just fine. We're going to clean and get some sterile equipment before I get started."

"Well, then. I can see I'm not needed, but first…" He walked out of the lab and came back with a small brown paper shopping bag. "I thought if you were anything like your father, you might need this."

He held out the bag and Melissa placed it on a table. Inside there was a small box covered in deep maroon wrapping paper. She undid the wrap to reveal a brass Seth Thomas clock. She held it up so Sebastian could see it. "Isn't this beautiful?"

"Yes. Very thoughtful," he said, a forced smile on his face.

Edward chimed in with, "Your father always lost track of time. I hope this might help keep you from the same mistake."

"Thank you," she replied, thinking she wouldn't make the same mistake her father had made in trusting his old friend. Despite that, she gave him a hug. She suspected the clock was bugged, much like the frame in her office.

After Edward left, Melissa closed the door and turned to face Sebastian, holding out the clock for his inspection. "What do you think?"

Sebastian accepted the clock and examined it carefully. Sure enough, there was a hint of something in the small hole that was supposed to mimic the look of a winding mechanism. "Beautiful. Let's put it somewhere special."

He placed the clock on a table, but in a position that left him and Melissa free to move about a large portion of the lab. Grabbing his knapsack, he extracted his laptop and sat down in a metal folding chair at the far end of one table. After powering up, he quickly searched the various frequencies until he got a hit. "This one has the transmitter hidden inside," he said as he tapped into the signal coming from the clock.

While staying out of camera range, Sebastian checked beneath all the tables. "It's a strong signal so the receiver doesn't have to be in this room. He may have it stowed somewhere nearby."

Melissa glanced over his shoulder at his screen where the video from the lab was displayed. It was a much sharper picture than the one from the camera in her office. "The old prick. It is him. What do we do now?"

"It's illegal to video someone without their knowledge, but that's a minor charge. So we sucker him into something more." He turned the laptop until the screen was visible from the rest of the room.

"Sounding all law enforcement, aren't we?" she teased.

He took hold of her hand and led her back into the line of sight of the camera. Leaning on the edge of the table, he drew her close, all the time keeping a guarded eye on what was visible on his laptop screen.

"Sebastian?" Melissa asked as he pulled her against him and wrapped his arms around her waist. She, too, shot a quick glance at the computer. "What are we doing?"

"Giving him the show he expects," he said, nuzzling the side of her face. "We need to act normal and dear Edward probably expects us to get back to what he interrupted."

There was something a little odd about being on exhibition, even if at their current position the camera only had a view of them from about their hips to their shoulders. Still, Sebastian's suggestion made sense and was, of course, highly pleasurable. She opened her mouth to his kiss. Enjoyed the slow, almost drugging way he made love to her with his mouth. Pulling at her lips with his. Dancing his tongue inside to tease hers to play. Which she did until she was shaking and breathless.

She grabbed hold of his shoulders, but he wisely kept his hands at her waist. No sense giving Edward too much of a show and feeling uncomfortable about what they were doing.

When Sebastian finally broke away from her, he brushed a hand over her hair. "I guess we should get to work."

Melissa looked at the mess in the lab once again. With a grimace and then a smile, she said, "It would serve Edward right if we took him up on his offer of assistance."

Sebastian slipped his hands around her waist. "Nah. Wait until we get the lab rats and *then* drive the old guy crazy."

Melissa's grin broadened. Sebastian was probably right. "Yes, let's wait."

The little bitch was playing games with him. He'd gone by the equipment room and seen her requests. Lab rats. There was only one reason for them—she was going to recreate Frederick's experiments. Which meant she knew the source of the unusual cells.

As he walked down the hall, he opened his PDA and quickly executed the remote camera's program. On came the picture from the lab. Very distinct and revealing. They were at it again. A bitch in heat. The possibilities excited him since, at his age, the options for recreational sex were rather limited.

Only nothing happened. He experienced only a slight sense of disappointment, which vanished quickly as he realized that they were cleaning and organizing the lab. Considering its sad state, it might take them a day or two to get it ready.

When they finished with their work, he'd be ready, as well.

* * *

"I've got news," Diana said.

The four of them had met in Ryder's kitchen after Melissa's return from her late-night shift at the hospital.

Diana and Ryder had presumably shared a night together since both were still in robes, Sebastian thought. He had spent the night working, then he'd picked up Melissa at the hospital. Although he'd finished scanning the journals, he knew he wasn't going anywhere. Except maybe Melissa's bed, he thought as she slipped her hand into his.

He smiled and twined his fingers with hers.

"Peter Daly called a few minutes ago," Diana said. "The tail he had on Sloan didn't produce any results, except for this—Sloan visited an oncologist in the hospital yesterday afternoon."

Ryder shrugged. "One doctor consulting with another."

Diana shook her head and joined Ryder by sitting on his lap. "That's what the detective thought at first, but he decided to confirm it. The receptionist wouldn't say much. Claimed that doctors couldn't reveal information about a patient."

Melissa's hand stiffened in his. "Edward was in some pain the other day when he visited me. Claimed it was a touch of arthritis. Maybe he's sick."

"Which gives him a personal investment in your father's work. He saw how your mother had improved and assumed whatever helped her might be able to do the same for him," Sebastian said.

Diana nodded at her brother. "That would explain why he was so over the top at the NSA. It wasn't just about 'super-soldiers.' It was about finding a cure for himself, as well."

"Desperation makes him even more dangerous." The concern in Ryder's voice was apparent, so it came as no surprise to anyone what he said next. "We can't expose you to that kind of risk, Melissa. We'll have to rethink the lab decoy."

"No way. It's the only thing that's worked so far. Thanks

to that, we know it's Edward spying on me," Melissa said, her voice growing more tense with every word.

Sebastian rubbed her back. "We need to pressure Sloan into making a mistake so Diana has enough probable cause to have her friend ask for a warrant. Without the lab, we're back to square one."

"I can't protect her at the lab. I'm not strong enough to be out in the sun," Ryder said, clearly uneasy.

Sebastian didn't know much about vampire physiology. But he did know one thing. "No one said you were the one who was going to protect her."

He met his sister's concerned gaze, waiting for her to contradict him. Instead she nodded and laid a hand on Ryder's shoulder. "I know you want to help her, *amor*. But your control of your vamp traits has been unreliable lately. If you were hanging around and slipped up while Sloan was watching…"

"I can stay with her and make sure she's safe," Sebastian confirmed.

A myriad emotions passed over Ryder's face as he glanced from Sebastian to Melissa. Finally, with a long slow nod, he acquiesced, but quickly raised his finger and pointed it at Sebastian. "But remember, I'll be close by."

"That brings me great comfort," Sebastian replied facetiously. In reality, knowing Ryder was nearby did bring a bit of relief.

Melissa rose from the table and tugged on Sebastian's hand. "Now that that's settled, I'd like to get some sleep so I can return to the lab late this afternoon."

Diana likewise rose and took a quick look at her watch. "And I should be back at the office to see what else I can find out about Sloan, or if Daly's people get any more info today."

Ryder warned Melissa, "If Sloan is keeping tabs on you, he'll know what you're up to in the lab."

"The rats arrive this afternoon. I've got a feeling he already knows about them."

"And if he does, he's bound to make his move soon, so please be careful." Diana gave both Melissa and Sebastian a hug.

"*Hermanita,* don't worry. Between Ryder and me, everything will be all right."

"And me. Remember me? I'm still here," Melissa added, waving her hand in the air, clearly a little annoyed at being left out.

"How could I forget you, *mi amor?*" he replied teasingly and embraced her tightly. "Let's go to bed. We need to get some rest."

Only as they walked into Melissa's bedroom, Sebastian wished rest would wait for a bit. As Melissa turned to him, her hand outstretched and a broad smile on her face, his wish came true.

Chapter 25

"We should call him Ben," Sebastian said as he stroked the brown-gray fur of the Norway rat.

Melissa eased the animal out of his hands and back into its cage. "Don't go all *Willard* on me. These are part of an experiment, and not pets."

"Yes, sir, Dr. Danvers, sir," he teased with a mock salute.

Melissa was hard-pressed to battle his infectious playfulness. With a smile and a wave of her hand to the far corner of the room, she ordered him away. "Go. Now. Before it's even harder to think about starting this work."

Doing a quick about-face, Sebastian strode to the spot they had set up for him in the lab, out of camera range. When he opened his laptop, Melissa turned her attention to the medical journal and her notes. Before her on the counter were blood samples from her patients who had responded to the experimental therapy. She intended to follow the procedures from the article and determine if the mechanism they noted was what had occurred with her patients.

She carefully uncorked the first blood sample.

"You shouldn't frown so," Sebastian said from his corner.

Her back was to him. For a moment, she was confused until she realized he was picking up the signal Sloan's clock was transmitting.

"And please lean over just a bit more, because with the way your blouse is gaping—"

"Stop, Sebastian." She turned and shot him what she hoped was a murderous glare. "I really would like to do this study."

"Do you need help with anything? Want to keep track of the results in a spreadsheet or something?"

She appreciated his offer. "Maybe later, once I'm a little further along. I may need to analyze the results of some of the assays I'm going to run."

At his nod, she returned to her work and presumably he was busy, as well, judging from the soft taps his fingers made against the keys. She had just moved a bit of the last sample from a pipette to the centrifuge tube, when there was a knock at the door.

She quickly capped the tube, tossed the pipette in a biohazard receptacle and went to the door. She wasn't surprised to find Edward Sloan. "Hello, Edward. How are you today?"

"Fine, thank you. I just dropped by to see if you needed any assistance." Without waiting for her invitation, he walked straight to the counter.

He paused, glancing at the test tubes and the rats. After picking up one tube and examining its label, he carefully placed it back in the rack. "Do you think your results will match those in the article?"

"Possibly. I'll know in a day or so when the more complex test results come back."

Edward picked up her notes and quickly glanced through

them. "Interesting. Very interesting." With a wave of her papers toward the cages with the rats, he asked, "Is this a new step you're adding?"

"I'm not sure yet. Maybe once I'm a little further along I'll find some use for them," she lied, and held her breath, hoping he would see it for the lie it was.

Edward examined her carefully and actually seemed a bit disappointed. "Well, then. Let me know how it goes." He stiffly walked out.

"Talk about feeling totally left out," Sebastian said from behind the lab door.

Melissa had gotten so involved in the moment she'd failed to realize Edward hadn't noticed Sebastian. "Maybe it's better that he didn't notice you," she said.

"Don't get hyper. I'm not in need of rescuing." Although there was a playful tone to his words, she sensed the underlying hurt.

She embraced him from behind as he continued typing. But she wasn't about to be ignored.

She nuzzled the side of his face and tongued the edge of his ear before tugging at the lobe with the little silver hoop that drove her crazy. While she did so, she ran her hands down to his midsection and pressed herself tight against him.

"If this is an effort to distract me—"

He didn't finish the thought. Instead he rose and turned until she was trapped between him and the wall. He was hard against her belly. She rubbed her hips against him and draped her arms over his shoulders.

"I guess it worked," she said. Her tone was bold and a little seductive. She wasn't normally the vixen type, but Sebastian had rocked her world and all her perceptions of herself. He'd let loose the spirit inside her that had been trapped for so long. And not just the sexual spirit.

"This is something new for you, isn't it?" he asked before he brushed his lips against hers.

She answered him with a hint of wonder in her voice. "Maybe. Maybe not. You let me be me."

Sebastian pulled back, feeling both amazement and that gnawing bit of fear he hadn't been able to dispel. "This is getting serious, you know. You and me."

She chuckled and smiled broadly. "I would hope so. I've done things with you I never even imagined were possible."

"But it's not just—"

"The sex. I know." Tenderly she ran her thumbs along the planes of his face, her eyes a dark sapphire-blue with emotion. "It's still a little scary, thinking this might last."

Sebastian knew what she meant. For days he'd been wondering how, with their crazy lives, things had gone so smoothly. Between scanning the journals and playing bodyguard and sharing her bed, he'd managed to answer calls from his clients and get some programming done. He'd meshed his life and needs with hers, almost too flawlessly. Perhaps he was avoiding what he knew he'd have to face: the true harshness of her existence. In the back of his mind, fear remained. Could he deal with the danger?

But right now, he only wanted to think of her. "We can last thanks to the wonder of power naps," he replied in a teasing tone.

"Do you always hide behind a joke?" Melissa asked, echoing his question from nearly two weeks before. It seemed more like years, thanks to all that had followed.

Shoving off the wall, he freed her and himself, needing the space. "You let me be me, as well, Melissa. I've never been able to do that with anyone else."

She took a few steps closer to him. "And that's bad because…?"

"Too much is going on right now. There are too many things messing with our heads and—"

"My life will always be like this, Sebastian. If it isn't this crap with Sloan, it'll be something else having to do with Ryder or the hospital."

As exposed as he felt, he realized her emotions were just as raw. He wrapped his arms around her. "I know, Melissa. I've been doing what I can to fit into your life."

"It's not easy—"

"No, it isn't, but…" He hesitated. If he couldn't be open with her, where could this relationship go? "I don't want to fail you."

"You won't." There was no doubt in her voice. No hint of hesitation.

Sebastian stood there, watching her as she intently resumed the experiment. When he returned to his laptop, he switched to the video signal of Melissa hard at work.

At some point she must have realized he was no longer typing, for she turned. He quickly shifted back to his client's program.

He forced himself to concentrate on the code, knowing he had to get the project done. But in the back of his mind, all he could think of was that she'd set the bar high with her unquestioned faith in him.

Which would make it that much harder a fall should he fail her.

Sebastian was determined not to fail her.

Melissa lay in her bed alone for the first time in the nearly two weeks she'd been with Sebastian.

Sebastian had gotten beeped while she was doing rounds. An important client with a major problem. After failing to solve the problem by remotely connecting to the client's computers, he had told Melissa he should probably visit the client. But he hadn't been sure about leaving.

She was almost done at the hospital and wouldn't be returning to the lab until the next day. There was minimal risk in her short walk home.

She told Sebastian he should go to his client. He'd given her more of his time lately than she'd thought possible. With it being dusk, Ryder had stood in Sebastian's stead, watching her from afar as she'd made her way to the apartment building.

It had been a little creepy knowing Ryder was there, but unable to see him. Despite that, she'd been grateful he was nearby.

By the time she'd arrived at the apartment, night had fallen. She entered to see Ryder stepping through the balcony door. "Just trying out some newfound skills," he said.

Ryder's experiments with his vampire side were a little troubling. How far would his interest take him? She hoped it would be good for all involved. His vampire power was strong and she worried it might lure him to a darker side of himself, one he would eventually be unable to control.

That was part of the reason she was lying in bed now, fully awake despite a long and tiring day. The other part—the much bigger part—was how much she missed having Sebastian beside her.

She'd come to count on his presence in her life much too quickly. Her insecurity made her wonder… Was she capable of keeping Sebastian in her life? Would the demands she made on him be too much?

She'd already had so much disappointment in her life. What would she do if this relationship with Sebastian didn't work out? What if their feelings weren't strong enough to bear the challenges of her daily life?

Melissa didn't doubt Sebastian was strong enough to deal with it. Her fear was that *she* couldn't deal with it. What if she was unable to balance all that was demanded of her with her relationship with Sebastian?

The last thing she wanted to do was fail him. He'd given her too much for her to disappoint him like that.

She only hoped that what she could give him in return would be enough to keep him in her life.

Chapter 26

The hospital cafeteria was teeming with staff and visitors, making it easy for Melissa to hide in plain sight. Not to mention that Sloan, elitist that he was, wouldn't be caught dead mingling with the masses.

She looked around and finally spied a small table for two in a far corner. "Over there, Diana."

They reached the table before another pair of diners, and cleared the debris from the earlier inhabitants of the space. The table was out of the way and private, yet allowed an unobstructed view of the entire dining area.

"Any chance of Sloan popping in?" Diana asked as she undid the napkin from around her cutlery.

Melissa shot a quick look at the busy dining room. "Slim to none. Edward never struck me as the kind who mingled with the rest of us."

"Good. I've got some news for you."

"Bad news," Melissa said, sensing unease in Diana's voice.

"Detective Daly had to pull his man off Sloan's tail. His captain wants him to shift his focus elsewhere. Possibly close the cases for now."

She leaned back in her chair, disheartened. "So we have *nada*. Zip. Zilch."

Diana laid her hand over Melissa's. "It sucks, I know. But we'll get something soon."

"How?" Melissa expelled the word harshly. "It's been quiet here and at the lab. Sloan seems to be one cool character."

Diana motioned to Melissa's plate of food. "Eat up. You could use it."

Melissa stared down at the turkey sandwich she had taken just because Diana had insisted. She wasn't really hungry. There was too much happening, or rather not happening. But when Diana picked up her own sandwich and again motioned to Melissa's, she relented and grabbed it.

Diana resumed her report. "I asked Peter to let the files sit on his desk for another day or so. I've got the feeling something is about to happen."

Melissa wished she could be as optimistic. "I hope so, Diana."

"Trust me. And keep alert. Don't let Sloan's apparent inactivity fool you." Diana finally took a bite of her sandwich and Melissa followed suit. The turkey was surprisingly moist and tasty. In response, her mouth watered and her stomach growled.

"Good thing I forced you to go to lunch," Diana teased with a smile.

Diana's visit to her office had been a surprise, Melissa had to admit. Although they'd known each other for months, up until recently, they hadn't really bonded. "Thanks for that. I think if left to my own devices—"

"You'd starve?" she teased again. "Good thing you've got Sebastian and me around now. Maybe we can even get some good Cuban food in you, put some meat back on those bones."

Melissa was a little taken aback by Diana's comments. "Why do you think I need more meat—"

"From the pictures you have in your office and back at the apartment." Putting down her sandwich, Diana leaned closer to the table. "Look, I know how hard it can be when you lose someone. After my dad died…"

"It's hard, isn't it?" Melissa was intrigued by the emotion visible on Diana's face. For the most part, she'd only seen FBI Agent Diana. Always tough and ready to rumble. This was a new side to Ryder's girlfriend.

Diana nodded. "Very. I was lucky to have Sebastian afterward. He was my rock. If it hadn't been for him, I'm not sure what would have happened."

Melissa knew just what Diana meant. If it hadn't been for Sebastian during the last few weeks… "He's my rock, as well. I don't know what I'd do without him."

Diana once more grasped Melissa's hand, but instead of pulling away as she might have a few months ago, Melissa joined her hand with Diana's. "I know you care for him and he'll be there for you. That's the way he is. That's the way I am."

"Thanks. It's been easier knowing that I'm not alone anymore."

Diana gave her hand a reassuring squeeze, and then returned to eating her lunch. Melissa did the same and they ate in companionable silence until Melissa asked, "This Detective Daly. What's he to you?"

With a small smile, Diana replied, "A friend and nothing more. For me, there's only Ryder."

Her answer eased a little bit of the disquiet Melissa had about Ryder's feelings for the detective. "Glad to know that, but Daly must be a good friend."

Diana shrugged. "When I first met him, I wasn't sure whether he'd be friend or foe. But we reached an understanding of sorts. He's come through for us, so I owe him."

"And what do you think the good detective will ask for in payment?"

"Not anything romantic, trust me. Rumor has it that Peter

got burned by his wife and has absolutely no interest in anything romantic. And he's aware that I am totally not interested."

"That's good to know." Melissa finished her sandwich. "So what do we do now?"

Diana glanced at her watch. "I need to head back to the office and try and get more info from my sources, not to mention work on a few other cases. In the meantime, if you can find out for me where Sloan is, I can unofficially tail him."

"Sounds like a plan."

After grabbing one last chip from her plate, Diana rose with her tray in hand and Melissa followed. Once out in the hall, Diana said, "See if you can locate our friend. Then give me a buzz."

"I will."

For a moment they stood there awkwardly, and then Diana reached out and gave Melissa a tight hug. It was that Cuban, being-physical-with-friends-and-family thing, Melissa thought. Surprisingly, she found that she didn't mind. She hugged Diana back and said, "I'll call you as soon as I have anything."

Melissa returned to her office and tried to track down Sloan, to no avail. He wasn't on the floor, according to the on-duty nurse. Calls to his home yielded only the answering machine.

Melissa reported in to Diana, who was clearly unhappy with the results.

"I'll call Peter and see if he has any ideas where else we can check. In the meantime, can you fill Ryder in for me?"

Melissa dialed Ryder and gave him the bad news about the surveillance and the pressure on Peter to close the cases.

"Seems to me there's only one thing we can do," Ryder said. "You need to make it seem as if you've started something with the rats. That might be enough to force Sloan to act."

"If I do that, we need to be careful. We can't take any risks."

"Sebastian and I will watch you. Do you want Diana to come by and stand guard, as well?"

Melissa picked up a pencil from her desk and nervously tapped it from end to end. She feared for the safety of all of them, given Sloan's past activities, and there wasn't anything Diana could legally do. "She's got enough for right now. Unofficially, of course."

"Melissa. Sloan is not someone to mess with, so expect me and Sebastian to be on you 24/7." He hung up before she could respond.

But who's going to watch after you? she thought, fearful that Sloan would eventually connect the dots from her to Ryder and decide to change his focus.

Or worse, that Sloan would realize Ryder was the source of the elusive cells. Her father had already placed them in enough jeopardy.

Melissa didn't want to do anything to make the situation worse.

Sebastian was exhausted and no amount of power napping was going to make up for losing last night's and this morning's sleep.

His client had had a major network failure. It had taken Sebastian and one of the client's technicians the better part of a day to set up a new server, get all the network users and rights reconfigured, and restore the data and programs from the backup tape from the night before.

But no amount of exhaustion was going to keep him from meeting Melissa in the lab. If he needed to, he could catch a few zzz's while he waited for her to finish up whatever she was doing.

At the door of the building, he was stopped by the security guards asking for clearance. Melissa was waiting for him at the door, a slightly worried look on her face. When she saw him, she motioned for him to enter quickly.

He rushed in and she hurriedly shut the door behind him. "Ryder called. Sloan is missing. Diana is trying to locate him.

I inoculated one of the rats to make it seem like I'm doing my father's experiments."

Melissa was wired, he thought. Maybe justifiably so, given all that was happening. Surprisingly, he couldn't muster the same kind of angst. Taking a step toward her, he touched her cheek and said, "Good night, good morning and—" he paused to look at his watch "—good afternoon. I missed you."

The worry evaporated from her face like a soap bubble in a summer breeze. "I missed you, as well. The bed was empty without you."

He wrapped his arms around her and kissed her, a brush of his lips that grew deeper with each kiss that followed. "Hmm," he said as she opened her mouth to him. "I can't wait until tonight."

She outlined the edges of his goatee, which had grown thicker over the past few days. "Me, too. But you look beat."

"I am, but I can get some rest here while you work, if that's okay." He inclined his head in the direction of his quiet corner of the lab.

"I'd like that. Plus, I just got the assays back from the lab and need to review them. Maybe prepare some other samples for analysis." After another kiss, she moved to the assortment of papers laid out on the black countertop before her.

Sebastian opened his laptop on the far side of the lab and tuned into his favorite version of MTV—Melissa Live and Uncensored. There was a rather earnest look on her face as she studied the lab results; it was followed by a knowing smile.

He liked to see her pleased with her work. Slouching in the hard metal chair, his duster wrapped tightly around him since he was still cold from his walk to her building, he managed to find a position that was comfortable. Crossing his arms, he tucked his hands beneath his armpits to watch her. Occasionally he would nod off, but he battled to stay awake.

Eventually, he lost the battle.

* * *

"You understand what you're supposed to do. Get the test tubes and the rat. Nothing is to get in the way." Sloan examined the young man's face to confirm that he did, in fact, comprehend his task.

The young man—a friend of a friend of a friend who spoke highly of Sloan's designer drugs—fidgeted before finally nodding emphatically.

Sloan was hesitating over this one. The man seemed a little too young and a trifle too desperate. But Sloan was desperate, as well, and had few choices. He should have kept his last associate around for a bit longer. He'd been more responsible.

Funny thing to say about someone willing to do anything for their next high, he thought as he reached into his pocket and held up a few bills in front of the man's face. "This is to get you there and back. Once you arrive with the goods, I will make payment with this," he said, holding up a vial containing a clear liquid.

The young man's eyes perked up and he rubbed his gloved hands together as if in glee. "Dude, I so understand."

Sloan examined him again, from the combat-style boots on his feet to the multiple piercings and tattoo marring what might have otherwise been a handsome face. He was tempted to call this off and find a more reputable minion, but it was too late. This Neanderthal already knew too much, which made him prime morgue material. But not before he did this one job.

"You should get going," Sloan advised, and his associate grabbed the bills from his hand.

"I'm on it."

Sloan turned his back on the young man and walked around the edge of the table that was a remnant of his old days in the NSA. He hadn't known what possessed him to keep the setup, but it had certainly proved worthwhile in the last year or so.

Suddenly he was uneasy. When he turned, he caught a glimpse of the man from the corner of his eye. Had his young associate pocketed something on his way out?

Sloan returned to the spot where they had both been standing and carefully examined the area. Nothing appeared out of order or missing. At least not that he recalled. One of the problems of his advancing years.

It was also one of the problems that might be remedied once the young man returned with the merchandise he'd been paid to steal.

With a slightly sprier gait and a lightheartedness he hadn't felt in some time, Sloan walked back to the lab table to prepare the payment for the young man.

A payment of the most final kind, he thought with a chuckle.

Sebastian was half-awake when he heard the creak of the door, the abrupt rush of footsteps and Melissa's startled cry.

A gaunt and very scruffy man stood in the center of the lab, barely a foot from Melissa. He had a knife in his hand and his stance was unsteady. "Get out of the way," he instructed, his speech slurred.

Melissa remained at her position by the counter, hands braced against the edge of it. Her body was poised for action, but Sebastian wasn't about to let that happen. He couldn't allow Melissa to be hurt.

The intruder hadn't noticed him. Slowly Sebastian rose from the chair and looked around for something he could use as a weapon. Nothing except the chair, which was too noisy to be moved slowly.

The man waved the knife about in the air. "Get the fuck out of the way, bitch."

Melissa stayed in place, staring straight at the young man. Her gaze wasn't fearful, but calculating, as if assessing the risks and what she could do.

The man lunged at her.

Sebastian experienced a weird sense of déjà vu.

To this day, he remembered vividly the seconds before his

father had been killed. The car had driven by in front of his sister, his father and assorted others. He remembered shouting at them, although not what he'd said. He'd run toward his sister and father, intent on getting them out of harm's way.

Only he hadn't been fast enough.

He wouldn't be too slow this time.

His senses slipped into hypermode as everything seemed to slow down around him.

His heart pounded, loud and fast, urging him on. The metal chair was cold and slick beneath his hands. His mouth dry, lungs almost painful when he took a deep breath, he sprung into action. The floor beneath his feet seemed unsteady as he grabbed the chair and, half running, swung it into the path of Melissa's would-be attacker, catching him across the legs.

The man went down in a sprawling heap.

Sebastian placed himself between Melissa and the intruder, keeping her trapped behind him with one arm.

The man recovered and awkwardly lumbered to his feet, knife still in his hand. With a ruthless leer, he lunged.

Sebastian blocked the thrust, but his attacker quickly recovered and wildly lashed out at him again.

Fire erupted across Sebastian's arm as the sharp blade bit through the leather of his duster and across his skin. That didn't keep him from landing a sharp punishing jab to the man's nose.

Blood erupted in a spray as Sebastian's blow connected soundly. The man grabbed his nose with one hand, but continued to threaten them with the knife.

Sebastian was about to strike out at the man again when Melissa grabbed a beaker from the table and threw it at the man's head. Their attacker ducked the missile and Sebastian seized the momentary distraction by lashing out a drop-kick to the man's upper chest.

Their attacker crumpled to the ground in a heap. Sebastian kicked away the knife, which the man had finally dropped. "Call Security."

Their intruder gave an odd groan and went into spasms. "What the hell—" Sebastian cursed.

Melissa hesitated on her way to the phone, but when the convulsions continued, she dropped to the ground beside the man and cradled his head in her lap. Forcing his jaw open, she pulled a depressor from her jacket pocket and used it to keep him from swallowing his tongue. She tried to hold him down as best she could. "Phone's by the door. Call for help," she instructed.

Sebastian rushed to the phone. After giving Security the details, he received a promise that assistance would be on its way quickly.

The man's seizures had almost completely stopped, but judging from Melissa's face, that wasn't a good thing. "What's up?"

"He's high as a kite on something. His pulse is too rapid and shallow. Breathing's very labored. He's not looking good."

She had no sooner said that when his breathing stopped entirely. "We've got to do CPR."

With Melissa instructing him, he helped her until Security arrived with the EMTs in tow. He and Melissa stepped away. It was then that she noticed Sebastian was hurt as blood dripped from beneath the cuff of his jacket and onto his hand.

"Let me see that." Sebastian eased off his duster to reveal the long, ugly gash along his forearm. Blood oozed freely from the wound and onto the white speckled tiles of the floor.

Melissa went into action, helping herself to some gauze and bandages from the EMT's tray. She bound his wound, but said, "I need to take you to the E.R. for some stitches and a tetanus shot. I'm so sorry, Sebastian."

Distress was clear on her face. She felt responsible and he worried how that might affect things between them. Striving to downplay the injury, he said, "I'm sorry, too. That was my favorite jacket."

But that didn't help the situation as one of the EMTs called out to Melissa, "Doc, we need you here. We're losing this guy."

Melissa stepped into the fray of trying to save the life of the man who might have taken hers without a second thought. Sebastian had only seen her in action once before—the night Ryder had been injured by the serial killer Diana had been tracking. He remembered her intensity that night and her perseverance. The cool competence that had impressed him so.

Melissa was no different tonight with this total stranger. She worked with the paramedics to stabilize her attacker, but to no avail. Whatever the man had taken was too potent for his body to handle. Nearly half an hour later, they pronounced him dead and called for NYPD and a coroner.

Melissa rose, defeat etched into the lines of her face. He held his arms open and she stepped into them, hugging him tightly. He returned the embrace, wincing slightly from the cut on his arm. She must have sensed his discomfort for she reacted immediately, advising Security that if she was needed they could call down to the E.R.

He reached for her hand, but she shied away from his touch, much as she had when they had first met. He knew then that her earlier look of defeat wasn't just about the dead man on the lab floor.

It was about them, as well.

Chapter 27

Detective Peter Daly arrived with his partner and Diana in tow. When the call came in about the attack and possible homicide, he'd grabbed the case and phoned her.

Melissa watched as both he and Diana patiently went over the crime scene, searching for clues. Sebastian stood by her side, ever vigilant and protective. A little jolt of fear went through her again as she realized how he had risked himself. All for her. He must have sensed her discomfort for he placed his hand on her shoulder and gave a reassuring squeeze, but she couldn't bear his touch.

She'd put him in great danger. He'd risen to the call, but she couldn't deal with putting him at risk again. Taking another step away from him, she wrapped her arms around herself tightly and gave her concentration back to the police work going on in her lab.

Diana and Peter got to the body after examining the surrounding area. They searched the man's pockets and seemed pleased with what they discovered. From one pocket, Diana extracted a bag and what looked like a key card for the building. When Diana opened the bag, she discovered that it contained a needle, syringe and rubber tie. Peter extracted a small vial of clear liquid from another pocket. Holding it up to the light carefully, he smiled and called out for one of the crime-scene staff to come over. "I think we've got a print."

"Probably not the perp's," Diana said quickly, motioning to the gloves the young man was wearing. The CSU tech dusted the vial and lifted a partial print.

"My money says it's similar to the batch that killed the other two," Daly said, rising.

"Easy money, Daly. Let's hope the print gives us something we can use." Diana came to stand beside her brother. "You okay?" She laid a hand on the white bandage wrapped around his forearm.

"Fine. The cut wasn't too deep—"

"You needed twenty stitches," Melissa said, and was surprised by the anger in her voice.

"I'm okay." Sebastian laid a hand on her shoulder, trying to reassure her.

Melissa took a step away from him and wished *she* was fine. She tightened her arms around herself, suddenly feeling cold now that the adrenaline coursing through her body was starting to wear off. Diana must have noticed she wasn't okay, for she said, "Maybe it's time you and Sebastian went home. Detective Daly and I will probably go to the M.E.'s to wait for a fingerprint match and the toxicology reports. Don't wait up."

"Call us when you have some kind of info." Sebastian placed his uninjured arm around Melissa's waist. As before, she shifted away as if uneasy with his touch.

Sebastian didn't know how to reach her. When she grabbed her coat from a peg by the door, he just stood there.

Melissa turned and said, "I'll meet you by the elevator." She didn't wait for his reply to leave the room.

Sebastian stared after her, both confused and hurt. He grabbed his duster off a chair where somebody had placed it. Diana laid a hand on his arm.

"Give her some space or you might scare her away."

Leave it to his sister to cut past all the bullshit to what was important. "I'll try. I don't want to lose her."

"I don't think you could."

Still unconvinced by her statement, he took a step toward the door. He stopped when Diana called to him in soft tones, "*Hermanito.*"

She smiled and laid a hand on his shoulder. "I'm proud of what you did today. The way you protected Melissa."

"You don't think I could watch you all these years and not learn anything, did you?" he said, trying to dispel not only his sister's concerns, but his own. What would it be like to live every day like this—the way Diana lived her life? The way Melissa did?

Diana hugged him hard and he returned the embrace, having a new appreciation for all that she did and all that she was. "I love you, *hermanita.*"

"I love you, too," she responded and before it got any worse, he walked out to meet Melissa.

Ryder was about.

Sebastian didn't know how he knew it, but he did.

He sensed the vampire's presence as he and Melissa left the hospital. Even though he searched as best he could, he saw no sign of the vampire. He wondered if Ryder was waiting for Diana or if he'd follow them home.

After a block or so of walking in silence beside Melissa, Sebastian realized Ryder had stayed behind to wait.

He pressed on, feeling strangely like a man walking to the gallows. Once inside the apartment, there was an awkward moment at the door, as if Melissa wasn't quite sure she wanted him to come in.

Cradling her cheek, he said, "Don't shut me out, Melissa."

When she looked up at him, her eyes were dark with emotion, almost glimmering with unshed tears. "Don't," he said, fearful of where she was going. Unwilling to accept that she wanted him gone.

"Sebastian—"

He cut her short with his lips, taking her mouth in an almost-bruising kiss. "We're okay," he said between kisses as he kicked the door closed behind him.

"You could have been—"

"So could you." At that, she broke away from him, her breathing rough and the tears finally spilling down her face.

"Sebastian, don't do this," she said, fists clenched at her sides and her body tight.

"Do what?" he challenged, walking toward her, his arms spread wide.

Melissa retreated until she could go no farther. "Save me. I don't need to be saved."

Sebastian stopped short of trapping her against the wall. He laid a hand over the middle of his chest and said, "So what if somewhere in this geek's heart there was a man who needed to be a hero? Is that so bad?"

Her tears had stopped, but her tone was hard enough to cut glass. "I should have handled it."

Sebastian smiled. "I suspect you could have kicked his ass. But what you're upset about has nothing to do with that and everything to do with the head trip your parents laid on you."

"This isn't about them." She slipped through the opening he'd left for her, striding quickly through the door to her room.

Sebastian grabbed the door, keeping her from shutting it. "But it is, Melissa. You're afraid of being saved from yourself. Of admitting that maybe, just maybe, you're someone that I truly care about. That scares the shit out of you."

Melissa battled with the door, but Sebastian's grip was too firm. The door was going nowhere. So she gave up the battle and stalked into her room. "Thank you, Dr. Laura. And what about you?"

Sebastian followed her in, closing the door just in case Ryder or Diana came home. He wanted privacy for this little discussion. "Me? What about me?"

Facing him, Melissa tucked her arms across her chest and narrowed her eyes. "When I asked you that night if you needed to be saved, don't you think I saw what you thought?"

Shrugging, he had to admit she had likely read him right. "You probably did, only things have changed, *amor.*"

She slashed a hand through the air to silence him. "And this miraculous thing—"

"Is that you made it possible for me to believe in me. To believe that someone as special as you could actually care about someone like me," he said earnestly, laying himself open to her.

His honesty was enough to defuse the situation. She closed her eyes and took a deep breath. When she opened them again, she laid a hand on the middle of his chest. In a tone that bordered on disbelieving, she said, "Someone like you? Don't you see what you are? How caring and loving and brave? I know you probably don't want to hear that last part—"

Covering her hand with his, he smiled and said, "Actually I do. Especially coming from you."

Melissa couldn't stop the grin that came to her face. He made it so hard to stay angry. So hard to stop wanting him in her life. But doubt lingered still. "Why?"

This time, his smile was tender. He cradled her cheek, his palm rough against her skin. "Because you're the world to me, Melissa. You've made me whole and without you…"

"This is just too difficult, Sebastian." Her voice was rough with the emotion she was holding back.

"Funny thing to hear from you. I've watched you deal with a sliced-up Ryder and a knife-wielding junkie who's OD'd."

She shook her head. "Easy to deal with because…" She stopped, afraid for a moment of revealing too much.

"Because what?" he asked. There was no avoiding him or the love that was so plainly obvious in his gaze.

"They don't reach me in here," she replied, motioning with her hand to the spot right above her heart. "Deep in here where the hurt is. Where I'm afraid of so many things."

"Of me?" he asked.

Surprisingly, she knew at that moment that it wasn't him she feared, but everything else around her. He had become her stability. Her rock in a sea of the surreal madness that was her life since she'd learned she'd been called to be Ryder's companion.

"Never you," she replied.

He pulled her into his arms and held her tight. She wrapped her arms around him and held him just as fiercely.

When they finally broke apart, he tentatively met her lips with his, as if uncertain of this new place in their relationship.

She returned the kiss, but couldn't hold back. He meant too much to her and she wanted him to know it.

Opening her mouth, she became the aggressor, empowered by his belief in her. He responded, meeting every kiss and caress. Undressing her with a haste that matched her own.

This time, it was she who backed him to the bed until he could go no farther, urged him onto its surface where she became his lover in ways she hadn't been before, emboldened by his passion for her.

As she took him inside her, she watched his face. Marvelled at the love that shone there and the happiness. He was grinning that devilishly boyish grin when he wasn't busy elsewhere with that wonderful mouth. And she was grinning back when she wasn't urging him on with soft cries as she reached her climax.

She was shaking, almost weak, when he reversed their positions and paused for a moment, gazing down at her, totally serious. "I love you. Forever, Melissa."

Melissa cradled his face in her hands and lifted herself up to kiss him. After, she braced her forehead against his and said, "I love you, too, Sebastian. And I won't let anything get in the way of us."

His answer was a rough groan and the powerful surge of his body as he drove into her. She slipped her hands to his shoulders, gripped them as she answered the call of his body and of his heart.

When it was over, she lay cradled in his arms, secure for the first time in her life that she was totally loved for who she was.

That she was finally happy.

Chapter 28

She was in love. Deeply and truly in love.

That could be the only possible explanation for why she was watching him sleep rather than getting in the shower and preparing for another day at the hospital.

He was sprawled indolently on top of the covers.

She'd discovered that from their many nights together. He was an on-top-of-the-covers kind of guy, when he wasn't busy beneath them with her.

Today he looked totally gorgeous as he lay there. The morning light etched the planes and hollows of his muscled body. His legs were long and perfectly formed. It wasn't fair that a man had such gorgeous legs.

She curled her fingers into fists, wanting to stroke her hand over him. Rouse him.

Taking a shuddery breath, she controlled the urge. She didn't have time. Work awaited her.

But despite that admonishment, she finished her perusal of

Sebastian in slumber. The goatee had finished growing in and the dark brown hair framed full lips he knew how to use to pleasure her. He had one arm tucked behind his head. The other was flung beside him as if reaching for her. Perfect, except for one glaring thing—the white of the bandage wrapped around his left forearm.

That forced her to move, but not toward the bathroom for her shower.

She sat on the edge of the bed. Laying her hand on his chest, she savored the strong beat of his heart beneath sleep-warmed skin. His muscles twitched as that slight touch woke him.

His grin was sleepy as he stretched. *"Buenos dias."*

"Hmm," she replied as she stroked the muscles of his chest. *"Muy bueno."*

Casually, almost as if unintentionally, she moved her hand down while keeping her gaze on his face. There was a perceptible hitch in his breath as she encircled him.

"And getting better," he said, his voice a low rumble.

"I have to shower."

He slipped his hand beneath the edge of her gown, unerringly found her breast and ran his thumb along the stiffening peak. "I can help with the shower."

The enticing vision of him sprawled on the sheets was blasted away by the image of him wet and slick in her hands. "I could use the help."

She slipped off her robe as she walked to the bathroom. Sebastian eagerly trailed behind her. As she adjusted the temperature of the water, he pressed against her back and ran his hands along her shoulders and down to grasp her hips.

Melissa swatted at him playfully. "Not yet. The water temp is so all-important."

"I love it when you get commanding." He playfully rubbed himself against her.

"Stop," she said, but with a laugh as she pushed him away.

Sebastian nipped at her earlobe. "That wasn't what you said last night."

She finally turned to face him, hands on her hips. "We're wasting precious time here. Let me get the water right so we can get in the shower."

He copied her stance, hands on his hips, his erection magnificent to behold. "Why didn't you just say so?"

The look on his face was full of amusement and passion. An odd mix, but then again, making love with Sebastian was fun and pleasurable and satisfying and unpredictable.

With a wag of one finger, she returned to the faucets. When she finished adjusting the water, she stepped into the spray of the dual showerheads.

Sebastian loved the sight of her. The water slipped over her body, the heat of it raising a rosy flush against her skin. Droplets clung to the rigid peaks of her nipples and the dark blond nest of curls between her legs.

They were both breathing roughly from wanting each other. He didn't waste another second.

Stepping into the shower, he licked the droplets from her breasts, then followed the trail of the water down her body to the juncture of her legs, where he dipped his tongue inside for a taste.

"Sebastian, I can't wait." She grabbed his shoulders.

He couldn't wait, either. "Turn around, *amor.*"

Melissa did as he asked, facing the back wall of the shower. The heat of the water from the jets on either wall warmed both sides of her body. The heat of his body bathed her back as he pressed himself against her.

She held her breath at his exquisitely slow penetration of her from behind, which filled her vagina with his hardness. It was almost too much to bear, the way he stretched her. Almost too much, but not quite. Maybe not enough, she thought, biting her lip and shifting her hips slightly so that his penetration went even deeper.

He braced his left forearm, the one with the bandage, on the shower wall above her head to support them and trailed the other hand to her breast. Tenderly, he fingered her nipple while slowly withdrawing then slipping back in. The water sluiced over them and between their legs, almost as if in a caress. She moaned. He whispered against her ear, *"Te gusta?"*

Melissa knew enough Spanish to understand his simple question. "I like. A lot." As he moved in her again, her breath caught in her chest. She held it and closed her eyes, ran her hands back to grasp his buttocks as he drew in and out of her, slowly at first, then increasing his tempo as their passion grew.

His breath was rough against the side of her face as he strove for their completion. He kissed her neck, whispered Spanish words of love, the tone of his voice husky. Arousing. She turned her face, kissed him back. Her own breath was choppy, more unsteady by the moment as his movements drew her to the edge.

When he slipped one hand between her legs and ran his finger over the swollen nub buried in her damp curls, she lost it. As she cried out her completion against his mouth, his own hoarse shout echoed in the humid air of the shower stall.

"We've got him. We've got a partial," Diana said after reading off the results of the fingerprint match from the M.E.'s office.

"So what do we do now?" Ryder asked as he, Melissa and Sebastian gathered around the speakerphone in his office.

"This is Daly's collar so we need to stay in the background. I'm meeting him at the hospital first."

Sebastian considered his sister's news and how that changed their plans for that morning. "And then what, *hermanita?* If he's not there—"

"His brownstone. The most important thing is that you not let your guard down."

"You can count on that." Sebastian looked at Melissa. "You need to go, right?"

Melissa glanced at her watch. "Definitely. I'm going to be late as it is."

"Are you sure this is what we should do?" Ryder asked.

"What's wrong?" Diana replied.

"The sun. It's early morning now, but by midday I don't know how much help I can be," he said, frustration evident in his voice.

"Meet us at the hospital. We can decide what to do there."

"Done." He hung up.

Sebastian looked at Ryder. "We'll be okay. Just follow when you can."

Ryder nodded, but Sebastian could almost feel the vampire's anxiety pouring off him.

But as Melissa slipped her hand in his and gave him an almost beatific smile, it was impossible to keep thinking about the bad things that awaited them.

Chapter 29

Melissa was nearly half an hour late for work, for the first time in her life. As she thought of the reason why and shot a shy glance at Sebastian, she smiled.

It had definitely been worth it. She gripped Sebastian's hand tightly.

It was a good feeling to have first thing in the morning, she thought, waving at Sara as they walked past the nurses' station. Her friend gave her a knowing look and a wink.

Heat blossomed across her cheeks, but that didn't stop Melissa's smile from growing broader as she strolled down the hall and around the bend to her office, Sebastian beside her. She paused at her door, tried the handle. Still locked, she thought with satisfaction.

She unlocked the door and stepped inside.

That was when she heard a loud thud followed by the forceful closing of the door.

She whirled. Sebastian lay on the ground, an ugly bruise already forming on the side of his face. Blood trickled from a cut along his brow. Standing over him, a gun with a silencer in his hand, was Edward Sloan. "Good morning, my dear."

His manner was calm in a way that was disturbing.

"What are you doing?" She took a step toward Sebastian, but stopped short as Edward aimed the gun in her direction.

"I think you know, Melissa. The lab. The rats. The fake blood," he said in tones so sedate that it was frightening.

Somehow she mustered bravado, trying not to reveal her fear for both herself and Sebastian. "You didn't think I'd use the real deal, did you, Edward?"

"I was hoping you'd be foolish enough, like your father—"

"The only foolish thing he did was trust you."

"My, my. We've grown some spine, haven't we?"

"Yes, we have," she answered, irritated by his demeanor and inexplicably filled with a new sense of power. The worst had finally happened and she was ready for it.

Edward lowered the muzzle of the gun toward Sebastian's head. "Do you know what a .22 does inside a person's brain?"

At her silence, he continued, "Most people think it's the shot itself that kills, but it isn't. It's the way the bullet ricochets around inside the skull, scrambling the brains until there's nothing worthwhile left."

He bent a little more until the muzzle of the gun was barely inches from Sebastian's head. "Then it kills them."

"What do you want, Edward?" She surprised herself at how calm she sounded.

He rose, but kept the gun trained on Sebastian's head. "The blood and the process."

"You have the journal, don't you?" She placed her arms across her chest.

"But that doesn't tell me anything." The words burst from his lips. He dragged a hand through his thinning hair and strands came away in his fingers. At her shocked expression, he said, "Surprised? You of all people should know what chemo can do to a body."

"Is that why—"

"Would that help ease your pain? To know that I did it because I was dying?"

That would have made it a little easier for her to reconcile the Edward she had known for so long with the murderous coward now standing before her, she thought. But she didn't need to hear his next words to know the truth.

"At first I wasn't dying. It was about the power and the money. The NSA didn't believe me, but I knew there were others who would pay handsomely for something as wondrous as what your father had stumbled upon."

He paced as he continued with his story. Melissa heard his words, but she wasn't listening. She was wondering how she could get Sebastian out of harm's way. Maybe if she moved slowly enough, she could reach the cell phone clipped to her waist and alert Ryder. At the slight movement of her hand, Edward regained his focus and aimed the gun straight at her head.

"Scrambled, remember?" He lowered the gun to Sebastian's head. He pulled the trigger. There was a muffled pop. The bullet ripped into the carpet barely inches from Sebastian's head, leaving a small but deadly looking hole. "Take that as a warning. Next time I won't miss."

Melissa inched her hand away from the cell phone. "What next, Edward? If we stand here all day, eventually someone will walk through that door looking for me."

"And we wouldn't want that. We have enough dead bodies already don't we?"

"So where do we go from here?"

"Somewhere more private." He motioned with the gun toward the door. When she moved, he grabbed the raincoat off the arm of her sofa. Draping it over the hand holding the gun, he stepped behind her and jabbed the muzzle into her back. She was about to open the door when he said, "Hold on a minute."

Edward reached to her side, unclipped the cell phone and tossed it on the couch. "GPS chips are a wondrous thing, aren't they?"

Shit. Of course Edward would leave nothing to chance. He hadn't left any clues so far and the body count was up to five.

"Please open the door. Go to the stairs. I've got a car waiting for us at the curb."

She did as he asked. Knowing that he wouldn't take her by the nurses' station made her alternately grateful—she didn't want to expose Sara to any possible danger—and angry—since no one would know which way they'd gone. Except maybe for the surveillance cameras, she thought and made sure to look straight up into the lens of one as they passed it. She wanted Security to know it was her. And, just in case, she wanted to leave one last message.

She slowed her pace and mouthed "I love you, Sebastian."

Edward jabbed her in the back with the gun and she had no choice but to move on.

Ryder slipped on what he could to protect himself against the sun. Jacket. Hat. Gloves. Sunglasses.

Hurrying to the basement level, he went out through the back door of the apartment building. That side of the street was in shade at this time of day. He stayed away from the strongest rays of the sun, hurried across block after block, always keeping within the shade created by the buildings lining the street.

He moved as quickly as he could, accelerating beyond human speed to the vamp velocity he had only recently discovered and had yet to fully master. With that speed, he slipped unnoticed by the security guards and entered the stairwell. Maintaining that preternatural pace, he hurried to the door of Melissa's office, expecting to find Melissa and Sebastian waiting for him within.

The smell of blood instantly assailed him. He had to shake

himself to curb his natural vampire urge. It had been harder since his injuries to maintain the line between demon and human. He closed his eyes and through sheer force of will he controlled the beast and let the human rise to the surface.

When he opened his eyes, Sebastian was lying on the floor, a trickle of blood trailing down his face from a ragged cut at his brow. There was a large purpling bruise on his temple directly above the cut.

Sebastian had been coldcocked with a gun. Ryder hurried to his side, concerned about the extent of his injuries and Melissa's whereabouts. "Sebastian." He gently shook the young man's shoulder in an effort to rouse him.

Sebastian's reaction was minimal. A groan and a slight flutter of his eyelids.

Ryder shook him more forcefully. Sebastian's eyes opened, but they were unfocused.

His helplessness sent anger surging through him. He took a deep breath and hurried to the nurses' station. "I need help," he said to the young Latina woman behind the counter. "In Dr. Danvers's office." The woman immediately swept into action.

"Is Melissa okay? Sebastian?"

The nurse clearly knew Melissa, but Ryder didn't have a clue who the young woman was. Guilt swept over him at the realization that he knew so little about Melissa's life. But he didn't have time to beat himself up about it now, not when Melissa's life might be at risk.

He followed the nurse back to Melissa's office.

She dropped to Sebastian's side. Removing a flashlight from her jacket pocket, she opened his eyelids and shone the light into his pupils. Sebastian moved and the young woman reached for the phone on the table beside the sofa.

"Security. Alert all the guards that Dr. Danvers might be in trouble. I need a gurney in her office stat to take someone to the E.R. Male. Late twenties. Possible skull fracture. Definite concussion."

Ryder didn't have time to be impressed by her actions. A second later, Diana and Detective Daly appeared at the door.

"Sebastian." Diana rushed to her brother's side.

Ryder nodded at Daly, who asked the nurse, "Did you see who did this?"

"I saw Melissa and Sebastian come in about half an hour ago. But I didn't see you go by," Sara said, and pointed to Ryder.

"I used the stairwell," he explained.

"Did you see Dr. Sloan?" Diana asked.

"No. Not for days, actually. Is Melissa okay?"

"We don't know." Daly grabbed his cell phone. "I need an APB on an Edward Sloan. Male. Caucasian. Gray hair, about six foot. Late seventies." He paused. "He's armed and dangerous. Sloan's wanted for five homicides, assault and kidnapping. He may have a hostage—white female. Early thirties. Blond hair. About five foot three."

Ryder stepped away as Daly gave additional details to the dispatcher. He kneeled beside Diana and laid a hand on her shoulder as she tried to comfort her brother. "He's going to be fine. Melissa's going to be fine."

She looked at him with determination on her face. From the fire in her eyes, he knew Edward Sloan would be one sorry man when Diana got her hands on him. "I know," she said.

The moment was interrupted by the arrival of Security and the E.R. personnel.

Diana and Ryder stepped away. As the staff wheeled Sebastian to the door, Ryder could see Diana was conflicted about what to do. He grabbed her hand and gave it a reassuring squeeze. "I'll make sure he's fine. You find Melissa."

With a last touch for her brother, who was lying motionless on the gurney, Diana nodded. "You make sure he's okay."

"I will. Take care and hurry."

Diana watched Ryder follow the gurney, then pulled her

ID from her jacket and flashed it at the security guards. "Special Agent Reyes. Is there surveillance on this floor and if so, where can we view the tapes?"

"Right this way, ma'am," one tall, overly muscled guard said.

Diana met Peter's gaze. "It's personal now. You understand, don't you?"

Peter gave a curt nod and followed her out the door.

The tapes had helped in numerous ways. First, they confirmed Sloan had taken Melissa. Second, they got a partial plate off the photo of Sloan's Jeep. The photo also confirmed the existence of an EZ-Pass on the Jeep's windshield, an electronic system for the New York area toll booths that would allow the vehicle to be tracked, and a third person behind the wheel. Likely another of Edward's junkie associates who would soon end up on the medical examiner's table.

Peter called in the description of the car and partial plate and asked for a trace on the EZ-Pass activity.

The tapes had also revealed yet one more thing. Something she would keep to herself until Melissa was found. Diana couldn't imagine having to relay that message if what Melissa had obviously feared came to pass.

With all the information at hand, she and Peter drove to Sloan's brownstone, although she doubted he'd be stupid enough to go to such an obvious place.

She only hoped she could figure out where Sloan was taking Melissa before it was too late.

His head felt heavy and large. Sebastian opened his eyes, but the light was painfully harsh. He raised his hand to block the glare, but something pulled it back. He tried to rise to see what was going on, but a firm hand on his shoulder stopped him. "Take it easy, Sebastian."

"Ryder?" He turned in the direction of the voice, but could

only see a blurry outline. Forcing himself to focus, Ryder's face finally came into view. When it did, memory returned as well. "Melissa. Is she—"

"Missing."

"Shit. Someone hit me. I don't remember anything else." It pained him just to talk. Every movement sent shards through his temple and the words bounced around in his skull along with an equally distressing thought—he'd failed Melissa.

He couldn't just lie there, doing nothing. He gripped the rails of the hospital bed and tried to sit up, but again Ryder held him back. "You need to rest. You've got a severe concussion."

Like he needed Ryder to tell him. His head was throbbing and his jaw hurt. At the slightest movement, everything around him whirled. The remains of the coffee he'd grabbed on the way to the hospital with Melissa rose up in the back of his throat, but he forced it down. "Let go, Ryder. Now. Before I have to hurt you."

The words reverberated in his head, but he suspected they'd been barely more than a whisper. Nevertheless, Ryder not only complied, but helped him to sit up.

Once the room had stopped spinning, he said, "I can't just do nothing while she's in danger."

"Diana called a little while ago. Sloan's on his way somewhere, but so far, they haven't been able to track the car."

There was something lurking in the back of his brain. Addresses that he had seen, but couldn't quite recollect. "There was something in Sloan's file. A piece I skimmed, but didn't download."

"What was it?" Ryder asked.

"A list of his safe houses, I think. He may be taking her to one of them."

"How can we—"

"Help me get me out of here and to my computer," Sebastian said, swinging his legs to the floor. He nearly crumpled as he tried to stand.

"We need to get you dressed."

Sebastian glanced down at the blue hospital gown and frowned. "Please don't tell me they cut off my jeans."

"'Fraid so."

"No. They were Melissa's favorites." He tried not to think that she might not be able to help him pick out another pair.

Chapter 30

His laptop was in his knapsack in Melissa's office, where he must have dropped it when he'd been clobbered. Once he'd powered up the computer and connected to the Internet, he surfed to a Web site that had a host of webcam locations. Thinking out loud, Sebastian said, "It's been about half an hour. Given typical traffic, there's a few places he could be by now."

With Ryder looking over his shoulder, Sebastian checked three of the webcams, but there were so many Jeep Cherokees it was impossible to ascertain if one of them was Sloan's. "Damn. That model is way too popular."

Ryder's cell phone rang. After a look at the caller ID, he said, "It's Diana." Answering, he asked her, "Anything?"

Sebastian waited expectantly, hoping to hear some good news, but it was not meant to be.

"No tracking with the EZ-Pass. Sloan must have taken it off the windshield," Ryder repeated.

"So we have no clue where he's gone. But I know where we can get more information."

"No way," Ryder said to Sebastian. He explained to Diana about Sebastian's suspicions about the safe houses.

Ryder was silent while Diana spoke to him. Sebastian heard the low murmur of her voice on the cell phone. Finally, Ryder faced him. "She doesn't have that info in her file so she's going to call her friend. The one who got her the rest of the NSA info on Sloan. In the meantime, she and Daly are on their way to Sloan's brownstone and, if need be, to Westchester."

Sebastian nodded. A bad mistake. The room whirled and he had to grip the cushions of the sofa for stability. Taking deep breaths, he managed to control the nausea that followed. When he opened his eyes, it took a moment to focus again. "If her friend can't get the info—"

"We'll worry about that when it happens. In the meantime—"

"You need to get your van so we can head to Westchester."

Ryder nodded. "Diana thinks he's near the scene of the crash."

"I remember her mentioning once that most killings happen close to where the killer lives. Sloan might not live there, but he's got to have a place nearby. He knew the area. Where to have the car go off the road for the most damage." After he spoke, he brought up a screen with cameras that were located along the Saw Mill and other Westchester parkways. Again, the Jeep Cherokees were plentiful and the pictures were too grainy to see beyond the windshields of the vehicles.

"Anything?"

"Nothing." Sebastian looked up to see concern in Ryder's gaze. Ryder shot a quick glance at the windows. The sun was way too strong for him, Sebastian realized. With a quick peek at his watch, he confirmed it was just past noon.

"You can't go out to get the van."

Ryder cursed beneath his breath. "Can you get downstairs?"

Sebastian wasn't really sure of what he could do in his current condition. Just getting dressed in the scrubs Ryder had scrounged from a supply room had taxed his strength. But Melissa needed him. He would deal with his injuries.

"I can do whatever you need," he confirmed.

Ryder nodded and rose from the sofa. "I'm going to get the van."

"Are you sure?"

"I will do whatever I need to so Melissa is safe. Have your cell on. I'll call you when I'm downstairs or when Diana has news."

"I'll be ready," Sebastian said, but was certain that doing so might take all of his resolve.

Pacing himself, Sebastian managed to get his cellular modem set up on his laptop and pack the computer so he could meet Ryder, who'd called about ten minutes earlier to say he was on his way.

As he rose from the sofa, the ground beneath his feet wavered unsteadily, as if he were on the deck of a pitching ship. It was just his legs being wobbly from the blow to his head. If Ryder could head out into the noonday sun, Sebastian could somehow make it to the elevator and down to the lobby, even if he had to crawl.

He managed to get out the door and halfway to the nurses' station before a wave of dizziness assailed him. He closed his eyes and leaned against the wall for support. Sweat bathed his body and nausea rose up again, stronger than before.

"Easy," he heard and a cool hand passed over his forehead.

Opening his eyes, he realized Sara was slipping beneath his arm to offer support. "We need to get you back to the E.R. They've been wondering where you went."

"Can't," he said; his tone determined. "Need to get to Melissa."

"You can barely stand," Sara countered, but even as she did, she was busy walking him toward the elevator.

"Need a favor. Two actually." He asked her to help him down to the lobby, and to get some blood bags. He wasn't an expert, but Sebastian suspected Ryder would be weak after his exposure to the sun and might need to feed to recover.

Sara gave him a confused look. "Blood?"

"Please don't ask. If you're Melissa's friend—"

"I am," she confirmed. Once the elevator arrived, she helped him in, but then stepped away. "I'll meet you in the lobby."

Sebastian nodded and forced a smile. *"Gracias."*

"She's like a sister, *sabes*. I couldn't do any less."

The door closed on Sara, and Sebastian gripped the wall as the elevator began its descent to the ground floor. Luckily the movement was smooth, allowing him to maintain his faulty equilibrium.

When he reached the lobby, he slung his knapsack over his shoulder and gingerly made his way to the doors. Long minutes passed with no sign of the van. Traffic was heavy on York, which didn't bode well for how it might be on the more well-travelled streets.

If traffic was like this all the way uptown…

He wouldn't think about the fact that every minute they lost was a minute Melissa came closer to harm.

He was so intent on looking for Ryder's van that he failed to notice Sara until she laid a hand on his arm. "I could only get two," she said, handing him her knapsack.

"That's great, Sara. It'll help." He took the bags from her.

Sara shook her head. "I won't ask how, but make sure she's safe, Sebastian."

He battled his natural inclination to nod and stiffly replied, "I will, Sara."

There came a short honk, followed by another longer, more irritated one. Ryder, Sebastian realized. His van sat at the curb, but the windows were so tinted that it was impossible for Sebastian to see the vampire in the driver's seat.

"Let me help you out." Sara once again slipped under his arm, providing support as they went through the doors and out onto the sidewalk. At the curb, she steadied Sebastian as he climbed into the van.

Once he was seated, she was about to close the door when she looked at Ryder. "Are you sure you can drive? You don't look too good."

Sebastian glanced over at Ryder. Sara's comment was an understatement. Ryder was paler than usual and sweating profusely. "Ryder?"

"I'll be fine. Let's get going."

"Are you sure?" Sara asked again. "I can drive."

Sebastian reassured her. "He'll be fine once he gets some fresh air."

Although she appeared unconvinced, Sara nodded and closed the door. Sebastian examined Ryder more carefully, worried about his condition despite his assurances to Sara. "Will feeding help?"

Ryder leaned against his headrest. "Probably, but I didn't get a chance to get—"

"I did." Sebastian reached into the knapsack Sara had given him and pulled out the two blood bags. "Can you drive and feed?"

As Ryder saw the blood, he transformed instantaneously and hastily grabbed one of the bags from Sebastian's hand.

Sebastian was grateful for the heavy tint on the windows, which would keep passersby from seeing the spectacle. Ryder sank his long fangs into the bag and greedily sucked down the blood. In less than a minute, the bag was empty. Ryder held his hand out for the second bag. After Sebastian provided it, Ryder drained the bag just as quickly.

Tossing the empty bags onto the floor of the backseat, Ryder leaned against the headrest and took deep bracing breaths. Blood stained the edges of his lips and his fangs were tinged with it, but as Ryder's breathing grew longer and steadier, the fangs slowly receded. When they were totally gone, Ryder licked his lips and turned to look at Sebastian.

Ryder's eyes still gleamed with an unnatural light and his look was a little too intense, making Sebastian worry that Ryder was sizing him up as a snack. "Thanks and sorry. It's been harder and harder to control myself lately," Ryder said.

"Well, try. I'm not dessert."

"I know," he answered, but there was an animal-like rumble to his voice that unnerved Sebastian.

Luckily, Sebastian's cell phone rang, breaking the tension of the moment.

"Sebastian? Where are you?" Diana asked. There was roadway noise in the background, making it difficult for him to hear.

"We're getting ready to head to Westchester," he answered, trying to hide his unease at everything that was happening.

It didn't fool his sister, who asked, "Are you okay?"

Taking a look at Ryder, who had yet to return completely to his human form, made him hesitate. At his prolonged silence, Diana questioned again, "Sebastian, are you okay?"

"Ryder went out into the sun."

This time there was a long pause on the other end of the line. Sebastian heard her worried sigh before she asked, "Is he all right?"

"He had to feed. I—"

"He didn't feed off you, did he? You're all right, aren't you?" Her earlier concern for Ryder quickly changed to anger on Sebastian's behalf.

"He didn't, and as for me, I've got a whopper of a headache."

This time when she spoke, there was relief in her voice. "I was so worried about you."

"My concern right now is Melissa. Do you have anything yet?" he asked while checking out the roadways in the web-

cams he had accessed in the hope they'd spot a Jeep match-
ing the description of Sloan's vehicle.

"*Nada*. Peter and I are still going through Sloan's papers
to see if we can locate another address before we give up and
drive to Westchester to scope things out. So far, we've got
nothing and my contact came up dry."

"I've got my laptop with me."

Diana clearly knew where he was going with his statement.
She also knew they didn't have time to delay if they had any
hope of reaching Melissa before Sloan harmed her. Sebastian
could almost hear her gritting her teeth and quite frankly, he
had a sick feeling in his own gut about what he had just pro-
posed. This laptop wasn't really prepared for serious hacking.

A moment later, she said, "Call me when you've got
something."

He checked the modem on his laptop, trying to configure
it for optimum performance. Not the best of transmission
speeds, but he couldn't hope for better in a moving vehicle.
They had no choice but to continue to move if they were
going to make up the time Sloan had on them.

Concentrating on the screen was tough between the motion
and the occasional bouts of double vision that assailed him.
The double vision in turn triggered nausea so strong that Ryder
had to pull over to the side of the road so Sebastian could vomit.

He was in rough shape, but couldn't let that stop him. He
assigned a spoofed IP address to his laptop and connected
through a remote server, hoping it would be enough of a distraction, knowing it might not be if he took too long on the
NSA network. Racking his brains, he finally remembered the
one user name and password, said a little prayer that it hadn't
changed and was on the system within minutes.

Bringing up the database program, he cursed beneath his
breath at how long it was taking to load thanks to the lower transmission speeds over the cell modem. If he lost the service…

He was sweating, counting the minutes until the log-in screen came on. Quickly he typed in the password and accessed Sloan's file. His memory was hazy as to where he had seen the addresses. He linked through all the different screens in Sloan's file until something at the bottom of one screen triggered a memory.

Sebastian couldn't wait to confirm if his recollection was right. He'd already been on way longer than he had been the last time. Highlighting the text on the screen, he copied it onto his drive and, with a few keystrokes, saved the text.

Then he broke the connection with the NSA server and quickly disconnected from the modem access. His hands were shaking badly as it occurred to him what he'd just done and how insecure it had been. He'd had few of the protections Len had provided. None of the ones he himself could have set up from home, given the time.

Time being something he didn't have. That Melissa didn't have.

"Well," Ryder said, apparently realizing that Sebastian was no longer typing.

"Give me a second." He was suffering through another round of double vision and closed his eyes to avoid the nausea that was sure to follow. It took several minutes, but he was finally able to retrieve the text he had saved and scroll through it.

Sure enough, at the bottom of the entry was a list of multiple locations, two of which were in Westchester. "Bingo. Now to see where these puppies are," he said out loud.

Before reconnecting with the cell modem, he changed his IP address yet again. If the NSA was tracking him at that moment, he didn't want to use the same one as before. Once he had the new IP address in place, he got back online and plotted the locations on a map.

Holding the laptop up so that Ryder could see it as he drove, he asked, "Which one is closer to the crash site?"

"Son of a bitch." Ryder quickly motioned to one spot on the screen. "It's barely a mile away."

Nodding, which he instantly regretted from the pain it created in his head, Sebastian unjacked the cell modem from his phone and called Diana.

"We think we've got him."

Chapter 31

The turnoff was well hidden on the little-used country road.

The small wood-frame building visible at the end of the turnoff would seem like stables to anyone who might have accidentally turned down from the main road. To the right of the building were some paddocks surrounded by whitewashed wooden fences. Behind the building, thick woods provided dense cover. The setting only needed a few horses grazing contentedly in the lush green grass to make the bucolic scene complete.

To the left of the stables was a gravel-covered parking area where a dark blue Jeep Cherokee sat unattended. Sloan's Jeep, Sebastian hoped.

Ryder stopped his van a good distance from where the road opened into the clearing. To go farther would be to risk immediate discovery.

"We need to go the rest of the way on foot. Through those woods and around the back where we've got some kind of cover."

Sebastian eyed the fairly dense thicket of trees through which they would have to travel. He wasn't sure if in his condition, he'd be able to keep up with Ryder, who seemed to have completely recovered after his little snack. He didn't want his weakness to hamper Melissa's rescue. "If you need to go on without me—"

"I will." Ryder didn't even look at him as he backed the van up a few feet so he could drive it into the underbrush along the side of the dirt road. By doing so, he'd leave the main road free for when Diana and her group of reinforcements arrived.

Which Sebastian prayed would be shortly. He and Ryder had planned on scoping out what was going on, but not going in unless it was absolutely necessary. The last thing either of them wanted was to get Melissa hurt by playing hero.

Armed with that understanding, they made their way through the stand of trees and toward the small building. It was slow going since the underbrush was thick and Sebastian's footing was less than stable. More than once he stumbled. When he stepped on a fallen twig, the noise seemed as loud as gunfire.

They paused then, waiting to see if anyone had heard and would come out from the building to investigate. Long minutes passed, but nothing happened. They continued onward.

Mindful of Sloan's background, they were careful to keep an eye out on the road and in the woods for surveillance cameras of any kind or booby traps. So far there had been none, but as they got closer to the edge of the building, Ryder held his hand up to signal Sebastian to stop.

Bending down, Ryder examined something low to the ground. Sebastian copied his actions and spotted the fine wire running all along the periphery of the woods. A trip wire, although Sebastian couldn't guess whether it was intended to warn Sloan or cause harm. Either way, it made them that much more cautious as they moved the last few feet and came to rest against the clapboards at the back of the building.

"How are you?" Ryder asked, looking at him for only a moment before scoping out the exterior of the building.

"I'm dealing." Surprisingly well, he thought. Maybe it was the adrenaline rush, but the double vision had finally cleared once he'd put away the computer. The nausea had abated once the van had stopped moving.

"There're no windows or entrances back here. We need to move around up front." Ryder struck out for the end of the building.

Once there, they crawled along the base of the building, keeping low to avoid discovery. The main entrance to the structure was a large sliding door like that to a livery. Someone had failed to slide the door closed all the way. There was an opening of about a foot and a half.

Large enough for them to slip through undetected.

Melissa's hands were numb from the tight ropes binding her to the chair. She wondered whether that was better than the pain from the rope chafing at her ankles.

Sloan's goon had done a good job before leaving with Sloan. For the last half an hour she'd been attempting to free herself. Not only were the ties secure, but the chair was strong enough to withstand her attempts to break a piece off.

So now she sat smack in the middle of the room, waiting for Sloan to return.

Two long tables ran along the wall before her. One held a few empty cages, one with a dead rat. A small refrigerator rested beneath that table, likely intended to hold samples.

On the other table was a large glass beaker and assorted filtering apparatuses. A low flame burned under the beaker, keeping the liquid warm, but not at a boil. Farther down the table was what looked like a small drying oven and an exhaust system of some kind. She wasn't sure if the exhaust was running since the smell of whatever was cooking was strong, as was the slight hint of ether.

She squinted, for the light in the room was not all that strong, and noted the glass storage jars on the far table. One was labelled Ether, which accounted for the odor and the slight dizziness she was experiencing.

Not good. She had to stay as alert as possible and ether was flammable. If fumes built up within the room, the flame burning beneath the beaker could ignite them.

"Ready for me, my dear?" Sloan asked as he slowly walked into the room.

"I don't know what you expect me to tell you, Edward."

He came to stand before her. Alone this time. She wondered where his associate had disappeared to. As if reading her mind, Edward said, "Oh, not to worry. My friend won't be bothering us again."

"Comforting. But since that's likely going to be my end—"

"Why should you cooperate?" Edward asked, but didn't wait for her answer. He walked to the table where the beaker simmered gently and picked up a small vial and a syringe. He motioned to the chemistry setup with the hand that held the vial. "Fundamental heroin lab 101. Lets me produce the basic drug."

With his free hand, he gestured to the filtration devices and oven she had noted earlier. "The key is in the cleaning process and what I mix in to make it injectable. Packs quite a punch."

Melissa remained silent as he stuck the syringe in the vial and filled it. When he was done, he replaced the vial on the table, capped the syringe and slipped it into the front pocket of his suit jacket.

"Is that for me?" she asked calmly, refusing to give him the satisfaction of seeing her fear.

He smiled. A cold snake's smile that didn't reach his eyes. "Only if you're good, my dear."

With that, he reached beneath his jacket and extracted the .22 caliber gun he had threatened her with earlier. "Now this." He held up the gun. "This is what I use if you're bad."

Melissa swallowed back the bile rising in her throat. In a voice much more composed than what she was feeling, she said, "You'd better be prepared to use it, Edward. You see, I've been a bad girl lately and am not about to stop."

Sebastian was moving down the hall when Ryder grabbed his arm. "I hear something."

There were a series of stalls, confirming that, at one time, this had been a stable. Slowly they inched past one empty stall. The sounds of thrashing reached them. Increasing their pace, they reached the noisy space, although the sounds had abated slightly.

Peering inside, it was obvious why as they watched the last spasms rack the body of Sloan's latest helper. His lifeless stare followed them as they shifted down a few more feet. They stopped at the sounds of Melissa and Sloan in conversation.

Hurrying their pace but keeping silent, they reached the opening to what at one time must have been the tack room just as Sloan struck Melissa across the face with the back of his hand.

"Don't make this hard on yourself, Melissa."

"Did you hit my mother this way? Did you?" she asked.

Sloan staggered back a little at the question and when he did so, Sebastian noted the gun he held. When Ryder would have charged into the room, Sebastian held him back. Using hand signals, he brought the weapon to Ryder's attention.

At the distance Sloan was from Melissa, Sebastian didn't think that even Ryder could reach her before Sloan could get off a shot. "We need to distract him," Sebastian said as softly as he could, as close as possible to Ryder's ear.

At Ryder's nod, he knew that the other man had heard. But Sloan hadn't. Sloan paced before Melissa, almost as if in distress. "She could have lived, you know. Your father had cured her. All she had to do was keep quiet about his death."

"You loved her," Melissa said, and Sloan grew increasingly agitated.

Sebastian slipped past the opening of the tack room without detection and hid behind a small stack of hay bales close to the opening.

"She was so beautiful, even with her illness. So full of life." There was regret and affection in the tone of his voice. "So much like you at times. Don't make me do this, Melissa. Together we can share this secret. Do wonderful things with it."

"What secret, Edward? That you're a sick old—"

It happened quickly. Even if it hadn't, Ryder and Sebastian would have been too powerless to prevent it. Edward backhanded Melissa again. Her head whipped back from the blow with a sickening snap, then lolled forward limply onto her chest.

Ryder rushed forward, moving almost too quickly to be seen. Sebastian realized it wasn't the human reacting, but the demon, angered and apparently out of control.

Edward whirled and opened fire at the blur of movement, emptying the gun. That didn't deter Ryder. Together, he and Edward crashed into a table holding beakers and a lit Bunsen burner. Glass shattered at the impact of their bodies. The table groaned and finally buckled with the weight of them and their struggle, for Edward was frantically trying to fight off whatever was attacking him. There was blood. A lot of blood as Ryder vented his rage.

Sebastian didn't delay to see what would happen next. He rushed to Melissa's side. Her face was bruised and a trickle of blood slipped from the side of her mouth. "Melissa," he said as he worked at undoing the ropes binding her ankles, aware of what was going on just a few feet away as Ryder and Edward continued their struggle.

The Bunsen burner was on its side, a small blue flame still spewing from it. Some of the jars had broken open. The liquid they had once contained oozed out onto the floor and Sebastian smelled a sweet odor. One he couldn't place at first, but when he did…

He had but a moment to throw himself over Melissa's unconscious body as the flame ignited the spilled ether. A small explosion ripped through the room.

After the initial blast, his ears were ringing and the heat of the fire that had erupted at one end of the room seared his back.

Ryder was much closer to the explosion, he thought with fear, but he couldn't wait to see if the vampire was okay. Using all of his remaining strength, he deadlifted Melissa, chair and all, and rushed through the opening, the fire chasing after him as the dried hay and grass ignited.

He burst through the sliding livery door and stumbled while trying to be as gentle as he could with his burden. He managed to place the chair on its feet before he turned to go back into the building for Ryder. He was surprised to see Ryder crash through the door behind him, a bruised and battered Sloan slung over his shoulders.

As Ryder dropped to the ground, Sebastian realized that while Sloan was bleeding a little, it was Ryder who had suffered the most injuries from the shots Sloan had fired.

A moan drew his attention.

"Melissa." He kneeled before her and cradled her cheek. She was coming to. He quickly worked at freeing her from the ropes still holding her to the chair. When she slumped as he released the last of her bindings, he steadied her.

That was when he heard the sirens and realized Ryder was still lying on the ground a few feet away, in the partial shade from the trees, but in vamp mode with assorted bullet holes in his body. "Melissa." As her gaze focused slightly, she seemed to understand the nature of his concern.

"Get Ryder out of here."

He slipped to Ryder's side and finally noticed that Sloan was busy crab-walking away from the vampire, a look of fright on his face. Before Sebastian could do a thing, Sloan stood and raced back into the burning building.

"Sebastian," Ryder said, gripping Sebastian's arm as he struggled to sit up.

"Hold on, Ryder." Sebastian eased his shoulder beneath Ryder's and helped him stand. Together, they did a shuffle-walk back into the woods and kept to the thicket of trees, working their way slowly back to Ryder's van. As they did so, the lights and sirens of assorted vehicles flashed by them.

Sebastian ignored them, certain Melissa could handle it, hoping Diana would be with the crew that had just arrived. Finally Ryder and he stumbled to the van. Sebastian helped Ryder crawl onto the backseat. "What can I do?" he asked, although it seemed as if there was already less blood coming from Ryder's injuries.

"Go back. Help Melissa. Let Diana know what you can." Ryder's voice was tight and his face showed the strain of his condition. It made Sebastian hesitate for a moment, but then Ryder turned his electric gaze on him and said, "You did well, Sebastian. Now, go."

It hurt when he smiled at Ryder's words, but that didn't diminish how he was feeling. "We'll be back soon, Ryder. Hang in there."

He locked the van, pocketed the keys and returned to the dirt road, following it back to the parking area. When he arrived, Melissa was sitting on the chair. Diana and another man stood before her. As he approached, his sister rushed up to him and embraced him tightly. "Are you okay?"

"I am, but Ryder needs a little help." He inclined his head in the direction of the road. "Up a ways. He's in his van."

Melissa was seated and giving her report to a tall blond man. Sebastian noted the NYPD Detective's shield and assumed it was Peter Daly, Diana's friend. A moment later, a local sheriff approached, his pad in hand.

Diana chose that time to excuse herself. "This is *your* collar, remember. I need to go."

Sebastian handed her the keys and she walked off.

Daly watched her with interest. A decidedly interested kind of interest, Sebastian thought. When the other man's gaze accidentally collided with his, a flush came to his cheeks. "Detective Daly, I presume," Sebastian said and offered his hand.

"Sebastian Reyes. You look a lot like your sister," the detective said. "Are you as stubborn?"

Sebastian chuckled and kneeled by Melissa. When she smiled despite her bruises, he knew she would be fine. "You scared the crap out of me."

"I'm fine, thanks to you. Are you okay?" Melissa reached up and brushed back a lock of his hair, exposing the bruise and cut at his brow. She winced.

"I'll be okay once we know Sloan won't be bothering us again."

He glanced back to the stable, which by now was engulfed in flames despite the efforts of a number of men with hoses. "He ran back in there."

Peter tracked his gaze. "If he's in there, he's toast."

"Could he have made it to the woods?" Melissa asked.

"We have men searching the area now," the sheriff interjected and immediately launched into a series of questions.

Melissa slipped her hand into Sebastian's as she answered, and he knew all was right with them. Gazing back up the road toward the van, he hoped all was well with Ryder and Diana.

Chapter 32

Diana cradled Ryder in her arms. He was still bleeding and although healing, weak from his injuries. Very weak. From what she could see, at least four bullets had struck him. "I can help," she said, brushing back a lock of dark hair plastered to his pale forehead with the sweat that came whenever his system was taxed.

Ryder shook his head. "There's some medicine—"

"You know that's not what you need."

Gently she eased him up, a little afraid of what she was proposing, but undeterred by her fear. While she held Ryder with one hand, she moved her hair to bare her neck.

"What if I can't stop?" he said, his voice lower with the edge of the animal in its tone. Despite his question, he nuzzled the side of her neck and took a deep breath as if inhaling her scent.

"You've stopped before." She twined her fingers through the hair at the back of his head, bracing herself.

"Once," he replied, and licked the side of her neck, tasting her. "I had more control then. Not like now. Now…"

Diana didn't get a chance to reply as he sank his fangs into her. Searing pain blazed along her nerve endings. She gripped the back of his head tightly and called out his name. The pain was gradually replaced by a strange and wondrous languor that travelled along her veins and spread throughout her body.

"Ryder," she murmured again and clung to him. Passion replaced the pain, tightening her insides with need for him.

Ryder fed on the sweetness of her, drawing her life's blood into him, merging it with his. Her warmth spread throughout his body, recharging him with its energy. With each sip, he felt stronger, experienced a sensual charge. With each sip, her body grew more limp. He battled the desire to keep on sucking until there was barely any life. Until he could offer up his own life's blood and make her like him. Bind her to him forever.

He ripped away from her, stared down at her pale face and wide unfocused eyes. Licking her blood from his lips, he switched positions so he now held her gently, embracing her until the effects of his bite ebbed and she stirred.

"Ryder?" Diana sat up and gripped her head with her hands as she wobbled a little from the loss of blood. Taking a deep breath that steadied her, she ran her hand over the bullet holes in his shirt. Beneath the holes there was nothing but smooth perfect flesh. On the floor by his feet were the bullets his body had expelled during the healing process. He picked one up and handed it to her.

She examined it for a moment before meeting his gaze again. "Will it always be like this? This complicated?"

Ryder wished he could tell her that it would be different. That things would one day be simpler. But as much as he wanted to do that, he couldn't.

Just as Ryder recognized that Melissa couldn't tell Sebastian that their lives would one day be different. Be normal.

As Diana slipped her arms around him, seemingly in acceptance of their fate, Ryder hoped Sebastian would be as strong.

After much protest, the doctor in the E.R. released both Melissa and Sebastian, although he made an issue of telling them their leaving was against medical advice.

Detective Daly had hung around, waiting to make sure they were fine and to tell them that Sloan had never gotten out of the building. When the doctor let them go, the NYPD detective was kind enough to drive them back to the apartment.

As Sebastian followed Melissa in, he wondered if Ryder was okay and if Diana was upstairs with him. If everything was all right with them.

As if anything could ever be all right in the crazy world into which both he and his sister had landed. He must have paused, for Melissa turned and looked at him. "Are you okay?"

He tightened his hold on her hand and said, "This is what it will always be like, isn't it?"

Fear clouded the blue of her eyes. She slipped her hand from his. "Yes."

He took a step closer to her and cradled her cheek, knowing what she was thinking. "I was scared today. So scared."

"So was I," she admitted. "But Sloan is dead. Detective Daly said no one could have survived that fire."

"But the journal is still missing. And Ryder is alive, which means—"

"I'm still his companion and no closer to finding out what my father had discovered," Melissa finished. A heavy sadness stole into her at that realization, at the possibility that Sebastian also finally understood the nature of her life and all the hardships it presented. She wrapped her arms around herself and walked away from him. Better to leave of her own accord before he broke it off.

Sebastian tenderly grasped her arm to stop her flight. "I know you don't need a hero—"

"You *were* a hero today," she said.

"No, not today, Melissa."

Melissa gave him a confused look and Sebastian continued. "Today, I was just a normal guy doing what was expected of him. What any normal guy would probably have done in the same situation. But all those other days—the everyday days when your hours are long and things are tough, when I'm by your side and make you smile…. That's when I'm a real hero."

She did what Sebastian had hoped she would. She smiled. A bright, gleaming smile that brought a rich, deep sapphire color to her wondrous eyes. She finally understood that he was there to stay. "You saved me when you came into my life," she said.

"Then we're even, 'cause you saved me, as well."

Sebastian didn't wait for her answer. He scooped her up into his arms and took her to the bedroom.

Melissa slipped her arms around Sebastian's shoulders as he lay beside her on the bed. She ran her hand tenderly over the purplish bruise over his brow. Below it, two stitches held closed the ragged cut inflicted by Sloan's blow. "That's going to leave a scar."

He brushed his lips against hers and said, "Adds to the whole bad-boy mystique, don't you think?"

She smiled, and peace replaced the earlier sadness that had gripped her. With this man by her side, they could handle anything. In between kisses, she managed to say, "The E.R. doctor said we should wake each other every couple of hours."

He eased away from her, his grin broad. The dimple along his cheek deep. "Sorry, no can do."

Puzzled, Melissa asked, "Why?"

Sebastian said nothing, just rolled her beneath him.

He didn't plan on letting her get any sleep.

Melissa could think of no better way to celebrate the start of their new life together.

* * * * *

*Don't miss the next exciting vampire
tale from Caridad Piñeiro,
TEMPTATION CALLS.*

SPECIAL EDITION™

At last!

From *New York Times* bestselling author

DEBBIE MACOMBER

comes

NAVY HUSBAND

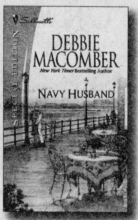

**This is the final book in her beloved Navy series—
a book readers have requested for years.**

The Navy series began in Special Edition in 1988
and now ends there with *Navy Husband*,
as Debbie makes a guest appearance.

Navy Husband *is available from
Silhouette Special Edition in July 2005.*

If you enjoyed what you just read,
then we've got an offer you can't resist!

Take 2 bestselling
love stories FREE!

Plus get a FREE surprise gift!